Touch of Lightning

A Mystic Waters Novel
Cavanaugh Sisters Trilogy, Book Two

JC Wardon

Mystic Waters Books, JC Wardon
Tennessee, U.S.A.

TOUCH OF LIGHTNING
Copyright © 2016, JC Wardon
Trade Paperback ISBN: 978-1-944454-94-4

Cover Art Design by Calliope-Designs.com
Editor, Kim Jacobs

Original Digital Release, March 2014
Rerelease, March 2016
Trade Paperback Release, March 2016

TOUCH OF LIGHTNING

Three identical sisters…
Three individual mystical gifts…
And three thousand years of warnings to never fall in love…

Millennia of tempestuous ancestral history forewarn Haven Cavanaugh to hide her ability to heal others with the heat from her hot little hands.

But…when she loses her gift, then it comes back in a darker, scarier form once Haven moves to Mystic Waters, West Virginia, she finds herself afraid to touch a man whose pull she can't deny.

Every time she dares…he ends up scorched!

Prologue

Blood chilled in his veins as his tension-strained body shook from both cold and uncontrollable fear.

Gavin knew what he was going to do was risky, but he'd been working for weeks on rebuilding his muscle-tone. He knew now his efforts were too feeble, as he hadn't gotten close to the shape he'd once been in when he played sports, and he was afraid his time was running out.

The weekly delivery of provisions he'd come to expect since first being kidnapped and imprisoned a lifetime ago now came with less frequency, and worse, with less food both in quantity and quality. Now his captor only brought boxes of cereal, candy bars, bags of chips, and beef jerky that made his teeth hurt when he tried to bite into it. Occasionally there were other things like little cups of pudding or custard he was forced to dig out with his fingers, and though he hated custard he ate it, knowing when those little cups ran out his supply was completely used up.

His seemingly stellar plan to take the time to get stronger before attempting to escape had backfired from the get-go. It was as if the kidnapper could read his mind and knew exactly when he'd decided to quit accepting his fate and would fight for his freedom. It killed him now to know the self-pity and fear he'd wallowed in, after his first attempt to flee, had allowed his once toned body to turn into nothing but flabby fat beneath sore skin.

The muscle tone he'd once rocked was gone, not just

from the lack of any exercise, but from the lack of nutrition his mother had always provided. Now, with only junk as his staple, he appreciated being forced to eat all those green vegetables when his life was normal, and he wished he could let his mother know he was sorry for the times he turned his nose up at the dinner table.

But she would never know, and he could never express his regret, as she and his dad were dead; murdered before his eyes a little over a month before he'd been captured and imprisoned in the hellhole he now called home. He wasn't sure, had no idea really, if the one holding him was the same one who had fired bullets into the dining room window killing his father immediately, before breaking into the house to kill and then molest his poor mother's corpse.

The man saw him but hadn't killed him, and Gavin knew it was because others had rushed the house and that cop decided to escape rather than finish the job. It sickened him remembering it all, but he needed the anger to give him the strength to do what must be done.

Gavin's biggest regret was waiting so long to get his head together. He wasn't nearly as strong as he'd once been, wasn't as brave either, but time had surely run out, and he knew he had no choice any longer but to try and make a break for it.

He heard the sounds—the muffled footsteps, the grunts, the occasional thuds—that always preceded the arrival of whomever it was who hit him with the car that night so long ago. Gavin had no idea how long he'd been in the hellhole; he only knew it seemed like he'd lived in dank darkness for all of his sixteen years.

Like a choreographed dance, their routine began with him lying back on the cot and remaining completely still until the person responsible for his present predicament shined the light in as they made their way toward him. He never heard a door opening or closing; never saw beyond the spot where the beam of the flashlight fell. Once the kidnapper was satisfied Gavin was blinded by the light, a box was placed on the dirt floor then pushed his way with a stick. His captor had known from the first just how far away from him to leave it, as he'd know exactly how long the chain was that was attached to the metal cuff encircling Gavin's wrist.

His body vibrated even more now as fear and anticipation raised the hairs on his arms. He averted his gaze as the bright beam of the flashlight was directed his way, knowing he couldn't allow it to burn his eyes if he was to have any chance at all. He was so over whatever game this person was playing, but he knew he had to be careful. In the beginning, when he still hadn't known what was happening and tried to fight back, it took him weeks to recover from the beating he'd been given.

Since he couldn't look directly into the light he attempted to determine the distance between his captor and himself by looking at the space of packed dirt that separated them. But the endless darkness in which he lived, and the brief amount of time he had to accomplish his goal, on top of nerves that had gone from fearful to panicked, made it impossible to focus his thoughts, much less his vision.

Gavin silently cursed himself for a fool. Somehow he'd convinced his brain he'd have a chance to reach his captor. Somehow he'd allowed his mind to forget that no matter his planning nothing would change unless the kidnapper moved closer to him than ever before. Anger took too much energy and he was getting weaker by the minute so Gavin forced his body from the cot and made his way to his feet. He wondered if the devil in the darkness noticed how badly he swayed and wondered, too, if he was now being slowly starved to death for its amusement.

Hesitating until he was certain of his balance, then straightening even more until he was completely erect, Gavin tried to hold back the nausea that didn't quite hurt his stomach but did make him feel seven shades of green, until he could breathe without the need to gag. He forced his shoulders back and held his chin up, determined to let the kidnapper know he had his pride even if he had nothing else.

He moved forward with rigid steps, determined not to stumble, afraid any sign of weakness would result in more than he could withstand. When he reached the box he didn't immediately bend over and lift it as he always had, instead he stared straight ahead, knowing his bravado could cost him his life. His captor said nothing, nor made any sound that indicated movement, and Gavin was certain he was being silently laughed at. Feeling defeated, and figuring he looked ridiculous, tears stung his eyes. With no other choice available, he gave in and retrieved the box then return to his bed.

As expected it was light in weight, and he feared had even less food than the last delivery. Instead of following protocol Gavin sat the box down and turned back. He held his hands over his eyes to shade them from the light, knowing it was now or never. He'd never dared speak after that first time, but it was obvious he wasn't going to make it out alive if something didn't change immediately.

Pulling on the strength of his upbringing, and remembering that his mother had taught him that you caught more flies with honey than with vinegar, he made sure his rusty voice was as conciliatory as possible. "Please. It isn't enough. I'm starving. You have taken such good care of me. But I'm starving now. Is that what you want?"

The flashlight went dark and Gavin's knees almost gave. He bowed his head and closed his eyes as he fought hard, but the tears fell anyway. It was clear he'd done the wrong thing and wished now he'd waited to get fresh water and to have his slop bucket emptied before he'd wagered it all. He took a ragged breath and wiped at his face as he waited for his captor to simply leave him to his misery.

"I'll try to bring more. But let's get this done now. I need your buckets."

Gavin's head jerked up at the sound of the woman's voice. It had never occurred to him a woman held him captive. The women he had always known were kind of heart. Mothers, aunts, teachers… With a clicking sound the flashlight was back on and the burning ray that followed stung eyes he hadn't realized he'd reopened.

He looked away quickly but halos of white floated before him anyway. He tried to ignore the results of being so blinded by the light and to clear his mind so he could do what he needed to do, but Gavin's thoughts were reeling with shock over the new information about his kidnapper. Dizzy with so much physical and mental overload, he tried to find his water bucket until he realized he was going in circles when the chain tightened around his legs. Once Gavin forced himself to calm down, he untangled himself and made his way to the cot to retrieve the bucket that held his drinking water.

Still blinking rapidly, he carried it across the floor until he reached the end of his chain. He left it there and went back toward his cot then veered off to the right and walked the length of his chain again since he kept the slop bucket as far away from his bed as possible. Holding it out the length of his arms Gavin retraced his steps back to the cot and then turned in the direction of his kidnapper. He'd walked around in the darkness for so long, using only his memory as a guidance system, it didn't occur to him to look toward the small circle of light the woman shined on the ground until he sat the bucket down and noticed, for the very first time, that it gave him a glimpse of her shoes.

Not sure if she was aware she'd finally allowed him to see a part of her, or wondering if she figured it didn't matter now that he knew she was a woman, Gavin returned to his cot and sat down to try and process all the new information.

When she returned, Gavin continued to wait at the cot, as he always had, until she pushed the first bucket to the spot that would allow him to reach it. Once she was gone again, he retrieved it, realizing it was the fresh water, knowing the next bucket would be emptied and cleaned. He sighed, wondering why he hadn't realized before that that was significant. If a man had held him captive, he probably would have just dumped the waste and not bothered to clean it, if he had even bothered to do that.

Gavin bit his bottom lip, wondering what to do. Talk to her? Beg her to release him? Not say anything more and hope she carried out her promise to try to bring more food so he could get some strength back before thinking again of escape?

When movement of the light beam indicated she was back, and then further and further away indicating she was leaving, Gavin ran forward until the chain jerked him to a stop, though his heart raced on. He grabbed the bucket that now smelled like bleach, as tears threatened again. Unable to let her go without saying or doing anything, he struggled with what to do. "Thank you!"

The movement of the light stopped and then circled around until it blinded him again. Gavin didn't look away this time although the pain made his eyes water as he squinted. He held his breath. Hoping she would say something. Hoping she expressed regret. Hoping for anything that would keep him from being all alone for however long she'd be gone this time.

Disappointment almost took him to his knees when the light swung back down to the dirt. It was clear she was done with him for now as the circle of light she held off to the side kept getting further away, and smaller, until he was once again in total darkness.

Gavin's entire body shook as he took the course back to where the slop bucket needed to go before returning to the cot where his legs gave out and he plopped down. He stared blindly ahead, wondering if knowing that she was a woman would make any difference to him, wondering if she ever planned to let him go.

Chapter One

Logan Hansen wandered his parents' house long after they'd gone to bed. His mother was still heavily sedated, and his father was so worn out and heartbroken over the loss of their youngest son he'd fallen asleep almost as quickly. He knew he should give in to his own exhaustion, but that meant going into Donny's room and climbing into his murdered brother's bed. He just couldn't do it.

He glanced at his watch and then looked around his childhood home once more before deciding he couldn't stay another night. Logan knew he would have to return at some point the next day to make sure his parents were doing okay, but it wasn't something he could look forward to.

Logan sighed, feeling guilty for wishing he was anywhere else, or the child of anyone else, but there was no point in pretending he was happy to be back in Mystic Waters. If it weren't for Rayne Cavanaugh offering him her rental cabin for the duration of his visit, he would be booking a motel room for the next week or so at least. Since she had, and he couldn't even stand the smell of his parents' house, he wasn't going to wait until tomorrow to go there like he'd originally planned.

It took only moments to gather the clothes he'd worn the past couple of days while they'd planned and made the trip from his Florida home to his parents' West Virginia home. He bagged his dirty laundry in one of the hundreds of small plastic shopping bags he'd found under the kitchen sink before grabbing the suitcase he'd planned to live out of until he was able to head back home.

Now that he was back in Mystic Waters, and after giving in to his mother's tantrums that he was obligated to stay for a few weeks to help her through this terrible ordeal,

Logan mentally calculated just how deep that obligation went. He shook his head, irritated he'd given in and now had to stay in spite of the fact that it was quite shallow. If not for seeing his best boyhood friend earlier, and meeting the beautiful woman Garrison was engaged to, he'd seriously consider reneging, and head on back to Miami before anyone was the wiser.

Logan sighed as he headed to the car with his belongings. He returned to the house long enough to leave a note saying he'd return sometime tomorrow, but he hesitated to specify a time, as he wasn't about to hurry over for more of his mother's dramatics, which had more to do with her than the child she'd lost, or his father's pitiful lack of reaction to any of it.

He left then, locking the door securely behind him. Chills washed over his body as he thought about what he was doing. He remembered as a kid it hadn't been a big deal if the door was locked, though his mother had always preferred it at night. But now it was a necessity, even during the daytime.

It looked like there was a possible mass-murderer hiding in Mystic Waters, killing off young men. Donny's body was the second one found, and Gavin White, Garrison White's nephew, was still missing, and, from what Garrison said, the police were starting to presume him dead, too.

As sick as he was over the obviously violent death of his younger brother, he was terrified for the nephew of the guy who was once his best friend, back when they were growing up. That poor kid, if he *was* still alive, could be suffering untold horrors. And after seeing the toll it was taking on Garrison, he was thankful, selfishly perhaps, to have not known about Donny's kidnapping and ultimate murder until it was all over.

Although he had no idea how he would have felt about it all, anyway.

It pained him to know he wasn't as upset as he should have been, given his much younger brother's brutal death.

He was horrified, of course, just as he would have been had it been anybody's kid. It felt like it had happened to someone else's relative, not his own brother.

Logan pondered these thoughts and his own lack of feeling as he drove toward the mountain road that would take him to the cabin Garrison's new fiancée had offered him. Rayne Cavanaugh was undoubtedly one of the most beautiful women he had ever met. She came to Mystic Waters recently, and even though Garrison had been in horrendous turmoil over his missing ward, he'd fallen in love, and now they were engaged.

Logan was happy for him. The poor guy needed someone to help ease the pain he was going through. And he knew Garrison well enough to know falling for a woman with everything else going on couldn't have been a comfortable fit. The guy had morals and loved his family above all else. Which meant Rayne Cavanaugh was something special.

Since Rayne decided to move in with Garrison, she had offered her rental cabin to him, for which he was eternally thankful. Though only thirty years old, he'd spent too many years practically estranged from his parents. First because they more often than not forgot he was around back when he was still a kid. Then he'd gone off to college, followed by medical school, topped off by the first year of his residency. During those years they forgot about him completely. It wasn't until he'd made a name for himself by becoming a surgeon that they remembered to make contact with him, and by that time he'd convinced himself he hadn't cared one way or the other.

Under the circumstances Logan couldn't help but feel bad for leaving them alone, but he hadn't felt like that house was his home since Donny's birth, and he couldn't make it feel like one now just because Donny was dead.

Jenna Hansen set the standard for all of their relationships all those years ago, and although she suddenly wanted and needed him, Logan couldn't manufacture feelings that didn't exist just because she was now hurting.

She'd just turned thirty when she gave birth to Logan, and Donny hadn't come along until ten years later. Logan accepted early on that his parents weren't as good at parenting as Garrison's mom and dad, but he'd quickly found out that wasn't the case at all after his brother's birth. With the new baby who grew into a terror of a toddler, they miraculously became doting and involved and generous, and it had been a slap in Logan's face to realize it wasn't that their parenting skills were lacking, it was they were lacking where he was concerned.

As an adult, now, Logan understood it wasn't uncommon for couples who had a child later in life to become better parents, but when he was younger there were times it hurt, even though he never believed his parents were aware they were slighting him in any way.

He'd convinced himself it hadn't been a big deal as he'd had his best buddy, Garrison White, as well as *his* family. The Whites lived on the next farm over, and if Logan didn't remember to go home for a few days, or weeks, neither family seemed to mind. If anything, Mary White lavished as much love and attention on him as she had her own sons and her only daughter, and Garrison Senior had treated Logan with the same affection and interest as he'd given his own kids, too. He'd even gotten to play sports because the Whites had sponsored him, and they'd been at the games to cheer not only their son on, but him as well. It had worked out just fine for everyone, and to this day he felt more a part of their family than his own. Even the years since, with no contact, hadn't taken that away.

After high school he and Garrison had gone away to college together, and every visit from his family included Logan. The contact had ended when they'd both graduated with their Bachelor's Degrees, but only because he hadn't ever wanted to return. Garrison had eventually moved back to Mystic Waters following a stint in the military. Logan had moved on to a whole new life, but by putting Mystic Waters behind him, he hadn't ever formed a bond with

Donny. Now that his baby brother was dead and gone at such a young age, Logan felt the tentacles of regret reaching out to sting him.

That still didn't change how he felt about his parents. Not at all.

Mentally exhausted and physically deflated, Logan pulled into the long driveway that led to the hidden cabin, relieved to be so close to having his own space and a bed that wouldn't hold the ghosts of opportunities missed.

****

The key wasn't where Rayne said it would be, which was just the perfect ending to an absolutely horrible day. Not really expecting the door to open, Logan tried the knob anyway and was taken aback that it slid open without a sound.

Given the events in Mystic Waters lately, and that they had just buried his murdered brother less than twelve hours before, Logan entered the cabin with caution, allowing the light of the moon through the large uncovered windows to guide his way once his eyes adjusted to the interior. The complete silence helped him to relax a little, until he noticed the trail of clothing on the floor.

A smile lifted his lips when he spotted the preformed studded push-up bra and matching tiny panties, knowing his forever-neat friend was going to have a problem living with a messy woman.

Since the cabin was neat and minimalist otherwise, Logan shifted his suitcase to the other hand and picked up the clothes as he advanced, hoping Garrison didn't mind he'd touched his lady's sexy gear. He laid them on the arm of the couch and headed to the stairs leading to the loft. As soon as his foot hit the first step a humming and clicking noise started from behind, causing him to turn so quickly he nearly tripped over his own feet.

His mouth fell open as he watched the lightshow coming from the top of the fireplace's mantle. Blues and greens, purples and reds, yellows and oranges sparkled, twinkled, and shot beams of color onto the ceiling and walls as the bowl containing them vibrated its way to the center of the mantel.

With caution he advanced toward it, calling himself all kinds of a fool for being spooked by what could be nothing more than a weird, probably motion-sensor night light. Once he was close enough he inspected the well-lit mantel for any indication of wiring, but the thing must have been battery operated. Just as he was about to touch it, the bowl stopped vibrating and the lights went dark.

The instant darkness combined with the nightlight's colors and shapes still burned into his corneal memory, disoriented him. He stood with a hand on the mantel until there was only a slight outline of the varying sized crystals still blocking clean sight before he turned to shuffle his way to the couch.

He'd have to make sure Rayne took her nightlight. That thing creeped him out, to put it mildly, and he wasn't entirely sure how long it would be before the images it burned into his eyes would go away. He closed them but that made no difference. The jagged cluster of pointed rocks was still there, as if drawn in chalk upon a blackboard.

He blew out a breath and knocked Rayne's clothes back onto the floor before snagging a throw pillow to put in their place. He stripped down to his boxers and left his clothes on the floor next to hers before stretching out on the couch. To hell with climbing the stairs and going to bed for the few hours left before sunrise. He'd settle in tomorrow. All he wanted now was to sleep away the last forty-eight hours, and pray his vision was back to normal when he awoke.

Waking up after what felt like just closing his eyes, to the painful thump on his skull, was the last thing Logan expected. His panicked first thought was that his gun was still in his suitcase, as he raised his arms to deflect the next blow.

Another three hard hits were killer on his forearms, but he managed to grasp the club and twist his body into a sitting position before a fourth hit could land. He jerked what turned out to be a baseball bat out of his attacker's hands and threw it behind him as he scrambled to his feet.

A body hit him hard, taking him back onto the couch, as a much less painful fist found his jaw. His mind was still muddled, and he was certain the liquid running down from his hairline was blood, but he was able to process that the warm naked flesh that now straddled his barely covered lap had curved hips and globelike breasts bouncing in opposite directions at she continued to pound at his head.

Knowing now that he could easily overpower his attacker, Logan grabbed both tiny wrists in his hands and twisted until he had them pinned behind her back. She continued to buck against him as she struggled for freedom. Unfortunately it was making his body react in an inappropriate way given the circumstances. She broke her silence with an earsplitting scream before she started yelling at him.

"Let go of me! Let go of me you big oaf! Get out!"

"Stop!" As his eyes adjusted to the low light, Logan eased his grip so he wasn't hurting her, torn between mortification for her, and embarrassment that he would have to look his old friend in the eyes in the coming days. "Rayne! Stop moving! It's me, Logan. You're not supposed to be here!

"For God's sake, woman, stop moving!"

She instantly stilled though her breasts continued to heave at his eye level with each harsh breath she took. He looked down, but that was no better. He hardened even more at the realization she had only a thin line of hair leading to....

No! He would not go there. This was Garrison's fiancé. He would definitely *not* go there.

He opened his hands and she immediately scuttled back until she was on her feet. She ran from the room and he could hear her climbing the stairs, but he didn't dare look back. He had seen more than enough. The next time they came face to face in front of Garrison it would be horribly awkward for everyone.

That realization propelled him to his feet. Trying to ignore the pounding ache in his boxers as well as the one at his crown, while he frantically searched for the pants he'd worn to the funeral that had somehow gotten kicked across the room, Logan's sense of panic mingled with amusement at how ridiculous he must look. Within seconds he had them pulled up, which was good enough, and was heading for the door.

"Wait!"

Logan stopped with this hand on the knob, trying to catch his breath. He turned slowly then looked up. Rayne had pulled a sheet around her and was standing at the loft's railing looking down at him. He exhaled another breath before being able to speak. "I'm sorry. I thought you said you would be at Garrison's. I wouldn't have come if I'd known you were still here."

She stared at him in silence for several seconds before turning to walk down the stairs, one hand holding the sheet at her breasts, and the other lifting its tail so she didn't trip.

When she reached the landing, she crossed to the end table and turned on the lamp. Soft light filtered by the lamp's shade lit her to magnificent perfection. Logan turned to the door again, knowing he had to get out. He wasn't a man to lust after a friend's woman, no matter how amazingly gorgeous she was.

"Please, don't go."

Logan shook his head, unable to move in either direction. So he kept his gaze on the door. "Look, Rayne, I'm sorry. I have to leave. I have no idea how I'm going to explain any of this to Garrison and still keep my teeth.

"I like my teeth."

Soft laughter tickled his skin and he had no choice but to turn around then. He stared at her as she gasped.

"Oh, my! I've made you bleed!"

Logan just wanted to get out. This was going to complicate a friendship that, though dormant for several years, still meant the world to him. "Don't worry about it.

I'm fine. I have to go."

She moved behind the island that separated the kitchen space from the lounging area.

"I'm not Rayne. But I'm glad you know her, and know where she is *supposed* to be. I'm her identical sister, Haven.

"I'm so sorry for hurting you! Let me get a wet cloth and clean that up for you."

Two of them? There were two such beautiful creatures on the planet? All thoughts of the forming headache, and him leaving, vanished, as he returned to the center of the room. He looked her over as much as the sheet allowed and envied his friend more than ever. If the sisters were identical in every way, Garrison was undoubtedly in sexual heaven.

"I'm Logan Hansen. Childhood best friend of your sister's fiancé. I'm sorry about frightening you like that. Rayne said the cabin was vacant now that she'd moved in with Garrison."

Haven's mouth stayed open for several seconds before she closed it. "Did you say fiancé? Rayne is *engaged?*"

Great! I've done it again.

"Uh, yeah. Just happened. They haven't told anyone yet. I accidently told his parents yesterday. By accident. I didn't know...no one knew...." Logan knew he was babbling in fragmented sentences, but he couldn't help himself. Haven's shock regarding her sister's engagement made her forget she was holding the sheet in place, so it no longer was.

She must have realized his gaze had travelled south because she slowly reached to her midriff where it was trapped between her belly button ring and the countertop she was leaning a hip against. She pulled it back up and wrapped it haphazardly then looked up at him with an awkward little smile on her lips.

"Sorry," she said, not sounding sorry at all.

Logan shook his head, his brows not the only part of him raised. "No need to apologize to me."

She laughed then and the musical sound had his

already hard part stirring. He tried to ignore it, which was completely impossible.

"Are you okay? I hit you pretty hard. I can fix you up, if you'll let me. I hope there's ice. And I can get you something to drink." Haven turned to the refrigerator and opened the door, then glanced back at him. "Not much to choose from, but the bottled water looks good."

Caught staring, and hoping she didn't notice his fascination with the strange tattoo just below her left shoulder, Logan found himself wishing there was whiskey on hand. But water would do. "Water sounds great. And I don't need ice. I don't think." He reached up and touched the cut and tried not to react. It hurt like a son of a bitch. He pulled wet fingers away and looked at the congealing blood, then at her. "Maybe just something to wipe the blood away?"

She snagged two waters and set his on the island separating the kitchen area and the living room before opening her own. Then she searched several drawers before pulling out a hand towel. She poured water onto the towel then leaned over the island to hand it to him, making her sheet slipped a little. "I can do that for you, if you want."

Logan thought it better to keep his distance. Headache or not, the woman had his body on full alert, so he shook his head as he advanced only far enough to get the cloth. He turned, dabbing at the cut. "No problem. But I think I'll sit back down for a minute."

"So tell me what's going on here," she said as she appeared at his side. She sat one bottle of water down on the table by his side, and carried the other to the other side of the couch where she plopped down.

"I can't believe my sister is engaged and living with a man she hasn't even told her family about. But then again, maybe I can. She's impetuous. A free-bird, if you will."

"You don't seem to have all that many inhibitions," Logan said, then immediately wanted to kick himself. But she just laughed.

"Oh, you mean about my body. We were raised by a

mother who believed and taught that anything that is natural is normal." She grinned. "I'm pretty confident about all this," she said, waving a careless hand over her body. And I feel more normal since arriving here than I have for some time now." She frowned then, holding up first one hand, and then grasped the sheet with it before looking at her other hand. She glanced at him then and shrugged her shoulders.

"Oh, please ignore me. And have your drink."

Logan grabbed his bottle, opened it, and stopped just short of drinking it all in one long swallow, thinking there was no way any man on the planet could ignore her. Since sticking his foot in his mouth was becoming a new and unwelcome habit, he kept the thought to himself.

But, oh, she fascinated him on every level. Which was why he needed to get talking and stop thinking about how naked she was, and how close she was, and how amazing she smelled.

"I'll tell you what little I know. I just arrived a couple days ago after having been gone for years. It's a long story." Logan frowned before adding, "A sad story."

Haven pulled her feet up and tucked her sheet up around her toes. "Has something bad happened? Rayne told us, *forever ago*, that she met this guy that had a missing child. But we haven't been able to contact her for weeks and weeks. We've been worried."

Logan fleetingly wondered how big her family was, but he noticed she was looking at her hands again, so he did too. Clearly feminine, with long straight fingers that sported smoothly manicured, unadorned nails, they were covered in skin that looked so pale he'd swear they had never felt the heat of the sun. Since there were no marks or anything to indicate injury or concern, Logan wondered why she inspected them so closely, even though he felt compelled to do the same.

Mystified, as he'd never had a hand fetish before, he looked up and felt his neck heat when he realized she was looking at him questioningly with a tiny mocking grin.

Logan licked his lips before biting down on the top one as he stared back. He felt like an adolescent: awkward, untried, unsure, and completely under the spell of a first crush. It wasn't comfortable feeling like he was thirteen again, but it *was* intriguing, and exciting in a way nothing had been for a really long time.

He wasn't sure if it was the tension, or amusement, or a sense of anticipation that tightened his cheek muscles, making him grin. He felt almost giddy and wondered if perhaps he wasn't just a little punch-drunk. It made sense. The phone call about his brother, the endlessly long trip with a hysterical mother and useless father, the funeral, the horror of learning of all the rest... He was exhausted, yet somehow being in her presence had him strangely revved up. He had never, in his entire life, felt as alive as he did at this moment. "Just who *are* you?"

Fatigue *was* taking a toll, Logan decided seconds later, as he was certain her emerald eyes sparkled with gold flecks before she quickly closed them and turned away. His skull started throbbing again as she reached for her water and turned the bottle up for a drink, before she settled it back on the table at her side. She turned to him then, and he blew out a shaky breath. Though incredibly lovely, her eyes looked normal again, if one could call such an intriguing shade of green normal.

Logan lifted his hand and touched the throbbing spot on his head, then immediately pulled his hand away. Although there was still a little area that felt wet, for the most part it felt as if the blood congealed and was drying. He looked at the dark and lighter blood on his fingertips, then fisted his hand and held it down by his thigh when she gasped.

Deciding he was fine...*ish*, Logan felt bad for bring his injury to her attention. To distract her he searched his aching head, hoping to remember and pick up the conversation where it had fallen off. "Uh...yeah. Um, Garrison White is Rayne's fiancé. I just met her but have known him all my life. The missing child is his seventeen-year-old nephew, Gavin."

Haven glanced from his eyes to his injury and then back again, her frown deepening. "Oh, that is horrible! How long has he been missing?"

Logan shook his head as heaviness of heart returned. He took a chest filling breath then released it before answering. "For several months. In fact he would have just had a birthday if I remember right, but his disappearance isn't all of it."

Haven tilted her head as she studied him, seeming completely unaware her sheet was once again falling down. Logan looked away and focused on the greenness of a huge aloe vera plant displayed before the large front window. It didn't seem right to notice her barely clad body when talking about his best friend's missing nephew.

"There's something worse?"

Without looking at Haven, he nodded. "Yes. The reason I'm here is because my younger brother was—" Logan licked his lips and swallowed. It was hard to say it out loud. "He was murdered."

"Oh! I'm so sorry. I...I don't even know what to say." Haven's voice shook, as she repeated, "I'm *so* sorry."

Catching Haven's movements in his peripheral vision as she'd reached out to touch him only to quickly pull her hand back before making contact tugged at something deep inside of him. Logan knew what a psychologist would say about that, as he'd spent ten months bending one's ear while they'd tested out living together, but he doubted it was as simple as him needing, maybe even craving, human contact and comfort.

Kaye's constant need to assess his moods had ended a relationship that had been pretty good otherwise, but her inability to leave her job at the office and stay out of his past while at home killed his desire for her lovely face and body. The worst part was she'd been completely wrong.

She'd wanted to hammer the theory in his head that his affectionate nature with her had more to do with his lack of affection from his parents during his confusing teen years than with feelings for her. What she hadn't understood was it wasn't *that* at all. What he'd really wanted with her was what he'd learned from his best friend's parents' relationship.

Logan had always envied Garrison's relationship with his parents and siblings, and he would have given anything to be a child of Garrison Sr. and Mary White. The Whites were *his* picture-perfect example of a loving and affection couple, and if he'd been a writer of fairytales, he would have put them in the starring roles of how to live happily ever after. Having that kind of a relationship, that kind of family, was still a dream he refused to let go of. He'd promised himself long ago he'd die old and alone before he'd ever settle for—

"Logan?"

Realizing he was zoning out, Logan sent her a tired smile. Haven smiled down at him gently and with concern, making him realize he was slumped over enough that his head was near her sheet-covered hip.

"Are you okay?"

Logan nodded and pulled himself back up so he was sitting up straight again. "I'm fine…where was I?"

"Telling me about your brother. Then you said something about Kaye not getting it, but I didn't really understand that part. But you look about to drop. Maybe I'd better let you get some sleep."

Almost certain he had a concussion now, Logan shook his head slowly, afraid to move too fast. He had to stay awake. And that meant he had to keep talking. He smiled at her, at least he hoped he was smiling, and then was reassured when she smiled back, although he could still see the concern in her sparkling eyes.

Sparkling eyes?

Haven was mesmerizing and confusing in equal measure. It seemed like they were talking and acting on two different planes. He watched her luscious lips move in slow motion, but heard no words. Her eyes really *were* sparkling with flakes of gold that shot out minute sunbursts as they twinkled like the stars in an emerald sky. He could smell the scent she wore; something hot and sensual that made him salivate so much he had to swallow to keep from drooling. It was a little nauseating to be both ultra focused, and dizzily distracted at the same time.

Determined to stay conscious he picked up on his story. "It's awful to admit, but I barely knew Donny. Did I already tell you my brother's name?" Logan frowned, not sure what he'd already said, but decided it didn't matter. "He was a lot younger than me."

Logan pressed his lips together as anger took hold, helping to clear the fog a little. "It gets worse, though. Donny's body was the *second* one found. One of Garrison's cousins was murdered, too. And, for that matter, so were his older brother, and sister-in-law. And now their son is missing on top of everything else."

Logan bit his bottom lip to hold back saying more as his head started throbbing again. It was no wonder. Somehow he'd convinced himself if he could distance himself emotionally from what was going on in Mystic Waters, it wouldn't hurt as much. But the truth was it made him want to cry like he hadn't since he was a little kid. His friends were murdered. His brother was murdered. A child he knew was missing, and there was nothing anyone could do about any of it.

He saw the shock and horror marring Haven's beautiful face and regretted unloading on her. "I'm sorry. I shouldn't burden you with all this."

"Oh, please. It's okay. I'm the one that's so sorry. How horrible this must be for you all. I just...*ah*—"

The tone of Haven's sharp gasp strung out before trailing away. She grabbed her sheet and untangled her feet before rising. As she walked to the fireplace Logan wondered what had captured her attention, but all he could do was watch with appreciation as the sheet overlapped and pooled just below the two dimples of her lovely lower back.

She stood with her completely exposed back to him for several seconds before she tilted her head and reached up to touch the nightlight that had scared the crap out him earlier. It flared to life and she jerked back.

Reflexive fear propelled Logan to his feet and though the quick jarring movements made him a little dizzy, and his head pounded with pain, he was at her side in seconds. He placed his palm over the wound and applied pressure, hoping that would help, but all his thoughts were on Haven. She looked like she'd seen a ghost. "It's okay. It must be battery operated and either heat or touch activated. It scared the pants off me when I first got here, too. I guess it's Rayne's nightlight, but I seriously doubt that Garrison is going to like it any better than I do."

Haven turned to him and opened her mouth and then shut it without say anything. She nodded then. "Of course. A nightlight. Rayne likes whimsical things."

He frowned. Even though Haven turned her gaze toward him, Logan was certain her mind was somewhere else. It was as if she was looking right through him. Even as ill as he was feeling the need to capture her notice took hold, and held. He lifted his hand to place a finger under her chin so he could direct her attention back to him. "Haven?"

She blinked, and the sheet slid to the floor. "What?"

Logan looked away abruptly. "Uh, you dropped the sheet again."

"What?"

He looked back at her, focusing on her sparkling catlike eyes, wondering if she was suffering some kind of a seizure or if his injury was such that he was seeing things that weren't actually there. "Are you okay?"

She blinked again. "I think so. I feel... Um...hmm." Haven focused on him, *really* focused on him, with an almost desperate stare. "Can I touch you?"

Thoroughly confused, Logan nodded before glancing down the length of her until his gaze rested on her sparkling, glittery-gold painted toenails. He looked back into her eyes and tried to ignore the fact his head wasn't the only thing throbbing. "Of course. But you might want to pull your sheet back up first."

She glanced down and then looked back at him with a frown. "Do you really care about that right now?"

What could he say? "Not if you don't."

Haven nodded as if satisfied with his answer. She took three deep breaths, inhaling through her nose, exhaling through her mouth, causing her nostrils to flair before her full lips pursed and parted. Logan waited, wondering what she would do next, wondering too if she was a little off her rocker.

Or if he was.

As strange as she was, he wanted her like he had never wanted a woman in his life. It was a little scary for someone else to have that much control over him, but maybe it was due to his injury. He started to step back because the pull of her was starting to unnerve him.

"Don't move! No matter what."

Logan froze immediately, not even finishing his half step back, nor did he question what *what* was. It took him a second to realize he couldn't move even if he tried.

Haven glanced at the nightlight before she held her hands out over either side of his head. When he realized she meant to touch his wound, Logan opened his mouth to protest, but she moved too fast. A flash of white light buckled his knees, and he felt himself sinking to the floor. Vaguely he realized she still had her hands covering his head until he gave in to what felt like a sleeping potion, before blacking out.

Chapter Two

"It worked!"

Haven couldn't move except for the shaking of her entire body. She finally removed her trembling hands from the sides of his head and settled back on top of the sheet. Tears of relief slid from her eyes and down her cheeks, landing with a plop on her breasts. She looked down, realizing she was naked.

Of course he had told her that. Several times. But it hadn't quite cleared the fog she'd been in since realizing the crystals might be calling to her. It was the last thing she'd expected. She'd feared magic had left her forever, had even forced herself to consider what her life would be like without it. The denial, followed by fear and anger, then finally devastating acceptance, was what had propelled her to this place. She had lost herself, her job as a nurse, and now any semblance of modesty, though she'd been honest with him about her mother's opinion about such things.

But Celestia Luna Cavanaugh was gone now, and had been since Haven and her sisters were fifteen years old. The ache that accompanied any thoughts of her mother, and the way in which they had lost her, was still as overwhelming now as it had ever been. But the hurtful memory and the agonizing lessons learned were why she and her sisters had always tried to hide their gifts. Not only hide them...resent them.

Now, with the renewal of hers, she knew Destiny's gift of intuition, Rayne's ability to talk with ghosts, and her own gift of healing were something to be treasured, not hated and feared.

And yet she would have to explain things to Logan without letting on her touch had done anything to help him. *If indeed it had.*

Haven wiggled while she pulled the sheet from under her and then pulled it around and over her body until her nudity was covered. She studied his face and even breathing, glad he was still unconscious. Since settling back she had let her legs fall open leaving herself *completely* exposed, and that would have been a little too much for even her to handle without blushing.

After binding the sheet at her breasts, she rolled onto her knees and leaned toward him. Just to make sure her heat was spent she poked a finger at his arm. Since there was no reaction for either of them, she very gently slid one hand under his head and used the other to turn it so she could see the wounded area.

Mixed feelings warred within her as she studied the long scorched scar. She cringed. His beautiful dark brown hair was thick and shined with health everywhere except for the broken-off area just around the wound. There, tinged with white, the barely-there strands were curled as tight as Christmas ribbon stripped with a sharp blade, and they were smoking a little, giving off an unpleasant scent.

Had her gift returned as before, there would have been little if any indication there had ever been an injury, and certainly not the burned flesh she was looking at now. On the other hand, at least it was cauterized. Which was something.

Haven blew out a breath of relief. Since the day she had tried to help the child with the failing kidney and realized she had lost all of her power, she had feared it would never return. Now she would have to figure out what was happening... Was this an indication her powers were striving to return, or was this bastardized version of healing all she now had?

It was a scary thought. She couldn't go around burning people.

Haven released his head, gently placing it back on the floor. She stood and turned to the mantel to look at the crystals. She would have to get with Rayne as soon as she could and ask her about their origins and what she knew about them. Was it possible they should be separated in order to do good not harm? Or were their powers only attuned to harm?

Crud! I should know these things!

Unfortunately, she hadn't paid much attention to the lessons her mother and aunts attempted to teach regarding the purpose of the different crystals. All she remembered was the one her mother had worn was a diamond she'd said was as old as time and that it magnified the powers of the one it chose to own. Her mother had been a true white witch, one capable of casting and conjuring. She'd been able to make things out of nothing, or change the chemical makeup of an object to make it something else altogether. She'd been able to defy the laws of gravity and take flight on any object she cast a spell upon. The things she had sworn to never do were force love between people where there was none, and revive someone who had died, as she believed both were works of evil. Free will was sacred, she'd said often, and to raise the dead was taboo. A soul once departed from its host body was already destined for another place, whether that place was good or bad.

The crystal that chose Aunt Lune Brille was as ancient, mined by cave dwellers according to her, and was a multicolored turquoise that assisted in the regeneration of all earthly things. If there was a devastating forest fire, like those who preceded her, Aunt Lune Brille went to the area affected and cast her regeneration spells and life began anew. Of course scientists had always thought it happened naturally.

Lune Brille Cavanaugh and the generations of Cavanaugh women and the female Kavanaugh ancestors before them had always been the keepers of the forest and the glade, as well as the oceans, rivers, springs, and streams. But over the centuries, the last one in particular, mankind had done such a stellar job of overpopulating and destroying the earth and sea that even Auntie's efforts were sometime futile.

And then there was Aunt Soleli. Haven had been

fascinated most with her crystal, and in truth, with the woman herself. The Citrine crystal allowed Aunt Soleli to travel through time and space metaphysically. Her spirit could leave the physical world and travel to abide with those from the time of ancient history to the time of history to come. She'd recorded her adventures in her own diaries then shared her stories of visits with the cave dwellers, with the Vikings, and with the horrible King Henry the Eighth, with Haven and her sisters, making them all laugh until their sides would be aching horribly.

Although she also had the ability to go forward in time, Aunt Soleli had only done so once, professing that to know the future was never a good thing. Haven had wanted to pick her brain about that, but Aunt Sole, as they sometimes called her, had refused to talk about it all those years ago and still refused to this day.

Now both aunts were off somewhere living their lives to the fullest. And it was nothing less than they deserved after raising Destiny, Rayne, and her following Celestia's murder.

Haven hung her head. It always came back to that. As wonderful as it would be to have her gift return in full, she had to always remember her very life could depend on her keeping it a secret. Her sisters' lives as well.

"Uhhh…"

Haven's attention was drawn back to the man who had so unexpectedly come into her life. She pasted a smile on her lips as he opened his chocolate brown eyes. He was still disoriented and just lay there looking around before finally seeming willing to test his ability to move. First his hands lifted from the floor to go immediately to his eyes and his wound. He lowered the hand covering his eyes then glanced over at her.

"What happened?"

This was good. *Very good.* If he didn't remember then she could make up any story she wanted. "I think you passed out. Are you feeling okay now?"

Logan struggled to a sitting position, and although she

wanted to help him, she was afraid to touch him while he was conscious, in case her hands decided to shoot fire again.

"I think I was struck by lightning."

Haven almost laughed when there was an immediate distant rumbling of thunder then a loud boom. Instead she just shrugged. "I don't think that's possible, or that it could come down the chimney without me seeing it."

Logan turned to look at the rock fireplace as if he'd forgotten its existence. Then he looked up and she held her breath, wondering if he had somehow made the connection that the crystals had something to do with his being on the floor. She breathed a sigh of relief when he looked back at her. "I may need help up. The mantle is too far for me to reach from here."

Haven looked down at her sheet, wondering if she could somehow cover her hands to help him, but before she could move he was already struggling to his feet. She rose too, and lifted the tail of the sheet to wrap it around the arm and hand closest to him.

Placing her well-wrapped hand under his arm, she led him to the couch, and then helped him settle there. "I'll get you some more water," she said, heading for the kitchenette.

"I still have a little."

Haven took the new bottle of water to him as he finished off the first one. "That's good. Here, drink more." Holding the bottle by its cap, she tilted the base of it toward him. He took it and held the empty one out to her. Trying not to be obvious, Haven took it by the lip and headed back toward the kitchen.

"I need to take a shower and get dressed and then I need to find my sister. She doesn't even know I'm in town."

Logan nodded. "Okay. I can take you. Maybe by the time you're ready and I've showered, I'll have my head on straight."

Haven felt bad for him. Here he had been nothing but

a gentleman and she had zapped him senseless. The aunts would have a field day with that, she was sure, but she felt bad all the same.

"I'm not sure you're going to be comfortable moving in on them though." He looked at her and grinned. "Young love, and all."

Well, crud! She hadn't planned on leaving the cabin for good, any time soon anyway, now that she knew about the crystals. What if they needed to be where they were? Crystals had their own agenda, and their own sense of home. If this cabin was their home—their powerbase—and she moved them to wherever it was Rayne had moved, they might refuse to awaken again, and then she might not know if they had chosen her, and why or why not that was.

She looked at him with speculation, wondering if he was as nice as he seemed. He was certainly attractive, and he had already proven not to be a letch, or worse, a creep, but would he even consider... "Would you mind if I stayed here? With you?"

Logan's brows shot up, but he said nothing for several seconds. "Um, I haven't actually checked, but I expect there's only one bedroom and one bed."

Haven nodded. "Yes. But I can sleep on the couch. Just for a little while. *If* you don't mind."

Logan turned back and leaned into the couch, laying his head back. "It won't be a problem. I don't plan to be in Mystic Waters for too long, anyway."

Haven exhaled, relieved all the way to her toes, yet she felt strangely disappointed. "So, where are you from?"

"Florida. I have a practice there. Doctor."

Haven moved back in front of him, delighted with her success. "Well, Doctor Hansen, I'm Nurse Cavanaugh. Small world, huh?"

Logan's lips lifted. "Yes. It sure is. So you're on vacation?"

Though the question caused her heart to skip a beat the smile stayed on her lips. "No. I quit. I was tired of living in LA. So I thought I would come to Mystic Waters and check out this area of the country while visiting my sister."

Although it wasn't the exact truth, Haven felt nary a qualm at telling the little white lie. She had been trained since childhood that misinformation was the only way to survive in the world they lived in. And the Cavanaugh women were nothing if not survivalists.

Their mother had forgotten that only once.

It only took once.

And that was the biggest lesson of all.

****

It wasn't that she had ever been lazy, but Haven hadn't been prepared to traipse through woods to go and visit her sister. For one thing she didn't own a pair of hiking boots and her three hundred and sixty-five dollar sandals were ruined. For another, there were mosquitoes the size of Volkswagens that thought new meat from California was their ambrosia.

"Not much further."

Haven kept herself from growling, *barely*. "That's good. Next time we take the car though."

Logan looked back at her with a smile. "City girl."

She wrinkled her nose at him. "Yeah, well, your tennis shoes look pretty expensive to me. I bet they haven't ever seen this side of a tennis court."

Logan laughed and turned back to lead the way. "You've got me. Hand, set, and match."

Haven grinned at his lame joke, swatted at another Volkswagen, and trudged on. She wouldn't complain anymore because she liked Doctor Logan Hansen, and she didn't want him to think she was a whiner. Besides, she was going to make him pay. Her bug bites would require a great deal of attention later, and she wasn't against playing doctor....

"Here we are."

Logan stopped and allowed her to catch up with him. She looked over the lovely log cabin with its stone chimney. The glossy finish spoke of hours and hours of handwork over and above the job of building the cabin itself. There was another larger building made of metal and an enclosed trailer that had *White's Handmade Furniture* in bold letters on its side.

An old truck sat next to a much newer car that had *rental* written all over it, figuratively speaking, of course. Figuring that was the car Rayne drove, excitement flooded Haven for a moment, but was followed by a case of nerves.

What if Rayne was angry with her for coming? They'd departed on good terms, but it was obvious to both Destiny and herself the day Rayne left California that she was setting out on a new course, a new life. What if she no longer wanted any part of her old life? What if she no longer wanted to bear the burdens of being a Cavanaugh? What if...she wanted nothing to do with the Cavanaugh name?

It had sort of been a pipe dream of all three sisters at one time or another to walk away and never look back. *Especially for me*, Haven remembered with regret. Until she lost her abilities. Now she wanted nothing more than to be what she was meant to be.

"Haven!"

Haven's head jerked up at Rayne's excited squeal, and they broke into a run toward each other. Identical faces slid cheek to cheek and they wrapped their arms around mirrored shoulders. Rayne finally leaned back and they smiled at each other before another tight hug ensued. When they pulled away again and turned, Logan and Garrison stood side by side looking at them with shocked expressions. The sisters laughed before Rayne walked over to Garrison and gave him a tight hug. "This is my sister, Haven. Haven, this is my fiancé, and *yes I know*," she said, looking pointedly at Haven, "I have a *lot* to tell you!"

I have a lot to tell you, too. Haven smiled, keeping her own thoughts for later. She looked at the man her sister had chosen, still stunned Rayne was actually engaged. Rarely did a Cavanaugh woman marry. The few times they had disaster quickly followed. She wondered if she should remind her sister of that, or wait and see what was what.

Rayne radiated so much happiness…so she would do nothing. For now.

Haven made her way to the couple and Garrison opened his arms. She grinned and hugged him as one would hug a brother. She knew whatever the consequences, if this man made her younger sister happy, she would do everything in her power to help them keep that happiness.

Thunder popped sharply and then reverberated with rumbling boom after rumbling boom in the distance. Startled, Haven looked to Rayne who was busily chatting with the two men. She didn't even glance Haven's way, or react to the noise.

Haven started to comment when another loud pop sounded, turning her attention in the direction of a swiftly developing storm. The wind whipped up quickly as the brewing clouds sped toward them. Swirling dried leaves lifted off the ground, and the tips of her long hair stirred with increasing speed. She continued to watch the sky, or what little of it she could see through the blowing branches of the thick canopy of those trees surrounding the cabin.

A shiver went through her even though the breeze was warm. Haven glanced at her sister again to see if Rayne felt it, too, but Rayne was still talking to the men. They *all* seemed oblivious… Not only unaware this was no normal rainstorm approaching, they acted like they were clueless anything at all was happening. Haven ignored them to focus on the startling surge of energy vibrating throughout her body. What was coming had power. Lots and lots of power… It made her skin tingle. It made her nipples tighten. It made her lower abdomen clench, and the palms of her hands heated enough that they glowed an orange-red with crackles of white sparks teasing the surface.

Haven looked from her firecracker hands to the sky directly over her head as lightning bolts blasted blinding light in triplicate, while the light to dark graying clouds changed to gunmetal blue. The wind increased, swirling now, throwing small sticks and dirt and other debris against her skin, but she didn't flinch. She stood entranced, allowing the magnetic lure to pull her hands skyward, away from her sides. She splayed her fingers, turned her palms up, and inhaled the power perfuming the air with the scent of hot metal. She heard her name called from afar but she ignored it, not wanting to release the power building within her.

She wanted to tell the others to run, to take cover, to allow her to absorb what was being sent to her. But Haven couldn't look at them now, couldn't hear them over the roar of wind and thunder as she waited for the lightning to find her. To fill her. To take her.

The hard shaking of her shoulders brought Haven back from the storm that engulfed her. Confused, she looked at her sister who was now standing directly before her. Rayne's gaze held a warning, her mouth set with grim purpose.

The wind died and the sky was back to a soft blue and was now silent. Confusion turned to understanding as she stared at her sister. Haven glanced at the two men who looked back, concern pulling their brows together making their expressions nearly identical. Rayne took her hand and led her to the men, making her realize she'd unknowingly moved away at some point.

"I'm sorry I shook you, but you had..." Rayne looked at her fiancé and shrugged her shoulders before turning back to Haven. "You acted like you were in a trance. You didn't answer when I called your name."

Haven didn't know what to say. Was she the only one who felt the wind? The only one who saw the churning clouds and angry lightning? If so, she couldn't let on.

"I think you may need an MRI. You did something similar earlier. I think you may be suffering from seizures. Have you ever been diagnosed with epilepsy? Or is there a history of it in your family?"

Concern sharpened in Rayne's gaze, but she said nothing. Haven shook her head and faced Logan, hoping he took her smile for embarrassment. "No. And no. I haven't and they haven't. I was just enjoying the breeze and was lost in thought. I'm fine, really." She turned to Rayne and put on her best smile. "But enough about me. Why in the world haven't we heard from you?"

The relief in Rayne's eyes told Haven she was glad for the change of subject.

"It is a long and complicated story. Why don't you come in and we'll catch up." She turned to Garrison. "Can I get you guys to run to the grocery store for me? I'll fire up the griddle, and we'll cook steaks and eggs, and maybe even those thick artery clogging pancakes you love so much."

"In other words," Garrison said, turning to Logan, "get lost and let us talk."

Logan smiled and nodded, though he still looked at Haven with concern. She just smiled at him before turning toward the cabin. She couldn't wait for Rayne to get the guys out so they could catch up. Rayne did have a lot to tell, but then so did she.

She took in the fine craftsmanship of the cabin knowing a lot more love had gone into its construction than the one she and Logan were sharing. But she didn't have time to catalog all the nice carvings and high gloss finishes. Instead she tried to act interested and not pace the floor while Rayne made out the list of things she wanted from the store.

Even in her agitated state Haven couldn't help but be amazed and horrified by some of the things on the list Rayne read off to Garrison. Since when did Rayne know the name brands of, or purchase things like, Martha White Corn Meal Mix, Bigg's Brothers Fatback Farms salt pork bacon, and Gilda's Gold Bond chunky-monkey ice cream?

Had Rayne completely lost her mind?

She glanced at her sister's midriff and couldn't see where she had put on even one pound, so maybe Rayne was trying to please Garrison but still following the healthy diet the Cavanaugh women were known for. Fatty foods? Processed sugary desserts? Seriously? And not one word about vegetables or even the multitude of fruits they liked to consume. But maybe she was just telling him about the weird stuff, assuming he could pick out apples and bananas without specific instruction.

Hopefully.

Finally the men were about to leave and now she could see what Logan meant about *young love, and all.* If Garrison had his tongue any further down Rayne's throat, he could extract her tonsils and dice them up. Pretending she was studying a picture that depicted the settling of the American mid-west, Haven kept her eyes averted, sending the guys a smile and a "Goodbye" as they were walking out the door.

Immediately Rayne was on her. "What the hell just happened?"

Haven pressed her lips together and raised her brows before responding, "I was just about to ask you the same thing."

Chapter Three

Haven and Rayne both started talking at the same time, then stopped, then started, then stopped, until Haven finally held up her hand. "Stop!"

Rayne nodded and kept her lips pressed together, but Haven didn't know where to begin. She glanced around the rustic but nicely put together room before turning back to Rayne, who still had her lips pressed together, but now had her head tilted and her brows lifted as high as they would go.

Haven laughed and shook her head. "I've missed the hell out of you!"

Rayne laughed with her and they hugged again before Haven stepped back. "I don't know where to start. Destiny and I have been sick with worry because we couldn't get you on the phone. And now I'm here and see that you are as fine as frog hair, and engaged to that gorgeous man. But *engaged*? Rayne, really? Do you know how dangerous that is?"

Rayne nodded. "I know but there is so much to tell and I am so crazy in love with that gorgeous man that I can't think beyond that, most of the time.

"So much has happened since I got here, well, before I got here actually but now I'm a part of it too. Garrison's nephew is missing. I've found the remains of two young men who were murdered, and the coroner thinks by the same person. So now we have a possible serial killer in the area. I lost my phone but was going to use Garrison's last night to call you two, then we got busy—" Rayne grinned. "Well, we just got kind of busy… So I was going to call you guys tonight, but now you're here."

Haven couldn't process the information fast enough to know if she should frown or smile, so she just nodded.

"Yeah, I get the *busy* part. And Logan told me about his brother's funeral, and Garrison's murdered brother and sister-in-law and their missing son. It's so scary. I hope you're safe here."

Rayne looked pointedly at Haven, her gaze sharp, her brows raised. "And now you, too. I'll ask Garrison if he minds if we let you use Gavin's room while you're here." She made a face and headed to the refrigerator.

"He's in the process of searching it right now, to look for any possible clues that might have been missed before regarding his missing nephew, but I can't imagine he would make me send you away."

Haven shook her head. "That isn't an issue. I'm staying in the cabin with Logan. We've already worked it out."

Rayne froze in the process of pulling milk and cheese from the refrigerator, and then she realized she had them in her hands and sat them on the counter between them. "What do you mean you've already worked it out? How long have you been here?"

Haven blew out a breath. It was time to catch Rayne up on a few things. "I got here yesterday evening. Worn out from the trip, as I'm sure you were if you remember. Stripped naked as I usually do when I want to take a nap. I hadn't meant to sleep the night away because I expected you to come home at some point, you know?"

Rayne nodded.

"But anyway, I climbed the stairs to hit the bed for a while. Well, I must have gone right to sleep because the next time I woke up it was as dark as a cave up in the loft. So now I'm figuring it must be middle of the night, right? And I hear this person downstairs moving around, and I know it isn't you because you move so quietly. So I grab your bat and I wait, hoping he will just leave and that will be the end of it.

"But *noooo*. This dude decides he is going to take a nap, too. Well, not on my watch, I thought, and not in my sister's cabin! What if you came home and he attacked you? You know? So I snuck down the stairs with the bat you so conveniently left lying beside the bed—by the way, doubt that would stop a serial killer but better than nothing I suppose—anyway, since I just thought the guy was a regular criminal and not a master criminal I began beating on his head."

Rayne's eyes were huge, her mouth hung open, making Haven laugh. "Oh, it gets better. The next thing I know this guy is wrestling the bat out of my hands. Then he stands up like he's going to do something to me, but I'm not about to go down without a fight and, okay, he *was* more than a little disoriented with the beating I gave him, so I tackled him back onto the couch."

Rayne held up her hands. "Before you go on, are you still naked?"

Haven nodded. "Yes, ma'am, as the day I was born." She ignored Rayne's groan. "So anyway, he starts yelling at me and I'm yelling at him, or the other way around, I don't remember, but anyway, he pins my wrists together behind my back and I'm jumping around trying to get loose until I finally realize he thinks I'm you, and he's freaking out because he's afraid your *fiancé* is going to knock out his teeth."

Rayne's eyes were huge as she shook her head. "Uh, uh."

"Uh-*huh!* Oh, yeah. So anyway, once I realize he knows you, and that you aren't supposed to be there, because he knew what I didn't, that you were here, I also realized he has this major hard-on and he's still yelling at me to be still." Haven frowned. "Or maybe I was already still at that point. Um… whatever.

"But anyway, he doesn't know yet that I'm me, and not you, so he is ready to hit the road, but I stopped him and told him I'm me and not you. So he stayed."

Rayne simply stared at her. Then she smiled. "So, are you still naked?"

Haven rolled her eyes. "No! I ran upstairs and pulled the sheet off the bed when he was trying to get himself together enough to get away, but I stopped him from leaving by telling him I'm me and not you. Haven't you been paying attention?"

Rayne leaned against the counter and folded her arms across her chest. "I'm trying. Go on. So how did you get from bashing in his skull to agreeing to live together?"

Haven exhaled then continued. "Well, let's see. That part gets a little dicey, because by this time I've noticed the crystals you left on the mantel—they were calling to me—at least I think they were, but not like Mom told us her diamond called to her, so I'm not totally sure about that, but anyway, I couldn't resist going to them even though I think I was in the middle of something else, and then I realize my hands are getting hot, *really* hot, and oh-*my*-gosh I was so excited because this is the first time since I'd lost my gift that I felt power in my hands again, and it made me wonder if I could fix his head—as I did hit him really hard—and he'd bled quite a bit.

"At this point I told him to be still so I could see if my healing had returned, but of course I didn't tell him why, just to do it, but I could tell from the look on his face he was starting to get a little wary of me so I grabbed his head really quickly and something strange happened. A flash of lightning pops over the top of me and hits where my hands are still holding his head then he falls to the floor almost in slow motion and then I realize I'd lost the sheet and was naked again, although he'd already told me that, but anyway, he's out cold and now his head is scorched."

Her eyes wide with horror, Rayne placed a hand on her forehead and stared at Haven from beneath it. "I barely even know where to begin… What do you mean *you lost your gift*? What about the crystals—you think they spoke to you? And what do you mean *his head is scorched*? Do you mean literally scorched as in burned? And would you *please* take a breath every once in a while?"

Haven shrugged. "Sorry. Okay… Anyway, it isn't a big deal. *Now* at least. I don't think he even noticed most of it. And yes, I think the crystals chose me, but I need to know more about them… I have no idea what it all means. I'm a little scared, but excited too. If you hadn't been so out of touch since coming here, you would already know that I lost my ability to heal, and I think Destiny is having trouble, too, but I don't know how much because she was getting all weirded out on me because, well, I *was* getting all weirded out on her first, so it makes sense that she was such a mess. But I'm not excusing her behavior towards me. I swear she is getting meaner all the time. I used to ignore it, but that was before LOP, you know, loss of powers. I actually left home without telling her I was going because I was afraid that she was going to have me committed if I stayed. She has no compassion, and since you abandoned us so completely I was afraid I would be locked up somewhere and no one would know or care."

Haven took a deep breath, frowning at Rayne. "What's wrong with you? You look pale."

Rayne closed her eyes and rubbed at her temples. "You're making my head hurt."

"Hi ladies! We got everything you asked for."

Haven and Rayne turned at the same time to see Logan and Garrison entering the door, both men's arms filled with paper bags. Since they looked like conquering heroes, Haven tried not to be annoyed they were already back. She moved forward with Rayne and took a bag and placed it on the countertop. She looked at the bags and then at the men who were awaiting further instructions. Then she noticed Rayne had that look she got when one of her migraines were brewing.

Haven turned to Logan and Garrison. "Looks like it will take too long to make all this. Why don't we all just go out to eat?"

Rayne laughed, but continued to rub her temples. "This isn't California."

Garrison stepped up to Rayne and ever so gently pulled her against him. "Are you okay? You look a little pale."

****

As it turned out, Mystic Waters was also capable of

providing morning fare, though Haven was certain she would die of a bellyache later. But it was worth it. She had never had three-inch tall biscuits slathered in homemade butter and homemade strawberry preserves, or bacon as thick as the bark of a tree. And the eggs, which came from real chickens Rayne told her, were richer in taste and color than any she had ever had before.

Of course she had asked for fresh fruits, a variety of nuts, granola, and sprouts when ordering, but the woman had asked her what a sprout was, and said they had peanuts but she would have to shell them before eating, and the closest thing she had to granola was Quaker Instant Oatmeal with dehydrated apples in it to add flavor. As far as fresh fruit, the still green bananas and the formerly frozen half-ripe strawberries left something to be desired.

So she had looked from her less than appetizing plate to Rayne's, and decided *while in Rome....*

And Rome hadn't been a disappointment at all. But she had no idea how Rayne ate this way all the time and hadn't gained embarrassing amounts of weight. She would have to have a word with her about it later, when they could find more time alone again.

Which needed to happen soon. There was still so much to talk about, and so much to discover, and now that she had some degree, however much it was, of her powers back, she needed Rayne's help in getting it all straight.

And they needed to call Destiny....

Haven took another bite of the crispy bacon bark and realized she was experiencing guilt. Since it wasn't something that happened often, she knew she needed to contact her sister right away...or at least soon.

Haven glanced over at Logan and caught him grinning at her, then at her nearly cleaned plate. Realizing she had plowed through her meal with little grace or much contribution to the conversation that had gone on between her sister and the two men, she grinned back. The speculative interest in his gaze warmed her, and Haven slowly placed her fork on her plate as she held the contact.

The man was a fine work of art. His thick, nearly black hair shined with health and was shaped to fit his strong angular features. His large chocolate brown eyes looked into a person, not just at them, and were nearly always lit with amusement. She'd learned from their first encounter just how hard his long lean body was....

Haven sighed. Everything about him was as appetizing as the meal she'd just consumed, and though she wasn't usually struck dumb by such things, she had to admit, for the first time in her life, she wanted to throw caution to the wind and....

Realizing all conversation had ceased, Haven broke eye contact with Logan, wondering if her thoughts were apparent to everyone sitting at the table. Trying to ignore the heat filling her cheeks she smiled and turned to her future brother-in-law.

"Would you mind if I stole Rayne for a couple of hours?"

With a slight grin and twinkling eyes, Garrison shook his head.

"I can't, Sis. Not this morning. Garrison and I need to look into some things about his nephew."

"I can handle it by myself," Garrison said, taking her hand into his own. "It's fine."

Rayne shook her head. "No. I need to go too. It's important to me."

Rayne looked at Haven in that way they always looked to one or the other when they were trying to convey a private message while in public. Haven made herself smile as if it were no big deal, wishing she knew what had Rayne so desperate to go with Garrison when she was so desperate for some sisterly advice. "So, where are you guys off to, if you don't mind my asking?"

Rayne relaxed back into her seat. "There was a scrap of clothing that I found some time ago out in the woods. At the time we weren't sure what to make of it, and really still don't, but knowing now about the other boys...." Rayne sent Garrison a concerned look before turning back to

Haven. "We think we should go back to where I found it and look some more. It's close to where Garrison's cousin was found, and that could be significant.

"We were going to head there this morning, but then I saw you and completely forgot about everything else." She glanced at Garrison again, then held his gaze lovingly and mouthed the words, *"I'm sorry."*

He lifted the hand he was holding and kissed her knuckles, allowing his lips to linger several seconds before kissing them again. Haven watched the interplay and eye contact they held until she had to look away. It was almost as intimate as watching two people making love. Gratitude toward Logan for allowing her to share his cabin grew so she turned to him, and smiled. When he grinned in response, she looked back at her sister again.

She'd never see Rayne look at a man with her heart in her eyes. Not even that jerk she'd thought herself in love with back in LA. She'd dodged a bullet when Jamison Frey dumped her following the exposure of her gift on that horrible day, and Haven was thankful and scared for her sister in equal measure. Rayne deserved happiness… Haven hoped the family curse didn't take it from her.

Realizing everyone was looking at her now, Haven nodded. "No problem. Maybe we could get together later?"

Rayne's smile was full of curiosity. "Absolutely. We have so much to catch up on."

Within minutes they were parting company. Since Rayne had loaned them her little rental car to come into town, rather than all four of them trying to squeeze into Garrison's truck or the small car together, Haven settled into the passenger seat and waited for Logan to round the car. She noticed several other couples were taking the same positions in their vehicles and decided she would drive next time, if there was a next time. After all, she didn't need a man to drive her anywhere, though she had to admit the courtesies of the men in this town seemed to go above and beyond. Logan had opened and held her door, then shut it once she was inside the car. It was obvious he'd done so without giving it a thought.

"Are you angry?"

Haven turned to Logan as he settled into his seat and grasped his seat belt. "No, why?"

Logan shrugged. "You just look like you're mad about something."

Haven smiled to herself. *What the hell...* "I just noticed that all the women are passengers in this town."

Logan looked from her out the windshield, nodded, and looked at her again. "I see." He grinned at her and unbuckled his seatbelt. "You want the wheel?"

Haven laughed. "No. But thanks for offering. Just next time I drive."

"No problem. I've never minded a beautiful woman chauffeuring me around."

Haven settled back in her seat and pretended to act more nonchalant than she actually felt then wondered why she felt anything. Men told her she was beautiful all the time. It meant nothing... "So, you think I'm pretty?"

Logan put the car in reverse but kept his foot on the break as he looked from the rearview mirror to her. "I think you are by far the most gorgeous woman that I've ever seen completely naked."

Though she usually would have laughed off such a remark and given him back Cheshire cat smile for Cheshire cat smile, heat now filled her cheeks. Haven swallowed and kept her gaze forward though she could have cared less about what was on the other side of the windshield. For some reason she was embarrassed, which rarely happened. "About that... I wasn't *exactly* myself."

"Ah...so I can forget this fantasy I have of you walking around our cabin naked all the time?"

Haven looked at him, taking in the slightly tilted teasing smile and gleam in his eyes. She shook her head, grinning. "Yeah, you might want to forget that."

"Well, darn." His grin deepened before he returned his attention to the rear view mirror again.

Haven shook her head at them both and relaxed into

the seat, *sort of.* The truth was Logan made her too antsy to relax completely…in a way no man ever had. He was such a cool guy. Relaxed. Easy going. Drop your heart to your knees gorgeous. And funny. It was the funny she liked most of all, as she was *normally* a happy person, and she loved happy people. In spite of everything going on around them his sense of humor remained intact. She'd witnessed it in the exchanges between him and Garrison and Rayne all through breakfast, and she knew firsthand he enjoyed teasing her.

Though everyone had tried to steer clear of the reason Logan was in town, that *reason* always hovered over those gathered. She'd seen the smiles and heard the laughter of both her sister, and the two men, but the smiles sometimes quivered and the laughter held an edge. When the conversation lagged, eyes became distant and held sorrow. When that happened Logan would find something else to talk about, and Garrison and Rayne would become engaged in conversation again.

Haven was amazed by Logan's strength and compassion even though he too was facing loss. His sharp mind and large hands healed damaged hearts, something she understood and admired, but she was captivated by *his* heart, his compassion, and his ability to touch her so deeply without touching her at all.

Haven secretly slid a glance Logan's way, wondering how he could handle the death of his much younger brother so well, even though she'd learned how little they'd known each other. Maybe he was in denial. Maybe he was deflecting. But she just couldn't fathom that he didn't care.

Not all families are like ours….

Haven wasn't certain where the thought came from, but she allowed herself to acknowledge the truth of it. Logan talked about anything and everything *except* his family. There is pain there, she realized. The kind that couldn't be mended as easily as a broken bone. She closed her eyes and turned toward the door, afraid to let him see how badly she hurt for him. Knowing the ache in her heart couldn't compare to the ache in his, she forced her sorrow away. It was the last thing he'd want from her.

She glanced at him again and couldn't help but smile. The man took caution to a whole new level, or maybe it was courtesy. As several other customers had left the diner both in front of them and behind them, the parking lot was filled with several cars attempting to make an exodus from the lot, and it looked like Logan was going to let everyone else go first. Since he was busily looking around to make sure the coast was clear before backing out of their spot, she took the opportunity to study his profile. Whether she'd stared for too long, or he'd felt her gaze, she couldn't help but grin when he suddenly turned her way.

"When a woman looks at a man the way you're looking at me, it gives him ideas."

Caught red-handed, Haven faked a yawn and reached down beside her seat hoping to find a lever to allow her to lay the seat back slightly. The fake yawn sparked a real one and with it the realization that, though it was still morning, it felt as if she'd been up for days.

After the chaotic early morning wakeup call...the blast of power from the crystals...the whole storm thing, which she had no clue if real or imagined, topped off by the high carbohydrate breakfast that had stuffed her stomach as fully as her thoughts were filled with the man at her side...Haven decided her sudden need to close her eyes was completely understandable.

She heard Logan's chuckle as she yawned again then closed her eyes as the seat gave and took her back to a more comfortable position. Knowing the items she'd mentally listed were strength draining on their own, combined they were taking a major toll on her ability to stay awake. But...not so major a toll that she could push away speculation about his fine doctor's hands rubbing away the tension he was unknowingly creating.

She breathed deeply, embracing the fringes of slumber, willing to be lured to the void of unconsciousness. Until she felt his hand on her cheek. Felt it glide over the curve of her ear before skimming feather-like down her neck. Her heartbeat increased, her chest rose and fell as his touch warmed the rise of a breast. She wanted to turn to him, to grasp his hand and make it cover her breast completely.

Haven's eyelids popped open and she realized he wasn't touching her at all. She slid him another secret look. He wasn't even looking at her. Nearly breathless, her heart beating wildly, she swallowed and closed her eyes again, not wanting him to look over and see the shape she was in. Falling into a dream so quickly had never happened to her before. She wanted to blame it on fatigue, or the meal, or even on the fact that she was conflicted about her strong attraction to him. But she had to face the truth. For the first time in her life, her hands weren't the only parts of her flashing fire.

What would he say if I propositioned him? The thought took her breath at first, but as she let it marinade it grew legs and she found herself justifying the possibilities. She *was* on vacation, *sort of,* and she *was* too old to still be a virgin although it had hardly bothered her before. Mostly she *really* liked him more than she had ever liked any man of short or long acquaintance. And damned if she hadn't always wondered… "You know, maybe I *will* show you mine again, if you show me yours."

The car jerked sharply. Haven smiled, though she couldn't make herself look at him, so she kept her eyes closed.

"*What?*"

Knowing now was the time to take it back and laugh it off as if she were joking, Haven took several slow even breaths and gathered enough courage to repeat herself. She was *not* taking it back.

"Princess, if you are talking in your sleep I think I'll kill myself."

Haven opened her eyes, looked at the amused yet sharp look of his, then laughed. "I'm tired, but I'm wide awake…*now.*"

"Well then," was all he said, though Haven could tell

by the pressure pushing her head back into the headrest that the car had gotten a lot faster.

Chapter Four

Martha Thompson found herself looking over the layout of the kitchen table and realigning Burt's utensils for the fourth time as she waited for him to get home. He was late, *again*, and it was starting to irritate her to no end.

She'd already freshened up her lipstick, checked to make sure every eyebrow was in place, and scanned her overall appearance in the full-length mirror three times to make sure there were no creases or wrinkles marring the lines of her dress.

Playing the submissive wife to his demands for years now had become a habit she'd gotten a lot of pleasure out of, mostly. But ever since he went just a little too far a few weeks back he'd barely attempted touching her, and he'd started coming home later and later and never once bothered to call.

That just would not do.

She knew it was partly her own fault for threatening him with her fictitious sister, but she had made those threats before, and after a short break of better behavior, he always went back to beating and sodomizing her when she made him mad on purpose.

But not this time, which meant she would have to shake things up a little. Maybe even break something he loved like one of those damned elk-head mugs. Or maybe she would taunt him about his weight, or about the size of his dick, though she appreciated that the size of his penis was not an issue for her. If anything it helped that it wasn't all that big, otherwise she might not have survived or even enjoyed his love of anal assault.

Martha looked down at the dress he'd picked out for her that morning and shook her head at the 1950s style that matched every other dress he laid out for her day after day.

She glanced at the rooster kitchen clock and then at the dried-out roast sitting in the center of the wooden dining table. Fury reared its ugly head, but Martha forced herself to quickly close it down. She never allowed herself to have feelings of anger for the mate she had so carefully chosen. *Not after what happened before.* But that didn't mean Burt could continue to ignore her without any consequences. She had willingly bent to his will for all these years and didn't deserve to be treated in such a way.

Grinning with sudden inspiration, Martha unbuttoned the dress and then laughed as it fell to the floor to pool at her low-heeled shoes. She stepped from the now crinkled material and kicked it out of her way. Pretending she didn't notice the surge of satisfaction invigorating her, she removed her bra and panties and the fake pearls he loved to see her in before flinging them to the corner where the dress had landed.

Turning her attention back to the offending table she grabbed the cookware holding what was once a juicy roast, perfectly cooked potatoes, and tender baby carrots and dropped it, crock-ware and all, into the garbage can. She did the same with the containers holding the green beans and the corn on the cob. It didn't matter that she had spent the better part of the day planning and preparing the meal. Nothing mattered but making Burt mad enough to punish her.

Martha took in the neatly displayed dishes, the properly aligned silverware, the faux crystal water glasses, and the napkins she had embroidered years before to please him. She dragged the thirteen-gallon garbage can to the side of the table and raked it all in, taking pleasure in the sounds of glass hitting glass.

Nearly hysterical with excitement she ran to her bedroom and opened the closet door. In all the years since she'd been with Burt she'd never once touched the box she had hidden at the back of the closet on the day she married Burt and moved into his house. For almost eight years her treasures stayed buried in her closet, forced into darkness, denied. Shaking now, Martha quickly grabbed the smaller boxes and set them out of the way. When she turned back, tears smarted her eyes. There, looking like a long lost friend, was the large round hatbox that held her heart. She lifted it gingerly, held it close, and carried it to the bed.

Martha's heart shuddered as she slowly pulled the ends of the thick ribbon until the large bow collapsed. She gathered the long length of silky material and gently placed it on her comforter then slowly ran her hand over the surface of the lid before hooking her fingertips at the dropped edge and lifted it, placing it to the side.

Her breath lodged in her lungs as she peeled back the tissue paper and saw the black patent leather bra adorned with spiked brass studs. She reached out and touched it lovingly and wondered how she had gone these many years without its comfort. She lifted it to her face, inhaling the scent, before reverently setting it aside.

Next she lifted out the matching crotchless pants and held the waistband so that the folds fell open. As much as she wanted to hang them to let the creases smooth out, she knew that once she pulled them on the skin tightness would render the folds barely noticeable. She gently laid them aside, also, before pulling out the spiked six inch heeled shoes she was no longer sure she could stand in, but she was dying to find out.

And finally, there at the bottom, were the toys that had always filled her life with joy. She lifted them out one at a time, caressing the leather bullwhip before grasping the solid braided handle. Martha flung her arm out quickly so the long tail snapped, making the cracking sound that had always heightened her feelings of power.

The horsewhip followed, its solid length stinging her calf when she held it down to her side and hit her leg. The spiked neck collar, shackles, and chains were examined and set aside as were the faux fur covered handcuffs.

She looked at the last item in the box for several moments before looking away, wondering why she had never disposed of the Taser. But she *knew*. It was kept as an eternal reminder of why she lived the life she had now. Why she could never go back to being a Domme, even though she would love to see the expression on Burt's face should she punished him for a change. She leaned across the bed, placing the stun gun as far from the beloved items as she could.

With tears filling her eyes she slowly, gently, reverently, repacked the toys, the pants, the heels, and finally, after one last caress, the studded bra. The tissue paper was once again folded over her treasures and she choked on a sob, knowing it would be a long time, if ever, before she'd pull them out again.

She didn't deserve to look at them. To touch them. To caress them.

She'd lost that privilege.

With sharp angry movements Martha replaced the lid and quickly tied the bow, then guiltily untied it so she could make the ribbon as pretty as it originally was. Her treasures deserved that. None of this was their fault. It was bad enough she'd condemned them to darkness and solitude. If nothing else, they deserved a pretty prison.

Disheartened she returned the box to the back of her closet and replaced all the items that had hidden the hatbox for so long before turning back to smooth the bedding. She released a shaky breath as she stared at the remaining item. Afraid it might bite her, more than it already had, Martha rounded the bed to retrieve the stun gun.

The weight of it was familiar, as if eight years hadn't passed since she last held it in her hand. She swallowed a sob as memories washed over her. The heat. The excitement. The glory. And then the tragedy. The agony...and finally, the fear.

Martha looked around her tidy room uncertain what to do with it, wishing she could dispose of it, but knowing it was her burden to bear. She lifted it close to her face, really examining it for the first time since that horrible day she'd buried it beneath her treasures. It still looked brand new, but that was no surprise. She had only just bought it on the way home to the little house they'd shared, so excited they had a new threatening toy....

"No!"

Martha marched to her dresser and shoved the Taser into the back of her top drawer then slammed it shut. She hurried to the kitchen, furious with herself for unlocking those memories. She quickly pulled her dress back on, not giving a damn that it was horribly wrinkled. She kicked the bra and panties further into the corner before dragging the garbage can back to the table's side.

Glasses, dishes, and utensils were hauled out of the trash and wiped off or cleaned as best she could and then placed back on the table with little regard for the tiny new chips here and there. The roast, potatoes, and carrots were still intact for the most part, so she lifted the deep crock, wiped at the outer edges of the dish and returned it too. The corn on the cob was quickly placed under hot water and put on a clean plate as the deep glass covered dish that had held it was badly broken. The beans weren't salvageable so she left them in the trash.

Martha reveled in the knowledge that nothing was where it should have been and that the food now looked a mess. She glanced at the rooster clock and growled, further infuriated Burt had caused her to do what she had done. If he'd been home on time or only slightly late, she would have never gone into her room and opened the door to the past. Her hard work wouldn't look like she'd been dumpster diving for their dinner.

Sure, she still would have wanted to be punished, but nothing like she did now. Now, she wanted him to tear her up. To beat her senseless. To nearly, *but not quite* kill her, only because then she couldn't be punished anymore.

It was nothing less than she deserved.

Finally, she heard the sounds of the squad car pulling up next to the house and she looked at the table once more. This mess wasn't *her* fault and she absolutely would not let him get away with ruining her night without getting something out of it!

Martha quickly unbuttoned and dropped her dress again before shoving everything on the table over to one side. She climbed up on it slowly, knowing Burt's fat ass would take forever to get out of the squad car and get into the house.

Shaking with renewed excitement, and yes, stimulating fear, she arranged herself in the table's center with her feet pointed toward the front door. She leaned back on her elbows and spread her legs wide before licking the fingers of her right hand to reach down and rub herself.

With each tick of the rooster's second hand, Martha's anxiety mounted and with it excitement of what was to come. She moaned with both the pleasure of her own masterful touch and the fantasy of Burt's reaction. *He* might be late or alter plans, but when he came home he expected dinner on a table set exactly as he'd taught her all those years ago. Otherwise....

Oh, thank goodness for the otherwise!

The table was set her way this time, and if he didn't like it... *Perfect!* It meant he'd bend to *her will,* though he would believe just the opposite was true.

Anticipation along with gratification grew as Martha slid a finger deep into her womanly folds. She cried out at her body's instant reaction. The sharp vibrations were a familiar precursor to climax but she was certain her instant arousal was more from the coming threat, than her stimulation.

Martha continued to rub herself, scraping her manicured nails against her vaginal wall just to feel the pain. She knew she was going to have to stop soon. Knew too, to stroke her clit once would put her over the edge. But it was too soon. It would ruin everything if she finished before Burt dragged his ass in the house.

She pulled her hand away and leaned back on both elbows, determined to keep control. But she'd done too much already and had to clench her lower abdomen and vaginal muscles against the orgasm threatening to overtake her.

Shaking in earnest at the threat of orgasmic euphoria, she ground her teeth together and attempted to smile as she heard the lock turning. It took everything she had to hold that smile as Burt pushed the door open.

Martha reveled in his reaction when he froze as soon as he saw her. Burt's eyes widened with shock and his mouth fell into a large O as his triple chin pooled over the top of his uniform's collar. And finally, what she'd been longing for. His puffy cheeks flashed red with fury, his eyes sharpened to a glare, and he dropped everything in his hands and reached to unbuckle his belt. That was all it took to ignite the orgasms that slashed through her like a double-edged sword.

Chapter Five

Rayne kept her eyes straight ahead, as she and Garrison traipsed through the woods. They had returned to his cabin briefly to retrieve the tiny scrap of material that had obviously been torn from a flannel shirt Garrison believed belonged to his nephew, before heading in the direction of the cabin now occupied by her sister and Garrison's closest childhood friend.

She still could barely wrap her mind around all that, but had no time now to try to decipher the crazy story Haven told her. All her attention and energy had to remain focused on finding Gavin.

Garrison's nephew had been missing for months now, and the only ghost who'd contacted her since the move to Mystic Waters was the Mashpee Wampanaog Native American named Qaqeemasq. He hadn't led her to Gavin's body, so she still held hope the seventeen-year-old was alive.

Rayne didn't bother looking around to see if Qaqeemasq was near. If he was and had anything to relay to her he would make himself known, just as he had the first time they'd met and he led her to the tree where the scrap of material was found, and then later, to the brutally dismembered remains of both Garrison's cousin, Anthony, and Logan's younger brother, Donny.

Since her arrival in the community known as Mystic Waters, where she'd taken up residence on Mystic Mountain itself, Qaqeemasq had turned into a friend *of sorts*. He'd definitely become a *confidant,* as he was the only one who knew she had the ability to speak to Spirit. But he'd also made himself something of a little terror once when he'd had the audacity to take possession of her body and mind to prove a point. She had made it clear to him *that* was never to happen again. He'd done it for a purpose. To remind her of both of their precarious histories, and the reason for the distrust he felt for her at first, as well as reminding her of the need for secrecy regarding her gifts. Which were all good reasons, but unacceptable and downright creepy all the same.

"Is this it?"

Rayne stopped as Garrison did and looked around, certain they were in the right place. "Yes. I found the scrap here," she said, pointing at the tree. "But we both looked around and found nothing already, where do you want to look now?"

Garrison's head lowered and she went to him thinking emotions had taken hold again, but then she realized he was looking at the ground. Sickened that he was ready to start searching for a body rather than looking for his living nephew, she wrapped her arms around him, pinning his arms down to his sides. "You can't give up."

Garrison looked up at her then, his eyes filled with resignation. "It's been too long. And now we know...." He bit his bottom lip and inhaled deeply through his nose. "Now we know that the likelihood is that he is another body to be found."

Rayne shook her head and pulled back enough to punch him in the arm with her fist. "Don't you dare give up hope! You have searched day and night for months for this child and we are not done searching yet! What if he is alive and is just waiting for you? What then?"

She burst into tears and Garrison pulled her into his arms, lowering his head to her shoulder. He just held her until she was gasping for breath. She looked up at him through tear-filled eyes, and saw that his were as wet. "I'm sorry. I know this is killing you. I shouldn't have yelled, but I can't let you believe he's dead. Not yet. Not until there is proof."

Garrison nodded. "You're right. I know you are.... It's just that Mom and Dad are losing hope. The rest of the family, too. When we gathered to observe his birthday, I found them out on the patio. Mom was crying and Dad was trying to reassure her, but I could hear the doubt in his voice. They think he's gone."

Rayne leaned back into him, wanting so badly to admit she could contact the other side and she had called for Gavin's spirit to come to her, and because he hadn't, she still held hope. Only she couldn't do it. Not only because she couldn't stand the thought of him looking at her like she was crazy, but also because now that Haven was in Mystic Waters, any revelations about herself could catch Haven in the crossfire that might follow.

Protecting themselves was what Cavanaugh women did, no matter what.

The vision of her dear mother, pale and lovely in the glass-topped casket Aunt Soleli and Aunt Lune Brille had chosen for her, was a never-ending reminder of the consequences of depending on love to overrule mistrust and hatred of the mystical.

Rayne lifted her hands to pull his head down to hers. Their lips met gently in comfort. After a moment Garrison raised his head and whispered in her ear, "There's a backpacker out there."

Rayne turned and saw the diminutive form heading even further away from them. Whoever it was carried such a large backpack that it nearly swallowed the hiker whole. Even from such a distance, she could make out the Red Cross symbol with its white square background. Rayne turned back to Garrison with a gentle smile. "See? People haven't given up yet."

Garrison nodded, gratitude shining from his eyes. "And if others haven't, then neither can I."

Rayne smiled at him and kissed his nose, her faith in humanity renewed.

****

Gavin felt sick to his stomach and had ever since his captor's last visit. Some days he wondered if maybe she was trying to poison him, then others he feared that a poisonous spider might have bitten him in his sleep. Or crawled inside his nose or mouth.

So he'd stopped sleeping, or slept so little that he was always weak and nauseated. And he was getting thinner, but not in the way he had hoped when he first thought about getting himself in shape again. He could lie flat on his back and not even have to suck in his stomach to know his belly was mere inches from the cot at his back.

Sometimes he tasted blood in his mouth and feared his gums were decaying and his teeth rotting. A tear formed and then ran down the side of his face only stopping when it was captured in the overlong dirty hair that he'd always kept neatly trimmed and clean.

The sounds indicating he was once again being visited didn't bring him the rush of excitement it once had. At the beginning of his ordeal, he'd reacted to the visits with fear, then anger, and finally resignation. Now he felt nothing. He knew his only chance of survival was to do what he was supposed to do, which meant he had to dance to her steps, but survival didn't taste so good anymore.

Not caring, Gavin didn't sit up like he was supposed to once the woman was present and shining the light into his eyes. He didn't even bother to look away because he knew that it might be the last time he saw light this side of Heaven.

"You aren't up."

Gavin hesitated a moment longer before attempting to pull himself up. As much as he wanted to just give up and die the painful grinding of his stomach as his body instinctively fought to live wouldn't allow it. But he was so weak he couldn't do more than roll over to slide off the cot. He landed on the ground on his knees, his face planted into the cot. The indignity was the last straw and Gavin began to cry. Not silent tears of hurt and misery, but the anguished tears of the damned.

"Stop that!"

Gavin tried to stop but it took several minutes before he could attempt to speak through the jarring shudders wracking his chest and stifling his breath.

"I'm sick. I'm *really* sick."

His captor was silent for a while, continuing to shine the light at his back. Finally she moved toward him cautiously, her footsteps barely audible, but audible just the same. He waited, wishing he had thought to act sick earlier when he still had enough strength to fight her, but he hadn't known then that she was a woman, and in reality it made no difference if she still carried whatever it was that she'd beaten him with before. She had all the advantages, always had.

"I'm going to touch you, but if you try anything, or if this is a trick, you'll wish you were dead by the time I get through with you."

If laughing were possible Gavin would, but he didn't even remember how. "I'm sick," was all he could say, almost hoping she would just cut his throat and be done with it.

Gavin squinted as light radiated from around the back of his head, allowing him, for the first time, to see stone and dirt walls in the distance. His heart thudded painfully inside an already aching body as he realized his home was nothing more than a large cavern within a cave. It made so much sense; the dampness that never abated, the chill he could never overcome, the utter darkness that never gave way until the kidnapper brought in her small ray of light.

Gavin flinched when he felt the cold hand touch his forehead, as much because it had been so long since he'd felt a human's touch, as because her fingers were so cold on his hot flesh. He remained as still as he could though he feared he might fall apart again. The evil woman who held him captive was doing the same thing his own mother had done with love anytime she thought he might be ill.

"You're burning up."

Again Gavin wished he knew how to laugh, and that he had the nerve to say, *duh!* But since both of those weren't options, he decided to try something else. "Will you take care of me?"

The hand slid away but he could tell she hadn't moved,

and hoped his childlike plea appealed to whatever womanhood she possessed.

"I have to trust that you won't turn on me."

Refusing to sag in relief, or let her see any reaction at all, Gavin nodded. "I promise. I'll do whatever you say."

He flinched again when the hand returned to stroke his dirty head. But he remained where he was, how he was, hopeful he had found a way out, after all.

Gavin made himself stay very still as she continued to stroke his head, although everything inside him cringed at her touch. He listened then agreed to her terms, which basically meant he followed her instructions and didn't balk at anything she told him to do. Knowing he had no choice but to bend to whatever whim she had, terrified him, but the truth was that there was little else he could do and survive.

"Very well. Put your hands behind your back."

Lifting the arm with the metal bracket weighed down with the chain took almost more strength than he had, but Gavin forced himself to do as he was told then nearly cried out when she locked something around both wrists. As he was about to protest he felt the heavier shackle and chain fall off to hit his calves, and though painful, his relief was such that he nearly fell face first into the cot. Her hand was on his head again, pulling his hair until his head was upright. He didn't cry out, not even when she placed a cloth over his eyes.

Gavin grunted against the pain in his shoulder as she pulled him to his feet. He allowed her to lead him and he knew exactly when they reached what was the length of the chain he'd been shackled to for so long. From that point on his steps were less sure, and pain shot up his ankle once when he stepped down and his foot landed on uneven ground.

He nearly stopped from fear and confusion when something swept all over his head, shoulders, and arms, but she pulled him forward and he kept going without comment, more afraid of her than whatever it was he'd just passed through.

Gavin knew the second they'd passed from the cave out into the open. The chilled air was replaced with warmth, the dank smells with the fresh scent of earth and pine, and the hard surface of the cave floor was now soft and spongy; he was certain it was moss.

Excitement gave way to exhaustion and pain as the soles of his bare feet traipsed over what felt like tiny broken sticks and sharp rock. He stubbed his toes a couple of times, but held the pain inside, not daring to cry out. He continued forward blindly for what seemed like hours before she stopped him. Thankful, as his strength was nearly spent, he waited to see what came next.

Gavin's nerves got the best of him as minutes passed without any movement or words from her. Finally she pulled him forward and his sore feet felt the difference in the surface below him. Softer ground changed to the sharp pebble sized rocks, which gave way to hot concrete or blacktop. He winced with each step until, blessedly, they stopped again. A dull popping sound followed by a squeaking sound registered before she finally spoke.

"You've done well. We're at my car now. You're riding in the trunk."

Gavin forced himself to remain calm at the thought of being enclosed in a small area, but he was grateful he'd finally be off his aching feet. He moved forward when pulled and allowed her to guide him over the lip of the trunk and onto the hard surface within. By the time the process was done, he felt bruised and had skin burns on his left arm from sliding over the rough material lining the small compartment, but he sighed in relief that he could finally lie down, even if it was curled up so his knees touched his nose.

Tired to the bone, Gavin wished sleep would overtake him, but he was too hot and too uncomfortable to give in and let go. The ride seemed to take forever, making Gavin wonder if she drove in circles in an effort to disorient him should he attempt to identify where he was being taken.

But she needn't have bothered. He had no idea where he'd been, and he was so sick to his stomach that his mind couldn't engage in anything so complicated.

Having to breathe his own stale air in such confined quarters while lying on his side nearly rolled into a ball as the car swerved one way then the other, and with what felt like a raging fever heating up the interior of the trunk, bile rose to choke him. Gavin swallowed it back down, afraid to anger her by releasing it and soiling her car.

Just as he was about to give up hope that she would ever stop, he felt a bump that made him think of the change from a road to the lip of a driveway. He was thrown into something when the car stopped abruptly, adding additional pain to his overall body, but mostly at the top of his head.

Gavin waited for what seemed like hours for her to open the trunk. When she finally did the rush of cooler air told him it must be evening, and he realized then that was probably her purpose in driving for so long. She hadn't wanted anyone to see her take him from the back of her car.

Which meant that there could be other homes close.

Gavin knew he had to control his excitement. Knew he could never let her see any signs of strength or that even as sick as he felt, he was able to process information. Had she suspected what he was thinking, he was afraid she would just go on and kill him or take him back to the hellhole where he'd spent what now seemed his entire lifetime. He knew he would choose death before going back.

No question.

Getting his legs pulled until they hung over the lip of the trunk sent sharp needle-like pains from his ankles to his thighs. Gavin bit his lip to keep from crying out, but he couldn't help the grunt-sounds that escaped. She told him to shut up, sit up, and that he'd keep quiet if he knew what was good for him.

Landing on the hard rough surface sent another wave

of pain throughout his body, but Gavin huffed his way through it rather than making a sound. The woman led him away from the car on such a solid surface he knew it had to be a concrete sidewalk but that was all he could process with every nerve ending in his body screaming for help. Before long she told him he had to lift his foot to walk up three short steps and then she made him wait as keys jingled followed by the sound of a door opening. For the first time in so long air conditioning hit his overheated body, taking what was left of his strength. She half led, half dragged him across cool flooring, huffing and complaining the entire time about not being able to bathe him before laying him on her clean sheets.

Gavin nearly melted on the spot at the thought of a real bed and clean sheets, but he forced himself to think of what was really important. Like how she had to be shorter than him because he could feel her shoulder pressing against his arm, almost dead center between his elbow and the deltoid muscles of his shoulder, while she tried to hold him up. The woodsy smell of her perfume, which she must have sprayed liberally to try to mask his decaying smell, was adding to the pain in his head. As well as the way she handled him with the businesslike ease of a nurse with a disgustingly sick patient. He filed it all away as he followed her lead, relieved when she finally stopped walking.

"This is a hospital bed. I'm going to drop the railing. Then I'm going to release your hands. If you so much as move a muscle before I cuff you to the bed, I'll kill you."

Gavin nodded, sickened to know he would be tied down again, but then he needed to lay down more than he needed to breathe, anyway. The only thing he wanted more was a bath. "I won't do anything, like I promised."

"Good boy."

Vibrating with nerves, he rushed on, "But I could wash off first, if you would let me. I won't try anything, but I don't want to make the bed dirty."

Silence followed his hurried words and Gavin wished he didn't care what her decision was. But he did. He had been filthy for so long it finally hadn't mattered as much anymore. But now it did. If there was even a chance she'd let him bathe he'd do anything she asked of him.

"That would be good, actually…. But you have to let me do it."

Gavin nodded, not sure what that meant, nearly delirious with joy.

"I'm going to take you to your bathroom and put you in the shower. When I take off your blindfold, you are to keep your eyes closed, and when I release your hands they better not move unless I move them. Do you understand me?"

Gavin nodded. "I promise."

"You'd better. Or I'll pop your eyeballs out with a spoon and cut your hands off with the very large knife I have on me at all times."

"I promise," he repeated, but this time his voice quivered.

"Good boy." She took his arm and pulled him a few steps to his left then to the right. After only a few steps more, she pushed him forward before pulling him to a stop. "I'm going to take off your clothes."

Gavin nodded, though the thought of her seeing him naked made him cringe. It wasn't that he was all that modest, but he'd always expected that the first time he got naked in front of a girl he would be a willing participant and in love, as his parents had taught him the value of his body as well as the need to respect a girl's. He had never imagined himself blindfolded and forced to concede all rights to personal privacy.

"Don't be afraid. I'm only doing this to get you clean. I've had medical training, so just think of me as your nurse."

He hated the relief he felt, but he was grateful for the assurance she didn't plan to take the advantage she so obviously had. So he nodded again, just wanting it all to be over with as soon as possible.

Gavin wobbled a little when she released him. The

sounds of a drawer squeaking open and closing preceded something cold touching his wrist. It took only seconds to realize she was cutting the shirt from his body.

"I don't think I can stand much longer," he said, as his body bobbled a bit more. "I'm too weak."

"Just give me a minute. I'm hurrying."

It didn't take her long to cut away the sweatshirt plastered to his arms and torso. As the cool air penetrated his skin, she grasped his bony arms and maneuvered him around and pushed him down, and he realized he was probably sitting on a closed toilet seat.

He sighed and tried to sit upright, although every muscle in his body wanted to give way. He felt her pulling on the legs of the sweatpants that were also moist from fresh sweat and weeks of wear. He lifted his bottom and allowed them to slide down. As his mind registered that he was now completely exposed and that he stank embarrassingly, she lifted one foot and then the other as she pulled the pants from his body.

"I know what you're thinking, but don't. I'm not interesting in looking at your parts at the moment and I won't. If I was interested in you like that, you would have already known it.

"Now we are going to get you all cleaned up!"

Her sudden cheerfulness made Gavin shiver, but he was so thankful to be wherever he was, and not still alone in a cold cave. He only wished he knew why she was *interested* in him at all.

Gavin forced himself to stand, almost grateful when she assisted him. He still wanted to cover his genitals but she hadn't released the bindings holding his hands together and he had a feeling it wouldn't have mattered if she had. Unless she told him to move, he knew better than to do anything at all.

"Now, this is when you get to prove yourself to me. If you do exactly what I say, we will *both* be much happier with the outcome. I'm going to release your hands and help you into the shower. It just has a little lip at the bottom you have to step over. Then I'm going to close the curtain and you can remove the blindfold so you can wash yourself. A washcloth and soap are already laid out for you. Shampoo too.

"When you're done, you're going to tell me and I'm going to give you a towel to dry off with, then hand you a clean blindfold through the curtain to put back over your eyes. Then I'll lead you to the bedroom where I have clean pajamas laid out for you.

"Once you're dressed you will get in the bed and lie down and let me put a strap on your wrist that is attached to the railing of the bed. If *even once* you do anything that you are not supposed to do, you will regret it. Do I make myself clear?"

"Yes."

"What?"

"Yes, ma'am."

Gavin waited while she turned on the water. The sound of clean water hitting whatever surface it hit took his breath, he was so excited. He allowed her to lead him forward until the mist from the spray tickled his skin then she made him stop long enough to cut the bindings from his wrists. Although he wanted to rub them, he reached forward instead and felt the water hitting his fingers. He stepped under the gloriously hard spray and heard the plastic curtain pull closed.

"You get ten minutes. No more. So get busy."

Gavin didn't say anything as he removed the blindfold. He cautiously opened his eyes and then blinked rapidly. Although they stung horribly he tried to keep them open. He placed his hands against the wall beneath the spray and let the water run over him and mingled with his tears of joy. Yes, his vision was blurred, but it felt like a miracle that he could actually see again.

Though he knew he shouldn't be surprised it was so hard to keep his eyes open after living in darkness for so long, he also knew his time of sight would be short lived, and Gavin couldn't stand to blink as it took seconds away from the time he had.

"Are you washing in there?"

"I'm sorry. It just feels so good. I will now…sorry." Realizing he still held the blindfold, he stuck it out through the curtain and released it when he felt her pull. Then he used one hand to steady himself as he turned to the ceiling-to-floor metal shelving that held a variety of shampoos and both liquid and bar soaps, as well as the promised washcloth.

He forced his eyes to focus enough to distinguish between the shampoo and the body wash then poured a generous amount of shampoo into his palm. He leaned against the back wall of the stall for support as he scrubbed his scalp and the long hair that his father would have hated.

Not wanting to think about the life he would never again have, Gavin rinsed out his hair then shampooed it again. He reached for the washcloth and body wash because he just didn't have the energy to deal with a soap bar. Gavin scrubbed his face and ran his fingers over the sprouts of whiskers now growing on his jaw before washing his body as quickly as possible. He was afraid his time was running out and he *needed* every part of his body clean. When he finished and she still didn't tell him that his time was up he vigorously repeated the process again, this time scrubbing his skin until the hot water hitting it stung; embracing every second of the experience.

Finally feeling clean from his scalp to the soles of his feet, he stood and allowed the water to wash over him in a soothing caress, hoping it wouldn't be too long before she'd allow him to wash again.

"Time!"

Gavin turned off the water and wrung as much as he could from his hair before taking the towel she held just inside the curtain. He dried his hair first then his body quickly before wrapping the towel around his bony hips.

"I'm done."

Saying those words were necessary, but he hated that he'd once again have to bind his eyes. He indulged a second of refusing to cooperate, of jumping out at her and tackling her to the floor, but only a second, as a long strip of dark fabric appeared just inside the curtain. Hating her, but knowing he was in no shape to help himself yet, Gavin took what pleasure he could in stealing precious seconds to look around the stall one last time. Resigned, for now, he placed the cloth over his eyes and tied it over his wet hair.

"I've covered my eyes."

The sound of the shower curtain sliding back preceded her hand firmly grasping his elbow to lead him out. They walked the short distance back into the room he now thought of as his. When she stopped him, she took his hand and placed it on soft material.

"These are your pajamas. I don't care if you wear the shirt or not. Beneath them is your bed. Do you have any questions?"

Gavin had several, but the most urgent had to do with the one part of him that was still not clean. "Can I brush my teeth?"

"Of course. I hadn't thought of that. I'll get you a toothbrush and some paste later today, and you can brush them when I get back. Anything else?"

Gavin knew that he shouldn't feel embarrassed about anything at this point, but he still did. "What do I do if I have to go to the bathroom?"

"You have a table that slides over the bed that will hold both water and your food. It also has a lower shelf that holds the urinal bottle for you to pee in. If you have to poop and I'm not here to take you to the bathroom, you will have to use a bedpan. It will also be on the second shelf.

"Anything else?"

Gavin wondered how he was supposed to handle all that blindly, but he *had* managed for months in the dark so he said nothing and shook his head. He bit his bottom lip as he lifted the soft cloth and slid it between his fingers. He held it up to his face and inhaled the clean scent. It reminded him of his mother. She'd had the habit of smelling the laundry after taking a basket from the dryer. When he'd made fun of her once, she'd laughed at herself, and held the towel out to him. "Smell this," she'd said, and he had, but he hadn't understood then what he understood now; the scent of clean was something to rejoice in.

"What are you waiting for?"

Gavin jumped at the sound of her voice, realizing he'd zoned out. The momentary escape into his past was a dangerous place to go. It would be so easy to let his mind stay there. He lowered the pajama bottoms and turned in the direction of her voice. "Would you mind turning around while I get dressed?"

She laughed at that, but he could hear the movement of her shoes on the wood floor.

"I've turned around."

Relieved she wasn't planning on ogling him, Gavin began the process of feeling for the waistband of pajama bottoms first. It didn't matter that she had already seen all of him. It was the principle of the thing, and it really creeped him out, too, that she could look at him and he couldn't see where she was looking. He slipped the pants on quickly beneath the towel and then pulled it away. "Would you tell me what the date is?"

There was a long hesitation and he sighed. "I guess it isn't important."

To his surprise she finally responded, but instead of trying to gauge how long he'd been held captive all he could think was that he was now seventeen. *Seventeen years old.* He couldn't say anything more for the knot lodged in his throat. He had missed his birthday.

Once he finally got himself under control Gavin held the towel out in front of him, and climbed onto the bed once she took it.

"Arms."

Gavin stretched his arms out to his sides and flinched when she immediately took his left hand and pulled it closer to her. He felt the leather restraint being wrapped around his wrist then heard the snap of what must have been a lock. The weight of it reminded him of being back in the cold dark prison, but he couldn't let his mind go there either.

"I'm going to get you some soup and something for your fever. And I'm leaving you a free hand. *But I'm warning you now*, don't take off the blindfold when I'm not in here. I have a camera on you and everything you do is being recorded."

Trying to hold in a sudden flood of fury that he really had no privacy at all, Gavin nodded. He took several seconds to make sure no anger came out before saying, "I won't. I promised I would do what you told me."

"Good boy. Why don't you just rest until I get back then?"

Gavin nodded again and felt a light blanket being placed over him. "Thank you," he said quietly as he heard the clicking of her steps leading away from the room.

Flies and honey. How many times had his mother told him that? Gavin hoped he could gain her trust and eventually she'd drop her guard. If he was patient, and sweet, and did nothing he wasn't allowed to do, maybe, just maybe, he would win in the end.

Flies and honey....

Chapter Six

Haven held the phone slightly away from her ear and tried to answer the rapidly fired questions, but Destiny was too angry to listen to anything Haven had to say. Resigned her sister would never change, she said the only thing she could. "I *said* I was sorry."

Haven pressed her lips together in agitation, relieved Logan went into the store without her to get the groceries they had agreed upon, and to give her some privacy. The last thing she wanted him to hear was Destiny's ranting, or her own explanations and justifications for her quick departure from LA, which sounded a little lame even to her own ears.

Finally having had enough, she interrupted her sister's tirade. "Des! Would you stop already? I said I was sorry. And you haven't even asked how I am. But I'll tell you anyway. Something is happening to me here. I think there is the possibility that my power is coming back...but it's more than that."

The sight of Logan heading across the parking lot toward her forced her to talk faster. "Can't say much now, but Rayne bought some crystals and I think I'm theirs. Not only can I feel heat in my hands again, they—oh crud— can't talk now! Gotta go!"

Haven hung up and smiled at Logan as he opened his door to pitch his billfold on the driver's seat. "Do you need me to get out and help?"

"No thanks. I've got it." He placed the paper grocery bags in the seat behind them before storing the cart and returning and settling in the driver's seat. "They didn't have some of the stuff on your list, but I improvised."

Haven raised her brows. "As in when I asked for tofu, you got?"

"Deli sliced turkey."

"Hmmm. Okay. What about my bean sprouts?"

"They had those."

"Good. And the rhubarb?"

"Nope. But they had turnips."

Haven frowned. "I don't like turnips."

Logan looked into the rearview mirror before backing out of the parking spot. "Good thing I didn't get them then."

Haven smiled at him. "Good job. So… just how many of the things *I* added to our list did they have?"

He glanced over at her with a grin. "You came in at about fifty percent. I didn't feel quite so stupid when the grocer didn't know what some of the items you asked for were either."

Haven frowned. "I didn't come from another planet."

Logan laughed. "Around here, California qualifies as another planet. Have you ever watched those television programs where they interview people on the street?"

Knowing she was being set up, Haven nodded. "Of course."

"And have you ever noticed that when they interview people in California that for the most part they have no earthly idea what is going on in the nation, or with our government, or anything about the history of this country and its geography?"

Haven didn't know whether to be insulted or embarrassed. She didn't know much about those things either. So, like any smart Californian, she knew a good defense was a good offence. "That may be true, but didn't someone say that you shouldn't judge a person by what they know, but by the content of their character?"

"Actually I think what you're talking about is a line in a Martin Luther King speech. If I remember right, he said, 'I have a dream that my four children will one day live in a nation where they will not be judged by the color of their skin, but by the content of their character.'"

"Okay, smart ass, but didn't someone say don't judge

other people unless you want to be judged by them?"

Logan slid an evil grin her way before turning his gaze back toward the mountain road. "I think you may be talking about the Bible now. If memory serves, I believe the King James Version of the first couple of verses in the seventh chapter of the book of Matthew says, 'Judge not, that ye be not judged. For with what judgment ye judge, ye shall be judged."

Haven glared at him. "What are you, a freakin' *Jeopardy* champion?"

Logan settled back, obviously enjoying himself. "Not at all. I'm just not a Californian."

Haven settled back as well, a gleam in her eyes and a smile on her lips. "And to think I was going to let you pop my cherry."

Logan's head turned to her quickly causing him to swerve toward the mountainside. His attention torn, he overcorrected, turning the steering wheel to the left, which took them close to the guardrail that bordered the mountain's drop off, so he overcorrected again and they fishtailed into the ditch nestled between the mountainside and the road.

As the car came to a sudden stop jerking them both forward, Haven started laughing. Once he could catch his breath, Logan grinned at her and shook his head. "You do realize, don't you, that you just about got us both killed?"

She shrugged. "*I* wasn't the one driving."

Logan sighed and looked out to see they had stopped at an angle, just inches from actually hitting the mountain. "It looks like we might have a wheel stuck in the gully, could have torn up the undercarriage."

Haven looked out, then back at him. "Yep. Bet Rayne's going to be thrilled when she has to call the rental company and tell them you wrecked the car."

He lifted one brow at her. "Yeah, well if her sister wasn't so lazy, and had walked back to our cabin to get one of ours, we wouldn't be in hers to begin with."

"True," Haven acknowledged, flashing a big smile at

him. "But if the doctor hadn't gotten all hot and bothered over a little thing like ripe for the picking fruit, we wouldn't be in a ditch."

He barked out a laugh at that. "Ripe for the picking, huh?"

Haven was having a ball watching as sweat popped out on his forehead, making a lie of his ease with the subject. "Fully ripe. Plump and juicy ripe. Oh so yummy, ripe."

****

Logan groaned and sent her an unreadable look before awkwardly exiting the car. For some reason he was about to pop. Well, he *knew* the reason; the two cups of coffee followed by two glasses of water, which was more than he ever drank at one time, was obviously the culprit. He didn't know why he was so thirsty, but he was, even now.

On top of that, Haven was making him crazy. Good crazy, but crazy all the same. He was fascinated with her. She was funny and sassy, and if he wasn't mistaken, she was equally fascinated, and daring, and… Yep, she was making him crazy.

Logan walked to the front of the car to assess the situation, and sighed. The front tires hung over the edge of road, making the frame rest on the gravelly asphalt. Fortunately the suddenness of their stop kept them from hitting the mountainside and doing more damage to the front bumper and hood, and possibly Haven and him as well. Thankful he hadn't hurt her, he climbed down into the ditch and looked back under the car as much as he could. It didn't look like fluids gushed or even dripped, but that didn't mean they wouldn't once the car was towed back onto its tires.

Since there was nothing he could do until help came, Logan glanced back up to see if there were any signs of traffic and to see if Haven was within sight. Pleased to see neither, he turned toward the mountain and unzipped his pants, and instantly felt better once some of the pressure of all those fluids eased.

"Hey there!"

Logan jumped at the sound of the booming voice then quickly finished and re-zipped. He slid a peek around the front bumper to see Haven exiting the car as the elderly man leaned his way and waved. Logan waved back and then grinned as Haven smiled at him, devilment abundant in the raised brows and sweet smile that told him she knew exactly what he'd been doing.

"I called Mr. Doogar's Towing, and I'm assuming this is Mr. Doogar."

The old gentleman's friendly smile was accompanied by a shaking of his balding head as he looked at the front fender where it rested on the pavement. "Hi," Logan said, relieved they would be able to get the car pulled out pretty quickly.

"Gotcher-self quite a mess here."

Logan nodded at the understatement. "Yeah. Do you think it will be a problem getting it out?"

"Nope. You see anything to be concerned about down there?"

Logan shook his head. "Not that I can tell, but I'm not an expert."

"No problem. I'll hook her up and we'll pull her out. If there's anything more to deal with, we'll take care of it then. My knees aren't what they used to be. When I was a young man, I would have jumped right down in there with you. Trying to get my boys to work with me, but they'd rather get an education and do something else. Can't blame them. No one wants to get their hands dirty anymore. But I don't know what folks'll do when they need their car towed. You know?"

Logan nodded as he climbed out of the ditch. "I do." He looked around for Haven only to find her standing next to the tow truck petting a big white dog, which was happily eating up the attention as he hung halfway out of the passenger-side window. He grinned, finding it charming she liked dogs. He turned back to Doogar. "What can I do to help?"

****

As much as she enjoyed making Logan laugh and letting him amuse her, Haven was glad she and her sister were finally alone so they could resume discussions the boys couldn't be privy to. But before he and Garrison went outside to inspect for any axle damage, Logan took his time making sure Rayne knew the accident wasn't his fault. He'd joked around and laughingly told Rayne that Haven was clearly at fault as she unapologetically distracted him while he drove. She'd laughed too and still thought it hilarious he'd omitted just how she'd done it.

"They've found another body."

Haven's amusement fled as she looked intently at Rayne. "They? Or *you*?"

She joined Rayne to glance out the large front window to the area where Rayne kept her rental car parked to see if the men were heading back yet. But they were still standing down there, their backs to the cabin as they looked over the damage to the car. Haven had to suppress a grin again as they looked like two manly men completely in their element. Her smile fell when Logan reached up and gently touched the wound on his head.

"Me. With the help of my Indian guide, if you want to call Qaqeemasq that. But I can't let anyone know it was me. After I led them to the last two bodies one of the cops looked at me in a way that makes me think she already considers me a person of interest, and I can't afford to be a person of interest."

"A woman? Huh! She's probably just jealous that you are prettier than her or some such nonsense.

"So when did you find the body? And how did you let them know?"

Rayne laughed. "You haven't even seen the woman. How do you know I, *we*, are prettier than her?"

"Let's see, since she acted like that toward you, and I'm not saying all women cops are ugly, nor that this is the least bit politically correct, but…is she built like a guy, have chopped off dull brown hair, and walk like she has a dick between her legs?"

Rayne laughed outright at Haven's description. "Yeah, sort of. But that's not a nice assumption. Women around the world wouldn't appreciate it."

Haven grinned. "Since when do we care what women around the world think? Most have wanted to stone or hang us throughout our family's history."

Rayne grinned back. "True. Can't argue with history." Her face relaxed. "But that doesn't change anything. I don't need her investigating me."

"So you haven't told Garrison."

Though it wasn't a question, Rayne shook her head and looked back through the window. "I've wanted to so many times. But, no, I can't. It isn't just my life at stake. And I'm just not willing to lose him."

"You know, some people do accept us."

"Some, yes, but not all. I'm afraid he's too steeped in reality to accept anything mystical." She turned to Haven. "He's such a great guy, but some things just go against people's beliefs and realities. I'm not willing to risk losing him over something that he may not be able to accept, even if he wanted to."

"I know. I could spout all kinds of things like, if he loved you…blah, blah, blah, but I know, so I won't." Haven touched her sister's arm gently. "You really love him."

Radiant light shined from Rayne's emerald eyes as well as her smile. "I really do."

"Well, that is that then. Mum's the word. So, what do you know about the latest body?"

Rayne turned from the window and headed to the kitchen. "Not much. It isn't anyone the White family knows, which is a relief, I guess. They've attended enough funerals and suffered enough loss lately, but I don't want to think about that right now.

"Want a drink?" When Haven shook her head, Rayne pulled bottled water from the refrigerator and took a long swallow. "Let's see, I guess I should start at the beginning.

"Qaqeemasq first came to me right after I got to

Mystic Waters. It was kind of peculiar, because I hadn't seen or been able to conjure any spirits since arriving. And after meeting Garrison, I tried to conjure his nephew but got nothing."

"I didn't even know you did that."

Rayne sighed. "I never had tried it before, and didn't know if I could, and still don't really because Qaqeemasq came to me on his own. But anyway, I tried and got nothing." She shook her head at the memory. "I was so happy because I thought maybe that meant that Gavin was still alive.

"Qaqeemasq led me to a tree where I found this scrap of cloth that came from a flannel shirt. When I showed it to Garrison, he thought it might be Gavin's. But I'm getting ahead of myself....

"Before I had the scrap I had already tried to convince him his nephew was alive, but because I couldn't tell him of my failed attempt to conjure Gavin's spirit he got really angry at me." Rayne glanced toward the window again then turned back to Haven. "And rightly so.

"He'd been searching for the kid for around two months at that point, I think, with no luck. And to him I was this crazy woman from California who stepped in and acted like I knew something he didn't. Which I didn't, and still don't. It was a stupid thing to do to him. When we first met, he wasn't the man you see now. He had lost all hope and looked completely defeated.

"I have to remind myself every time I try to contact his nephew's spirit that, just because he isn't coming to me, it doesn't mean he isn't dead."

Haven moved closer, hurting for her sister, but needing to ask a question that had plagued her long before coming to Mystic Waters. "You say you haven't encountered any ghosts since coming here, except for Qaqee—whatever. What does that name mean, anyway?"

Rayne smiled. "It is a mouthful, but I think it means Running Bear. I never quite caught all he was telling me the day we met, so I could be wrong."

"Well, like it or not, that's what I'm calling him from now on. So, like I was asking, you haven't spoken to, or seen, any other ghosts except Running Bear?"

Rayne shook her head. "But it's probably my own fault. I closed them all out on the trip over here."

"Do you think there is a possibility that even if you hadn't, that you might not be able to…you know, talk to ghosts?"

Rayne frowned. "No. I don't think so. Why would you ask that? What exactly has happened to you?"

Haven knew they would never get to have an entire conversation unless they spent a day out, on the pretext of shopping or something, as Logan and Garrison entered the door smiling at them.

"Well, it doesn't look too bad," Garrison said. "I'll call Jess and see if he'll give us an estimate on fixing the dings."

Rayne shook her head. "I'll have to call the rental company first and see how they want to handle it."

Garrison nodded and shrugged. "Okay. So, when are you going to get rid of that thing and get your own car?"

Rayne slid a glance at Haven. "Well, actually, I was thinking Haven and I could go look at some tomorrow." At his crestfallen expression she rushed on. "But I won't make a final decision until you go with me to look, too."

Haven almost rolled her eyes. *Good grief!* Did Rayne really just go all gooey, *-I-can't-do-anything-without-a-man's-input* on her? She looked to see what Garrison's reaction was and shook her head in disgust. The guy's shoulders had gone back and she was just waiting for him to put his hands on his hips, bob his head back and forth, bend his knees to strut, and crow loud enough to wake the dead.

"Well, great," she said, hoping she didn't sound nearly as snide as she felt. She glanced back at Logan, and darn it, he was playing with his wound again! To distract him she walked up as close as she could get without actually allowing her breasts to touch his chest, putting on the sweet seductive smile she knew turned men's heads. "Maybe we should go shopping, too."

Logan nodded and his hand lowered as if he'd forgotten the scorched cut and Haven almost laughed out loud at how simple men really were.

His gaze bore into hers, and there was a wicked little smile on his lips. "Yes. I think you said something earlier about cherries?"

Rayne spoke up from behind her. "I thought you guys just got groceries."

Haven ignored Rayne and kept her gaze on Logan. So he had her number, did he? She kept the smile on her lips, although this one was real. "Yes, I do believe I did."

Logan's eyes flared though he kept the rest of his body perfectly still. Aware of their audience, Haven did the same. But it took everything she had not to press up against him just to watch him squirm.

Though she didn't look, she knew Garrison had crossed to where Rayne stood. "Let's go."

"Go where?"

"*Rayne*, let's just go!"

As she listened to their departing footsteps, Haven couldn't help appreciating just how perceptive her future brother-in-law was. She moved forward and pressed her breasts into Logan's hard chest. Immediately his arms were around her, crushing her to him, as his lips devoured her mouth.

As many people as she had touched in her life, and as much heat as her body had transferred to others, none of it came close to the fire Logan ignited inside of her now. She accepted the onslaught, as eager to give as to get.

"Let's go home," Logan mumbled against her lips.

Haven couldn't even respond, but she was finally able to nod which separated his lips from hers. Logan's grin was just a little smug as he pulled her in the direction of the door.

****

Logan captured Haven's mouth and barely let go the entire trip back to their cabin. He was determined to pleasure her and not to give her a chance to cool down, knowing the hike back gave her plenty of time. He walked her backward over twigs, branches, and thickening undergrowth while he nibbled on neck and lips and tongue. He lifted her and spun her around with their mouths fused until she fell into him, dizzy and clinging. He pinned her against a tree when he could barely stand the need to take her, and devoured her mouth all over again, only pulling away before taking things too far just in case she had been serious about her chastity. If it really was her first time, he wanted it to be perfect.

It was a relief when the cabin was finally only a short distance away. He scooped her up so quickly she squealed and clung to his neck laughing, as he jogged the remaining distance and up the steps. Once on the porch, he set her on her feet so he could dig around in his way too tight jeans for the key.

His efforts to keep her hungry for him had backfired, making his hands shake so badly he couldn't insert the key into the knob. Haven placed her hand on his, presumably to calm him, but the result was a burst of static electricity that caused him to flinch and her to turn alarmed eyes his way.

He laughed at her overreaction and pulled her tight against his erection for a kiss he hoped singed her to her toes. The dazed smile on her swollen moist lips when he pulled back had him fighting the lock again and he nearly groaned out loud when it found purchase and he could turn the knob.

He pulled her in, kicked the door closed, and forgot all his good intentions. Slow and gentle was no longer an option. Thankfully she seemed to agree as she began pulling at his shirt as soon as the door slammed, her fingers fumbling over the buttons that wouldn't open, desperation sharpening emerald eyes when she looked up at him helplessly.

Logan slid his fingers at the closure and pulled, sending buttons flying. "Anything you want, baby. Anything," he said, allowing her to push the shirt from his shoulders.

Immediately her lips were on his chest, kissing him in wild abandon, causing him to grab her head, tangling his fingers in her hair.

He wanted to tell her to let the shirt fall as it was still hanging between his bare back and her hands. But before he could form the words, her teeth nipped his nipple, her tongue swirled around it then her lips suckled the small nub until the pull took the strength from his legs.

The groan escaped this time, loud and long, and he forced her head back so he could take possession of those lips to devour them before nibbling none too gently along her jaw line, and neck.

"The bed!" he growled, determined to at least get her there before he completely lost control of any sense of propriety. He started maneuvering them in the direction of the stairs while meeting her ravenous mouth with his own, knowing the hum in his head was directly related to the throbbing in his pants.

He half-dragged, half-pulled her up the stairs, having to stop every few steps as she nailed his body to the spot, or he nailed hers, as their desperation for each other overrode their ability to advance.

They finally reached the landing and Logan twirled them the last few steps to the bed. He took her down with him, maneuvering so she landed on his body, and immediately devoured her mouth again.

Haven met his ardor with equal force, taking and giving in equal measure. There was no reluctance, no indication she didn't know what she was doing with and to him, so he let the increasing vibrations filling his body take over and gave up trying to remember to go slow.

He rolled them over so he was on top and then ignored her groan when he pulled away. Once she was forced to release it, he threw the shirt she'd somehow managed to hold on to before stripping them both with no finesse at all.

When his naked flesh met her naked flesh, he felt her sliding a hand toward his hip. He pinned her wrist to the sheet and then clinched his body against the raging need that threatened to take him over the top. Biting into the pillow next to her head, he struggled for control, his nostrils flaring and collapsing with desperate breaths.

He was too close. If she touched him now he wouldn't last a second.

"Please…*please*, keep your hands where they are."

Determined to still give her all he had before taking what she willingly gave, he pulled back and looked into her eyes. Her trembling smile nearly blinded him as she nodded. "Okay," she finally said breathlessly. "But hurry!"

Her blessing was all he needed. He started at her lips but was soon moving down her body, determined to taste and torture every inch of soft flesh. She moaned and stiffened when he reached a breast then made little mewing sounds as he stopped there to suckle. Eventually he paid homage to each one then moved further south to lavish her sumptuous flesh, stopping once with his face in her soft belly while attempting to get his need back under control.

When she threatened to move, he shook his head and slid his tongue in her belly button then used his teeth to capture the bejeweled dragonfly that dangled from it. She bucked and he growled, and the room filled with her whimpering as he continued to move downward. Instinct, or the need to curl against his onslaught, caused her to draw her legs up as he approached the thin line of red hair leading to his target.

"*Logan!*"

Her desperation fueled his own though it needed no kindling as he was burning and out of control. The hands that had followed his mouth down her body were now pulled back so he could slip them beneath her legs. He wrapped shaking fingers around her thighs and pulled them further apart as his mouth roughly suckled her core and his tongue teased and tormented the tiny nub of pleasure.

As the humming in his head and body intensified, she screamed his name, and continued to do so, time after time, as her body writhed so wildly he could barely hold her. Her upper torso curled up and her thighs fought the restraint of his fingers in her body's effort to resist the building pressure but he was having none of that. He pulled one hand from beneath her and splayed his fingers on her stomach then slid his palm up to her chest for a gentle but firm push, sending her back to the mattress and forcing her to submit fully to his demands.

Logan ran his palm back down her perspiring flesh until his hand joined his mouth. He slid his middle finger into her only enough to intensify what his tongue was already doing. She bucked again; this time so strongly it forced him back, so he took the opportunity to move up her body as he cupped her bottom with both hands. He slid into her in one long motion as her screams matched the intensity of the vibrations overtaking his body and ringing in his head.

He felt the ripples igniting her orgasm, and he exploded into her as lightning burst around his head, singeing him inside and out, when her hands finally grasped his back.

Light and sound, colors and chaos, lasted the duration of his climax. Oblivion overtook him as the last drops of semen were milked from his body and he collapsed on top of her, completely unconscious.

∗∗∗∗

Haven accepted Logan's weight willingly, as happy and exhausted as she had ever been in her life, barely able to believe she had lived so long resisting the pleasures of the flesh and the experience of making love. Now she understood why writers waxed poetic about it, and why songs that touched so deeply were sung from the hearts of minstrels who already knew what she had only just learned.

She loved that he wanted to cuddle and that he couldn't bring himself to leave her but eventually his weight began smothering her. "Logan?"

When he didn't move, she nudged him. "Logan?"

He still didn't respond.

Annoyed that he had actually fallen asleep while she

was lying there feeling all mushy, she nudged him harder, but nothing. *Nada.* Haven closed her eyes in frustration but she didn't want to end what had been so magical an experience by getting angry so she decided to endure the weight and let him sleep just a little while since he had, after all, given her a most amazing gift.

Relaxing, she turned her thoughts back to the feel of his mouth and hands doing all those wonderfully wicked things to her body. She could hardly wait to experience it all again, especially those astounding last seconds of rapture right before the blinding explosion of pleasure overtook her.

Haven stiffened and her eyes popped open.

Blinding?

Explosion?

"Oh, no!"

Haven used every ounce of strength she had to push Logan's dead weight off her, terrified she had killed him, but he wouldn't budge. She eventually succeeded in sliding out from under his frame. As she jumped up quickly, determined to check him out, he began to groan. But knowing he was alive did little to make her feel better as she stared in horror at the handprints lightly burned into the flesh of his back.

Chapter Seven

Haven jumped from the bed as Logan struggled to wake up. She ran down the stairs, her heart pounding against her chest. She remembered seeing the huge aloe vera plant sitting in front of the large window gracing the front of the cabin, and headed straight to it. She had no idea if it would really help erase her blunder or not, but she had no other immediate options to choose from.

"Haven?"

Crap!

"Coming!" she yelled brightly, hoping he would stay put. She silently apologized to the plant as she broke off a large thick leaf at its base. Plugging the end with her finger, so the gel wouldn't leak out of the soft spiny stem, she put it behind her back and climbed the stairs. Thankfully, Logan was right where she left him. He turned his head her way and smiled a little dopily.

"I'm sorry. I didn't mean to fall asleep on you, but my God, *woman*, I've never had an orgasm like that!"

I'll just bet you haven't!

Haven approached him trying not to be obvious that she was hiding anything. When he attempted to rise, she rushed over and grabbed a corner of sheet before using it to push him back down. "Stay put! You've had your fun, now I'm going to have mine."

Logan twisted his head around quickly to look at her. His sleepy state disappeared from his eyes as he looked at her in horror. "I didn't please you?"

Well, hells, bells! Foot. Mouth."

She laughed at him, hoping it sounded sincere. "If you had pleased me any more I would have gone up in smoke."

Haven mentally slapped her hand over her mouth. *Crap! Crap! Crap! Seriously?*

Relief replaced his horror and she breathed again, glad he hadn't made any connection to his present condition with her last comment. Hopefully he never would. She just gave him another saucy smile, determined to keep him distracted. "I just want to explore your body some more and I thought I would start by giving you a massage."

Logan immediately relaxed back into the sheets. "Oh, well then, you aren't going to get any arguments from me.

"Explore away. I'll be right here."

Relief washed over her that she had finally chosen the right words. But it was short lived as she looked at the mess she'd made of his skin. She was glad it was mostly first-degree burns although there were a couple of blisters forming at the center where her palms had touched. Hoping he didn't feel any pain, she climbed on the bed then straddled his rock hard ass.

"Oh!"

Haven froze. "What? Am I hurting you?"

Logan chuckled deeply, making his entire body shake and rub against her intimately, and she grinned as she understood. "Oh."

He finally settled and was still. "Yeah, *oh*, although I can't believe I have anything left in me…."

Satisfaction that she turned him on so quickly was mixed with fear of how she would explain what looked like handprint sunburns on his back if he turned out to be one of those men who went shirtless in public. Unless it stung at some point, it was doubtful he would ever see the marks so close to his spine.

Though she hadn't been all that attentive when the aunts tried to teach her and her sisters about natural healing remedies—since she had been so determined to learn more conventional science while studying for a nursing degree—Haven did remember them spouting about the multiple uses of the plant she held.

She was pretty sure it would help with any pain that might develop, but she didn't remember them ever saying anything about it making burns disappear any quicker.

Hopefully she would have a chance to ask Rayne before Logan discovered she'd marred his skin.

Haven checked to make sure he wasn't watching and smiled when she realized he had closed his eyes as he awaited her touch. She bit her bottom lip and concentrated on her hands, hoping that the charge of heat had bled out enough that she wouldn't burn him again. At this point she had no idea if that was how they worked.

Since she didn't feel them heating up at all, she slathered her fingertips and palm with the gel and gently touched his back just below the handprints. He jumped, and her heart raced until he mumbled that it was cold.

"Sorry." *Anything but!* "It's to soothe you, not excite you."

Logan chuckled again, rocking her. "I don't think there is any way you can ever touch me and not excite me."

Haven had to agree that it worked both ways. Every time he laughed and his butt shook she was teased and tantalized at her very core, but she had a mission and she couldn't let a renewed ardor distract her. More confident it was safe, Haven put her hands on him again, this time rubbing over his burns with the lightest touch, afraid that if she pushed too hard he would finally feel what she'd done to him.

"You're supposed to dig into muscle and work over a wider area."

Haven raised up enough to swat his butt from behind her own, leaving goo on his butt cheek. He jumped and laughed. "Do that again and we are switching places."

"Shut up. My turn, remember?"

He relaxed into the bed again. "Sorry. But you're making this hard on me." He waited a heartbeat then tried to twist enough to grin at her.

"Oh, you're *hard*, are you? Too bad. Lay still and let me do what I want. You said no arguments, remember?"

"You are a mean woman," he teased, before taking a deep breath. "Okay. Your rules. But if you want to explore me you'd find more to explore if I turned over."

"I'll get there eventually. Now, shush! And be still."

"Yes, ma'am."

He sounded like a disappointed little boy, which made her laugh. "I'll tell you what, you mind me now, and I'll let you give me a massage later."

He settled in and said no more as she labored over the area that concerned her most before extending her ministrations outward. She found that touching him, digging in as he'd suggested warmed her in ways that didn't pose a danger to him, though she wasn't so sure about herself.

She hadn't meant for this time with him to be anything other than a new and wonderful experience. And she'd certainly got that. But while he'd played with her and made love to her and even when he teasingly made her look stupid, something inside of her shifted, and though she didn't think it was love, she was afraid it could turn into just that.

Haven sat back and looked at his goo-covered skin, thankful the aloe had arrested the burn areas, as they didn't seem any worse. She leaned over him and gently kissed around the burns then shifted back and rose, taking the shredded stem with her. She looked down at him a second longer as she turned for the stairs.

"Whoa! Where are you going?"

Logan was half turned and had risen enough that his erection was clearly visible. She looked away and turned her back to him. The nicest thing she could do for him would be to leave. "I decided I don't want a massage."

Haven hurried down the steps and went straight to the little bathroom. She shut and locked the door, her slick and sticky fingers making it take a few seconds more than should have. By the time she released the knob, Logan was trying to turn it.

"Haven? What's going on?"

Taking a deep shaky breath Haven pitched the plant into the small trash can by the sink and paced the small space. "Can you give a girl a little privacy?"

"Sure, but what's wrong?"

"Why do you think something is wrong? I just need to use the bathroom!"

A heartbeat of silence.

"Okay... So why are you pacing?"

Haven froze immediately. "I'm not pacing!"

"You're not now, but you were, and you still haven't peed. I would have heard you."

Haven opened her mouth then closed it without saying anything. Then she smiled. "I'm taking a poop, okay? Do you want to know what color it is, too?"

Logan's chuckle coming through the door had the same effect on her as it did when he'd been between her legs on the bed.

"I'm a doctor. Those kinds of details don't bother me. So tell me what's bothering you?"

Haven unlocked the door and flung it open. She pushed past him and walked to the mantel then turned to face him. "Okay, you want to know what's bothering me? I'll tell you. I made a mistake. This whole sex thing was a mistake. Is that what you want to hear?"

Logan shook his head. "I didn't take you for a liar."

"That's a hateful thing to say."

"Not if you're lying to me. Which you are. You enjoyed me every bit as much as I enjoyed you."

"That isn't the point."

Frustration finally cracked his composure. "Then what the hell is the point?"

Haven shook her head. "I—"

"Am scared," he finished for her.

Haven shrugged. "I'm not afraid of you."

Logan smiled. "I know. You're afraid of you. You feel something for me."

Haven shook her head again. "Don't be ridiculous. Somebody is sure full of their self. I barely know you!"

"You've known me a short time, true, but you've known me as intimately as anyone does. And you like me. And it is scaring the fire out of you."

Duh! Literally! "You're wrong."

"You kissed me."

"So what? I had sex with you, too. People do it every day."

"I don't mean before. I mean just now, before you came downstairs. You kissed my spine and the area around it like you were cherishing me. That isn't casual. That is about as personal as it gets.

"And I feel the same way. I like your smartass sense of humor, and your sexy body, and even your disrespect for knowledge," he added with a grin. "Don't run from me. I really like you."

Haven had no response because she was afraid she was going to cry. He had hit the nail squarely on the head. She was afraid. Terrified, actually. If she allowed something serious to develop between them, there was no way she would get around revealing who she was.

"It can't work."

"It can."

"I live in California and you live in Florida."

"One of us can move if it comes to that. I'm just asking for a chance to see. I'll be here a month. You said you quit your job so you don't have to hurry back. Explore this with me."

Haven had no arguments left. She wasn't going anywhere anytime soon. She had too much to learn about the crystals, but even thinking that, she felt like the liar Logan said she was. She wanted to explore everything with him. She would just have to do it knowing when he went back to Florida she would likely end up breaking both of their hearts.

"Okay. But no promises. Let's just enjoy each other without any expectations."

He smiled and walked toward her, taking her into his arms. "See? That wasn't so hard."

If only you knew, Haven thought, as the palms of her hands began to warm.

Logan sighed, suddenly looking very sad. "I guess I

need to shower and get dressed. I haven't even checked in on my parents today." He pulled back and looked down at her. "I won't ask you to come, unless you want to. They aren't in the best shape right now."

"Thanks, but no, you go and spend whatever time you need with them. I have some things I need to take care of, too."

Hoping to see him smile she added, "Like birth control."

Instead of smiling his gaze sharpened. "Oh, Haven, *damn*, I'm sorry."

Haven laughed. "I'm sure it's fine. We've only done it once."

Logan looked like he was about to say something but didn't. Figuring he was about to say something mundane like *it only takes once*, she was glad he'd kept his thoughts to himself. The last thing she wanted to think about at the moment was an unexpected pregnancy, not that she knew if she would be the one of the three of them to ever have to concern herself with such things.

He just nodded, kissed her on the forehead, and entered the bathroom. Haven stood looking at the open door as sounds of spraying water indicated he had jumped right in. As much as she wanted to join him, the heat still radiating from her hands nixed that idea.

Besides, she needed to keep her distance as much as possible and was glad for an afternoon of separation. She needed some answers from Rayne, and she needed them today.

****

"Well, I didn't expect to see you back here so soon."

Haven ignored Rayne's cheeky grin. "Where is Garrison?"

She tilted her head toward the front door since her hands were covered with flour and busy rolling out dough on a baker's pie form. "He's working in the shop, but I should let him know that you're back." She laughed. "My future husband believed you and Logan were well on the way to some serious sexual activity, but I told him he was wrong."

"He wasn't."

Rayne set the rolling pin down and looked up. "Well damn. I just lost twenty bucks." She really looked at Haven then smiled in sympathy. "So, it must not have been all that great if you are already back here. Don't worry, the first time rarely is."

"It started before we left here, was ongoing the entire walk back, and then it was crazy great to the tenth power once we made it into the bed. That's why I'm here."

"I don't understand."

"My handprints are burned into Logan's back."

Horror crossed Rayne's features so dramatically Haven couldn't help but laugh. "I didn't burn a hole through him!"

Rayne looked at her white hands and reached for a dish towel. "So he knows?"

Haven shook her head. "No. He hasn't said anything about the burns, and I don't think he'll ever find out. I put aloe vera gel on them as soon as I realized what I'd done. Fortunately, while we were both having some amazingly intense climaxes the lightning strike exploded over the bed and caused him to pass out again. So that bought me some time."

Rayne just stood there with her mouth hanging open as the hand towel fell to her feet.

"Come on, Sis! Help me out here! I need some answers."

Rayne slumped against the counter. "I don't know the questions. And what the hell do you mean by lightning strike over the bed? Is that figuratively speaking or are you being literal?"

Haven threw up her hands. "Oh, sorry, okay. Forget about the lightning for now because I think it's all part of the same issue.

"What I need to know is where did those crystals on the mantel come from? And what kind are they? And why are they helping me to have powers again, only this time

I'm hurting instead of healing? Does that mean they are evil or I just don't know how to use them yet?"

Rayne placed her hand on her forehead and rubbed, leaving a light streak of white. "You are giving me a headache again."

Frustration thinned Haven's lips. "Get over it. I need to know what you know."

"That's just it. I really don't know much about them except that they were mined locally. I saw them at a roadside tourist cabin and thought they were pretty. It wasn't until I got them home that they did anything."

"They did something for you? Why didn't you say so! I thought they chose me."

"They just hummed a little and danced across the mantel. That was it. I've stayed with Garrison for the most part almost from the beginning. I had actually forgotten about them."

"But you didn't get thunder and lightning and clouds swirling, right?"

Rayne shook her head. "No…are you saying that they allow you to bring weather inside?"

"No. Well, just the lightning in the cabin. But before, when we were all here together and you shook me I had just experienced the most amazing power surge. Didn't you see the approaching storm? The grinding and churning clouds? Didn't you feel the tornado strength winds and the debris beating against your body? And that spectacular lightning? It was fueling me as it got closer. Filling me up like petro in a gas tank.

"I was *absorbing* it all, Rayne. Nothing like that had ever happened to me before. I think the crystals are filling me with energy…of the *voltage* variety. That's why I'm attracting storms and it's why I burned Logan's head last night and his back just now."

Sadness softened Rayne's gaze. "But there was no approaching storm or wind or lightning. It was all in your head."

"No. It. Was. Not!"

"Haven, look, Destiny and I talked on the phone right before you got here. She's concerned you are…ill."

"Right! Sure! That's what she wants to believe. But it isn't true. I'm evolving here. Aren't you? Since moving here don't you feel the energy? The power?"

Rayne nodded. "Yes, there's definitely something here. I can't deny that. But I haven't come close to what you are describing."

Satisfaction settled inside of Haven. "Good, it isn't yours to experience. You are mystical just like Momma was. Only you conjure the spirits of those who have passed on instead of casting spells for the living. But I'm not sure that's all you can do.

"We never wanted any of this, remember? Momma died and all three of us turned our backs on learning more than what was forced upon us. Sure, you've studied our history, but have you ever studied her book of spells? Have you tried to use magic?"

"Um…no." Rayne shook her head.

"And I am elemental like Aunt Lune Brille. She repairs the damage done to the earth and waterways, and I think I may be developing the power to nourish or destroy them both. But all I've ever done was grudgingly use my gift when there was no other choice, hiding my hands away in shame and fear. I actually hated them at times so I refused to consider what else the power source inside of me was capable of doing. I think I'm getting a taste of it now."

Torn between fear and excitement but absolutely certain of her sudden revelation, Haven pleaded for understanding from Rayne with her beseeching gaze as well as her insistent words. "I know I'm right. I mean I *really* know it. I just don't know why I never realized any of this before."

Rayne was silent for long seconds, her indrawn brows and uncertain gaze an indication that she was processing Haven's words. She finally blew out a long breath. "You're right. Oh my, I've been so stupid. I've hated my gift, too. And no, I haven't done anything more than pretend to learn who we really are. I avoided Momma's book of spells like it was the serpent in the garden.

"Everything you are saying confirms what the diaries revealed and I was too dumb to catch.

"In each generation of Cavanaugh triplets we have had these repeating mystical themes—the Enchantress who is capable of casting or conjuring, the Regulator who is capable of controlling all natural elements, and the Divine whose spirit is free to discover truth—though for each subsequent generation the individual gifts are distinctly different. I can't believe I didn't catch this before. It's so clear now!"

Rayne inhaled and smiled, sharing Haven's excitement. "That means Destiny is—"

"Divine," Haven finished. "That's why she can enter people's spirits and read them, just like Aunt Soleli spiritually travels through time and visits other civilizations. I bet Destiny would be a lot more interested in all this if she could do what Aunt Sole does, but I don't want to tell her yet. I want this next month without her around. I know that sounds mean, but I need some *me* time.

"Is that selfish, or do you understand?"

Rayne nodded and looked at Haven pointedly. "Yes, I understand. I enjoyed *me* time while it lasted.

"And you don't need to worry about Destiny coming before the wedding. She was quite clear that she has no interest in moving to *some hick town*, I believe she called it."

Haven was too busy thinking about all that had been revealed to her to catch Rayne's meaning, so she just nodded. "Good, let her think that.

"We're right about all this, Rayne. It finally all makes sense."

"What does?" Garrison asked, walking in the door.

The man had the worst timing was all Haven could think as Rayne smoothly told him a lie. Knowing her talk time was up for now she smiled at Rayne. "I should be getting back, but we are still on for tomorrow, right?"

"I'll come by about ten after Garrison and I go on our

morning hike if that works for you."

It was clear Rayne's smile was more for Garrison's benefit, as there was compassion in it. Though frustrated, since her most immediate concerns hadn't been addressed much less dissected and tackled, Haven conceded the later time than she had hoped for. She knew they spent every morning looking for his nephew, come Hell or high water.

Like a puppy spying a bone, Garrison headed to Rayne's side to snack on the apple slices she had marinating in cinnamon and sugar for the apple pies she was obviously making. Haven could hardly believe Rayne was baking the sweet, but she nodded and mouthed silently, *It will have to.*

Chapter Eight

Logan sat in the living room that hadn't changed at all since he'd left home to head off to college all those years ago. It had, in fact, not changed at all since the Christmas after Donny was born, and their ecstatic parents had decided they needed to remodel the entire three-bedroom house and start the transformation by moving Logan out of the room that had always been his.

His parents were quite matter of fact about it all and told him it was ridiculous for him to get upset about giving up the larger of the two rooms all those years ago. After all, Donny would grow into the room, and Logan wouldn't be living with them nearly as long anymore.

For Logan that was the beginning of the end. He'd lost a lot of respect for his father for allowing his mother to do that to him, and he'd lost his mother by default. She'd only had eyes for her new son, which made him jealous, and he'd had no use for the baby at all, and in truth, his parents either.

Sitting in the living room now pretending like he mourned the brother he barely knew made him feel like a fraud. The truth was he was more upset over the bigger picture. Grey and Joy, Garrison's brother and sister-in-law, were good people and were once close friends. Their son was always a funny kid who knew how to behave even back when he was a little tike, unlike the brother he'd always thought a spoiled brat.

Logan hadn't known their cousin Tony all that well, but he'd been a member of the White family, too. And Logan had long ago adopted the White clan as his own.

Mary White had known his pain even though she never once said anything about his situation at home. She had coddled him like she did her own children, and once, when he'd been hurt for the hundredth time by his mother's neglect and his father's indifference to it, she told him he should have been hers.

Logan had secretly agreed.

His own parents only started showing an interest in his life after he became a wealthy surgeon. At first he bought into it and was willing to forgive and forget, figuring he must have been too young to fully understand. So he started sending them tickets to visit him in Florida and they went, but they hadn't really been there to visit him. They took the money he'd placed at their disposal and took Donny to the beach and amusement parks, to zoos, and anywhere else the kid wanted to go.

When they were done vacationing, they would stop back by and spend an afternoon in his condo to tell him about all the wonderful things they'd done before heading back to Mystic Waters. It wasn't until after their third visit that Logan ran into an old friend from back home only to learn his parents made a habit of going back to Mystic Waters and telling people of their wonderful visit spending time with him.

At first he got angry, more with himself than them because he should have known better than to have expectations where they were concerned. Eventually he didn't care and was secretly grateful they stayed out of his hair while allowing him to fulfill his obligations as their son.

But now he didn't think he could stand being around them any longer, as his mother was either out cold from the prescriptions he'd written for her or bawling her eyes out until she vomited. The house smelled horrible from the garbage can she kept close but refused to have emptied.

His father wasn't as bad, but nearly, and neither of them even cared how any of this affected him. It had been too many years since they cared he was once their little boy too.

"Well, I'm heading out. I'll see you soon."

Jenna Hansen looked up when he stood, her swollen bloodshot eyes sad. "When will you be back?"

Logan shrugged, uncomfortable now that she was looking at him. She hadn't the entire two hours he'd been sitting on the couch. "I don't know. Soon…."

Anger twisted her lips. "What? You can't sit here and mourn Donny's passing with us?"

"Jenna," his father began, but Logan had truly had enough so he held up his hand to stop his father from talking. It was too late for him to offer anything, whether it was an opinion or a reprimand.

Logan studied his mother, wishing he felt anything at all for the pitiful woman. But they all knew his being there was equivalent to a lie. "I'm sorry for your loss. But it isn't mine. You locked me out of your heart and practically out of your house the day you found out you were pregnant with Donny. And you've never let me back in. Frankly, I learned to live with that long ago.

"So, no, I can't sit here and mourn with you. You took that ability away from me years ago, too." He glanced at his father, who didn't even have the guts to look back at him. Logan took one last look at the woman who had given him birth, before heading to the door.

"What about my pills? You only wrote a prescription for a few more days. What do I do when I run out?"

Logan stopped with his hand on the doorknob and shook his head. She hadn't protested his leaving, she hadn't denied his accusation, and she hadn't felt a moment's sorrow over losing the only other son she had. "I would suggest you call your family doctor." *I'm done.*

****

Garrison released the leg he just finished attaching to the final chair in Tom Whitehawk's kitchen set then stood back to look at it and then the other three. There was always a sense of satisfaction finishing a project, but there was also a sense of mourning that accompanied knowing that once finished, he would likely never see the artistry he'd put into it again.

Tom had commissioned the four different sets for his rental properties only days before Gavin went missing. He

105

had been more than kind in waiting so long for Garrison to get the backlog of orders he'd already had lined up completed and out the door before he'd started on Tom's.

After this piece, he would finally be caught back up. Though he knew others would commission his work if they thought he wanted it, he worried about having nothing more to do. It was a bittersweet problem. He'd have more time to look for Gavin and to spend with Rayne, but he'd have nothing to keep his mind and hands busy when he needed a break from it all, and Rayne was spending more time in *the cave*, as she called it, writing the novel she'd started soon after first coming to Mystic Waters.

"Hey!"

Garrison turned and smiled, glad for such a great distraction. He walked toward the doors of his shop and took Logan's outstretched hand. With his best friend back home, maybe some time off wouldn't be so bad. "Hey, yourself. What's up?"

Logan shrugged in the way he always had when he was bothered by something. "Not much. Just left the parents' house."

Garrison nodded, not needing to ask more. He was well aware of the relationship or lack of one between parents and son. Knowing what he knew made him love his parents all the more. So he changed the subject. "I've seen more of you today that I have in a hundred years. Wish you'd come by for dinner. You just missed the best piece of apple pie on the planet."

Logan's brows shot up. "Your mom finally got over that?"

Garrison snorted. "Not likely, but she had to concede when Rayne made some the first time she had dinner with us all and everyone devoured them like they hadn't eaten in years. Rayne made this one today just for me. And there's some waiting for when I get back in. I'll share, given it's you."

Logan grinned. "Lovely piece of work those two. And they cook too?"

"Mine does. I don't know about yours."

It was Logan's turn to snort. "I don't think I get to claim her. At least that's what she told me."

"Ouch."

"Yeah."

"Maybe it's your technique."

Logan burst out laughing. "My technique is quite superb, I'm told."

"By her?"

Logan laughed some more. "You're still a dick."

Grinning, Garrison agreed. It felt so good to laugh and cut up like they had as boys. It felt like they'd never been parted. "She was here earlier. I think she and Rayne are up to something, but I can't figure out what. Every time I walk in on them talking this look comes into their eyes." He frowned. "Like they are communicating silently."

"Well, maybe it's a twin thing. As I recall, you and I had the same type of system. I always knew what you were thinking and vice versa."

"Yep. You're right. I should have thought of that. Although I *am* the better-looking one in our case. They are identical."

"Says you," Logan countered.

"I got to claim the girl. Case closed."

"Yep," Logan said, still laughing, "Still a dick."

"You guys are nuts."

Garrison and Logan turned at the same time and smiled at Rayne. "How long have you been standing there?" Garrison asked, always taken aback by her beauty even though she had her hair in a ponytail and a pencil stuck over her ear. She looked at him and Logan like they were silly little boys.

"Long enough to know you two are talking about my sister and me."

Since she didn't seem upset, Garrison nodded. "Yep, I was just telling ugly here that I got the girl and he didn't measure up."

She smiled and walked into the arms he held open then

she turned to face Logan. Garrison loved the feel of her backside against him so he slid his arms around her and locked his fingers together at her belly. "So tell me, have you girls talked about us? Has Haven said anything about ugly over there?"

"I'm not supposed to disclose sisterly confidences."

Garrison grinned at Logan. "See, you were so bad Rayne can't even repeat what Haven said. She's afraid it will hurt your feelings."

"That is *not* what I said," Rayne said laughing, obviously tickled to be including in their foolishness.

"Then confess. Either throw him a bone or dash his hopes forever."

Rayne looked back and up, giving Garrison a wicked smile before she turned forward to face Logan. "Okay. I never repeated this, but her exact words were, 'It was crazy great to the tenth power.'"

Logan looked at her and then over her head to Garrison. He took his time allowing his smirk to form. "Told you."

"There you are! Where the hell have you been? I got worried when you didn't come home so I thought I'd come see if Rayne had heard from you because I can't get any damned cell phone service on this godforsaken mountain!

"I can't believe I actually walked all the way over here with it getting dark while you've been over here *visiting*! I ended up tripping over a damned branch and skinned my knee! And to make it even better I walked right into a tree and I think it may have broken my nose!"

Garrison, Rayne, and Logan froze, silently taking in the irate face of a disheveled and heaving Haven. No one moved or said a word, until they all burst out laughing.

Haven's jaw dropped and she growled before turning and leaving the shop. Rayne pushed Garrison's arms away and went after her sister. The two men looked at each other before Garrison raised his hand and Logan did the same. They high-fived each other, just as they always had as kids, when something went right in their world.

"Way to go, man," Garrison said, turning off the lights to the shop. As they left together, he closed and locked the door. He grinned at his brother-from-another-mother and repeated, "Way to go!"

****

"I can't believe I fell for a jerk!" Haven furiously paced around the living room twice before she realized Rayne was trying to contain a grin as she watched from the couch. "You think this is funny."

Rayne shook her head, though she was barely able to hide her amusement. "No. Of course not."

Haven glared at her. "You are supposed to be on my side."

"Always."

"Then why did you laugh at me? Look at me! I am bruised, cut, and a complete mess!"

Rayne looked Haven over then shrugged. "You have a few booboos. You'll heal, even more quickly than the rest of us. And you're not a complete mess, just a little messy. I'm sure Logan doesn't care that your hair has sticks sticking out of it."

Haven reached for her head immediately, feeling around. When she saw the grin on Rayne's face, she wanted to hit her. "Very funny.

"But I'm not talking about my appearance, I'm talking about sitting and waiting for a man who doesn't even care that I'm sitting and waiting for him. I'm talking about hiking across a mountain for a man who doesn't care that I like hiking about as much as I like being hit by a truck. I don't wait for men. They wait on me. They have always waited on me!"

Rayne nodded. "That's what this is about then. You gave Logan what you always made others wait for, without them having success, I might add."

"I should never have told you about that."

Rayne smiled. "I have to admit, I was a little surprised that you, um, well...."

"Oh, for Pete's sakes, just say it!"

"Okay, you've had long term relationships but never had sex with anyone. And then you had sex with a man you knew less than a full day. I was surprised."

"Yeah, well, so was I." Deflating, she looked at Rayne and sighed. "And those long term relationships I told you and Destiny about were not exactly physical. I was always afraid to touch anyone. Afraid they would feel the surge of power that used to heal. But men always took what I gave and never pushed for more. I think I intimidated them."

She shook her head. "And now I am so drawn to a man that it doesn't make sense, and every time I touch him, I harm him."

"Yet you were still waiting for him."

Haven nodded. "Yeah, I was. And the whole time I was trying to figure out how I could make the next month work."

Rayne's brows drew together. "The next month?"

"That's how long Logan plans to stay in Mystic Waters. We sort of agreed to explore this crazy attraction between us....

"I know it's a bad idea."

Rayne walked to her sister and put her arm around Haven's shoulder. "No, it isn't. It's a great idea. I know you'll find a way around blasting him with your super powers."

Haven chuckled. "Very funny."

Rayne squeezed then let Haven go. "You *did* laugh.

"But on a more serious note, Garrison is picking up that we have something going on...behind the scenes. I don't think it's anything to be concerned about because I overheard Logan telling him the looks we give each other are probably a twin communication thing." Rayne grinned. "Good man!

"I almost told them that we aren't twins, that we're triplets, but since they are talking about us behind our backs, I think I'll just let them learn that the hard way. When Destiny comes for the wedding I think we should find a way to have a lot of fun with it."

Haven nodded. "Good plan. At least with Garrison. Unless you plan on tying the knot soon, Logan will be back in Florida.

"Have you set a date?"

Rayne shook her head and sighed heavily. "No. We're waiting a little longer. Neither of us wants to, but there is too much misery going on in the community and for his family right now. It doesn't feel right to plan a celebration."

It was Haven's turn to put her arm around Rayne's shoulder and squeeze. "I'm sorry, Sis. Hopefully this will all end soon."

"Yeah, me too. I feel it in my bones that Gavin is still alive. But we are running out of places to look."

Chapter Nine

Gavin sat up in the bed and stretched then realized he was no longer tied down, nor was he blindfolded. Excitement filled him as he blinked against the bright natural light filling the room. *Everything* was white, blindingly white, so it took him a few minutes of shading and un-shading his eyes with his hands as he gave them time to adjust.

In the five days since he'd been relocated to the house, the woman holding him had changed, or maybe she just wasn't as big a monster as he'd made her out to be for all those months.

She hadn't let him do anything that first day, but she hadn't been particularly unkind either. Then on the second day he'd gotten braver and tried talking to her more, though he hadn't gotten up the nerve to ask her what it was he was supposed to call her. He tried ma'am and she seemed to like it, so that was that.

By the third day she was bringing him hot meals on a regular basis or left plenty of snacks if she said she wouldn't be able to get back until late. Of course he had no idea when she was home or not home as the radio played twenty-four hours at a time. Now that he could see and had time to study his room, he was able to confirm the speaker was set just below the ceiling on the wall facing the bed.

He'd been fortunate enough to be able to hold going to the bathroom unless she was present and so far was spared the embarrassment of being taped. He couldn't stand the thought of her watching him using the bedpan or bottle. It hadn't been pleasant having to take a dump with the bathroom door open, but he was fairly certain she at least left the bathroom when he was in there relieving himself.

So finally, before going to bed last night, he'd balled up all his courage and had asked her if she would consider letting him take off his blindfold when she wasn't home. Her response had been slow in coming, and in the end she told him she would have to think about it.

Apparently she had, and had removed the blindfold herself while he slept, and to his amazement the restraint too, which meant she was starting to trust him. He tried not being obvious about it as he took a slow perusal around the room, but he wanted to know where the camera was.

Gavin saw nothing that looked remotely like a camera and was afraid to look at everything again because it might look suspicious if she was watching from another room, or if he was alone in the house now, but she checked the video later. He climbed down off the bed and headed for the bathroom.

Thrilled that he was finally afforded full privacy, Gavin relieved himself, showered, and put on a clean pair of pajama pants from the stack left on a shelf in the bathroom closet. He looked around, but other than towels, washcloths, and the bedclothes, there was nothing more than a couple of unopened bottles of shampoos and bath soaps as well as a still boxed tube of toothpaste.

He turned to the sink and opened the tube of paste he'd already used three quarters of since getting to brush his teeth again. He loaded his brush before scrubbing at his teeth and gums, determined to get rid of the yellow line where they met. He was relieved to see that although he needed a good cleaning from the dentist, it looked like his gums were probably okay. He just hoped he hadn't developed any cavities. He'd never had one before and hated to think he might now.

"Good morning!"

Gavin froze before quickly rinsing his mouth out and his toothbrush off. He stood where he was, not sure what he was supposed to do. He took a breath then turned his back to the open door. "I'm in here. I don't have a blindfold on."

"It's okay. I wanted to let you know the way we are going to do things from here forward. Come on out."

Gavin braced himself to see the woman for the first time, afraid that if he knew her he'd lose it. Schooling his features in neutrality he stepped from the room to find her head covered with a hat blanketed in heavy black netting, and she carried a large brown paper in her arms. "Hi," he said, not sure what else to say.

Though he had no way of knowing for sure, he thought she smiled at him as a flash of white from behind the netting came and went quickly.

"I've brought you fast food fare this morning, Mc-things, because I don't have much time. I won't be back for lunch so PB&J sandwiches, chips and bottled waters are in the bag as well. I expect you to behave yourself while I'm gone."

"Yes, ma'am."

The flash of white appeared again.

"Well, I've turned off the radio because I figured you might want to watch some TV."

Only then realizing it was actually quiet, Gavin nodded, unable to contain the smile that pulled at his lips. "Yes, ma'am."

"Good. Well, I've got to go. But remember I'll be watching you."

"You don't have to worry. I'm really happy to be here."

She nodded and backed toward the closed door then stopped. "I'm glad you're here too. I've been waiting for you for a long time."

Gavin stayed in the spot just outside the bathroom door after she left and listened as her footsteps disappeared. He swallowed, afraid to move, in case she was watching. He didn't want to do anything that would have her running back into the room to tie him back to the bed, or worse, make her want to blindfold him again.

Even though his eyes hurt from all the light, he welcomed it more than the air he breathed. He moved to the dresser that the television sat on and lifted the remote lying on top. It was an older set, not one of the flat screens his dad liked. But he didn't care. For the first time in forever, he was going to get to know what was going on in the world outside of his own.

Gavin turned it on and instantly turned the volume down before flipping through the channels. He had no idea what time it was, or if there was any news on, but that was what he wanted to see.

His dad had always watched the local news to keep up with what was happening in the community, and Gavin was hoping he could find out something, *anything*, about his own case, his biggest fear being it had been too long since his kidnapping and he didn't know if anyone still looked for him or not.

When he could only find national news programs that talked about things he would care about if his life was normal, but didn't really care about now, he searched for something to entertain him, settling on reruns of *M*A*S*H*. Again his father came to mind, as they had laughed at the show together, even though his mom had thought some things about the show inappropriate.

Gavin settled back on his bed and opened the big bag. He unwrapped and devoured the *McBreakfast* sandwich in five bites, not caring that it had gotten cold.

****

She hurried to pull off the hat that was necessary to hide her identity and changed her clothes, putting back on the outfit she was forced to wear to get through her duties. She was coming to hate it, but the outfit reflected who she was to the world, and kept her private life a secret. No one, not even the man she answered to on a daily basis suspected a thing.

And she had to keep it that way.

Renting the house had been a stroke of genius, even though it had taken forever before she found the right one to live in. It was too bad she'd had to go through so many males but it was what it was. Now that she finally had the right one, she didn't mind paying that hippie freak of a landlord for its use. She just hoped he never called in his right to inspect the property or she would have to figure out how to dispose of him, too.

She wouldn't be stopped now that she finally had everything perfect.

In a year or two, once the boy was well into manhood, he would love her as she was meant to be loved. But in the meantime she would train him, first to depend on her and her alone, and then finally to fulfill every fantasy she could conjure. But he had to be ready, and she had to be patient because she was no pedophile, just a woman who had particular needs.

Satisfied she had everything headed in the right direction she glanced at the monitor, glad it was trained straight on the kid. Yes, she knew the name his birth parents had given him, but she would never call him by it. Maybe next time she came to the house she would try the name he had to live with in order to live. Maybe not. She'd think on it.

It would be the ultimate test.

The others had chosen that moment to defy her, and it had cost them their lives. They hadn't wanted to be her Jimmy.

But her patience won out this time and had worn this one down until his health had taken a really bad turn. Then she had improved his living conditions so drastically that he would never want less.

She hoped.

She didn't want to end up having to kill him too. It was getting harder to dispose of the bodies and people were watching their kids more closely. It was a shame she'd had to settle for guys so young, but she didn't think she could control one any older.

It didn't matter that he would remain forever younger than her Jimmy would have been. As long as he would be her Jimmy.

She finished putting herself together and looked in the

long mirror for only a second. Satisfied with the results she waved to the monitor, laughed, and headed out the door.

*****

"Where the hell have you been, woman?"

Martha stopped just inside the door, surprised to see Burt home. Though her heart was pounding, she tilted her head back enough that her chin was up slightly. "I've been out paying bills. I didn't know you were going to be off today."

"I'm not. I had to take a dump and I was doing traffic duty about a quarter of a mile away. Why did you leave the house without permission?" Burt began unbuckling his belt.

Martha sighed. She really wasn't in the mood. *Not at all.* The game had played out as far as she was concerned. "I got my period this morning and I was short on supplies so I went on and took care of other things too."

He released the belt buckle and she sighed again, this time in relief. Since the beating following her little performance on the table, Burt hadn't touched her, or even paid her any mind, so why, when she could finally get a reaction out of him, did she just not give a damn?

Martha knew the answer, but she couldn't smile.

"It's only been a couple of weeks since you were on the rag. Is something wrong with you?" He looked at her with real concern.

Martha hesitated, confused by his reaction. Burt *never* expressed concern for her. *Ever.* Since she hadn't fully thought out the lie, she could only hope he didn't notice that she wasn't carrying in any bags. Not sure what else to do, she moved toward the kitchen determined to distract him before his brain started working. The only thing he liked better than battering her was batter on his fried chicken.

But she didn't have that kind of time. "It's close to lunch time. Would you like me to make you some sandwiches?"

His pig eyes lit up. "Sure." He glanced at the big black watch on his wrist and she waited for him to tell her it wasn't anywhere close to lunchtime, but he didn't, he just went to sit in his chair at the kitchen table.

"It's a little early, but I don't mind."

Martha wasn't sure what to make of his mood. He seemed almost...solicitous. Was he picking up on the changes in her? That she was bored with him? That she wanted something different now and could finally see attaining it? She hoped not, she wasn't ready yet. "I'm sure it's nothing, but I'll call the doctor if you think I should."

Burt looked at her in panic before shaking his head. "I'm sure it's nothing. I'd give it another month or so...."

Martha nodded then turned her back to him before grinning. She knew he feared her getting an examination. Between all the ripped flesh and scarring she was certain there would be a lot of questions, and she had made sure he knew it years ago too, just in case he ever got any ideas of his own.

She slapped together two large sandwiches just the way he liked them, added chips and a large glass of milk. Martha bit her bottom lip as she stepped up to his side, wondering if he would slide his hand up her leg so he could play with or abuse the bottom he expected to be bare.

It was his habit to do so when he ate lunch at home. Sometimes she had liked it, sometimes she simply endured it, but because he knew she hated him doing it when she really *was* on her period, he nearly always did. Only this time the surprise would be his. Not only wasn't she bleeding, she had on panties.

She sat the plate and glass down quickly but gently and then backed away. He immediately started eating, ignoring her. She went back to the counter and started to close everything up to put it away, but stopped and looked at the back of Burt's fat head.

Martha took a deep breath and pulled out a piece of bread, added meat and cheese, and then mustard. She folded it over, wondering why she had put up with him for so long. But she knew the answer.

And she knew it was time to start the transition that

would lead to their end. Time to take charge in small steps, and now was as good a time as any. She carried the sandwich to the other side of the table and sat down to face him.

Burt looked up at her and frowned then continued chewing. Martha kept her gaze on him as she took the first bite, chewed slowly, and then swallowed. She continued to watch him watch her as she repeated the process of eating, wondering what was going through his head. She hadn't sat with him for a meal in years, always standing back and waiting for his instruction.

But now she was taking back control of her life. She had paid for her sins, and she would sin no more now that everything else she had worked so hard for was falling into place. Burt didn't know it, but he had always played by her rules, taking her when and how she wanted though she would make him believe it was his idea and that he was in control. Or, if he started getting suspicious, she would just endure his abuse as she always had but only just long enough to get everything else solidified. And now everything was coming together nicely, so she would wait a little longer. The time would come when she would know it was right to start her new life without him.

Then game over.

And if she had to, she would sin one last time.

Chapter Ten

Glad his hands were insured for a ridiculous amount of money since he'd busted his knuckles twice, Logan helped Garrison carry the four handmade tables with their sixteen matched set chairs from the shop to secure them inside the back of the cargo trailer. Wrapped and stacked they nearly filled the enclosed flat bed, but it was clear Garrison knew what he was doing as everything fit with room to spare. They each grabbed a barn type door and closed them before Garrison slid the bar home. Finally they snapped the padlocks into place.

"Bye, guys!"

Logan turned and smiled at Rayne and then sent Haven one as well, but she still wasn't talking to him and didn't smile back. He turned to get in the passenger seat of the truck since two could play that game. He sure hoped she came back from helping Rayne shop for a car in a better mood. Living with a woman you desperately wanted to taste again who gave you endless hours of the silent treatment was worse than living alone.

He watched as Garrison's woman planted a long deep kiss on her man, and he felt a moment of envy and then decided he was being a shit. If he was going to fix this, and he sure as hell wanted to, he was better off doing it now, rather than later. Logan stepped back out of the truck and walked past the couple who had turned to watch him. Garrison had a grin on his lips. Rayne's gaze held a warning that said he was biting off more than he could chew.

Logan ignored both and approached Rayne's rental car. Haven sat in the passenger seat and looked at him like he was lower than slug feces. He overlooked that as he was on a mission that had him pulling her door open, grabbing her arm, and pulling her out of the seat. Since he figured he probably deserved it, he also ignored her less than ladylike protests.

But enough was enough. He locked her in his left arm and captured her jaw with his right hand before taking her mouth with his own and holding on until she stopped fighting him. When he felt her relax he eased up, and then changed the kiss from dominating to adoring, hoping she got the message.

The blinding pain that forced him to double over only made sense when his knees hit the ground. He cupped his balls and choked back the bile rising up his throat as he moaned and rocked. He looked up at Haven in too much pain to express himself. Garrison and Rayne were instantly over him blocking her from view.

"Get *her* out of here!"

Logan saw the hurt and shock in Rayne's eyes, and wanted to tell Garrison not to bark at her like that, he just couldn't form any words yet. He shook his head, trying to communicate, but neither one was looking at him. Garrison was instantly contrite and apologetic, but Rayne ignored him as she climbed in the rental car and told Haven to do the same.

Without another word to either of them, she backed out of her parking spot and shortly disappeared down the road. Garrison blew out a long breath then reached down to help Logan to his feet.

"Looks like we are both in it up to our knees now."

Logan took a deep breath before finding his voice. "I'm sorry, man."

"Don't talk yet. You sound like a cartoon character."

Logan laughed and then cursed as pain slashed through him. "Need to sit down."

Garrison walked him the ten feet to the shop and then leaned him against the outside of the building while he hurried in for a chair. He was back out in a second and helping Logan into the seat and then went back in to get another. Logan looked over at him and apologized again.

Garrison waved the apology away. "I need to call Tom

and tell him we won't be able to deliver the furniture until tomorrow…" He looked over at Logan and grinned. "Or maybe the next day."

Logan felt like an idiot. He had singlehandedly ruined everything. "Damn. I thought I could make her remember what we had. And all I did was screw things up for you.

"I'm almost afraid to try, but we have to fix this, at least for you. What should we do?"

Garrison leaned back in his seat and stared straight ahead. "I think a lot of groveling will be required."

Logan nodded, finally starting to feel almost normal again, although he was sure his balls were the size of grapefruits that were filled with molten lava. "I'm sure.

"I can bake."

Garrison choked out a laugh. "What?"

Logan grinned. "You heard me. It's relaxing after a long day in the operating room. And I cook pretty well too over and above the standard steaks on a grill. But baking is my specialty."

Garrison nodded. "The baking would be good, and I can flip the steaks. You know how to make anything wicked with chocolate? Rayne doesn't know I know, but she is a secret addict."

Logan nodded. "Sure do. It's a super chocolate cake with a ganache poured over it and then I pile grated chocolate and chocolate curls on the top for decoration and taste.

"Of course you want to eat it sparingly; it's about five hundred and fifty calories for a thin slice, but the women I've made it for were very grateful."

Garrison grinned. "Was that before or after you all went shopping in your pearls for purses and high heels?"

Logan leaned back and crossed his arms over his chest, his smile smug. "Sure, make fun of me. But when I said the women were grateful…I meant *really grateful.*"

"Okay, I would settle for forgiven, but *really grateful* is better. I'm in. By the way, I've been meaning to ask you how you burnt you head."

****

"That fathead!"

Haven bit her bottom lip. "I didn't mean to cause trouble between you and Garrison. As for Logan? I guess I regret that, too. Garrison isn't a fathead. He was protecting his friend. I overreacted because I was already feeling pissy and I don't like being manhandled."

Rayne slid her sister a glance, wondering how Haven had managed to recover from her anger so quickly when she was still smarting over the way Garrison had talked to her. "Of course not, no one does."

Haven smiled. "Have to give credit where credit is due though. He handled me pretty good the other day."

Rayne grinned as she spotted a line of new SUVs that looked interesting. She turned into the Toyota dealership and gasped as men appeared from out of nowhere and started running toward her. It was obvious they were trying to beat each other to get to her first. She kept on driving, determined to get away, feeling like a dead carcass being circled by vultures.

They almost trapped her but she just shook her head at the one closest to her and nearly sideswiped him since he didn't take the message as intended. It was a relief to pull out of the lot and get back on the road. "I'm not feeling car shopping today."

Haven laughed. "Don't be too hard on them. A man's gotta eat."

Rayne conceded the point. "True, but I'm not feeling generous enough to be their breakfast. Let's do something else. Any ideas?"

Haven was silent a few minutes before nodding. "Yes. I want to investigate those crystals you found. Let's go back where you got them and see if the proprietor knows anything about their origins."

Rayne nodded, glanced in her rear view mirror, and made a U-turn. She hit the gas and they were flying back toward the mountain.

Haven settled back and sighed. "The area is so

beautiful. But, I can't stop thinking about Logan. I think I busted his balls pretty badly."

Rayne maneuvered a tight curve then glanced at her. "Yes, you did. I imagine they gave up on furniture delivery and headed straight to the hospital."

"Crap. Now I feel *really* bad. I didn't mean to knee him that hard."

"If nothing else, I'm sure he's learned his lesson."

Rayne glanced at Haven, who glanced back and they both laughed. Rayne turned back to the narrowing mountain road. "We'll give them a few hours to recover then go back so they can kiss our feet."

"I think that sounds like a fine plan. At least for you guys. Logan may be done with me." She frowned. "Saying the words hurt more than I expected. But maybe it's for the best. If we developed strong feeling for each other the complications could be too numerous to count."

"I doubt he's done with you. He's totally smitten."

Haven blew out a breath. "Yeah, me too. But it can't lead anywhere.

"Unless he thinks my wearing gloves every time we get intimate is sexy, I can't let myself go with him like that again. What if I stopped his heart or something equally disastrous?"

"It's a problem, for sure," Rayne agreed. Her mind worked the problem over furiously as she maneuvered a curve. "We'll call Destiny and ask her to overnight the books to us. Maybe there's something we can do. There are all kinds of instructions on how to counter things as well as create them.

"I've wished the books were with me several times since moving here, and had already planned to ask you both if I could borrow them for a while before your arrival. It just didn't feel right to take them when I left. They belong to us all. Not just me."

"It would have been fine," Haven assured her. "Neither one of us ever bothered to look at them, much less read them. I think they'll end up being yours to pass down anyway. The little I do know about our history is that only one of the three ever has children. I think you are the one for our generation, and then Destiny and I will get to play aunties to your girls just like Aunt Soleli and Aunt Lune Brille were for us."

"I've always wondered why that is. It isn't fair that it has always been only one of the three sisters," Rayne said, before honking at the car crawling along in front of them.

She knew Haven watched with her as it sped up then they smiled at each other. "Don't say it."

Grinning, Haven shrugged. "Are we talking about your road rage issues?" She laughed. "The thought never entered my mind," she added sarcastically. "But back to the subject at hand. I've wondered too. Sometimes I think I'd like to have kids, but I wouldn't want to take that opportunity away from you, or Destiny. But I don't believe it's ours to decide."

"You're right," Rayne agreed, as she sped up on the car again. "All that we are is decided for us. But I feel the same way…wanting to have some babies but not wanting to take anything from you and Dee."

"What do you think Garrison will think if you aren't the one? Or better yet, if you are. How will you train them and not let him know?"

"All good questions I don't have the answers to."

Rayne suddenly swerved and Haven braced her hand against the dash as Rayne pulled off onto one of the many extended shoulders that were built for cars needing to stop while traveling up the mountain roads.

"What's wrong?' Haven asked.

"I saw my friend, Qaqeemasq."

Haven looked out of the car windows as if she were looking for him, though they both knew she would never see what Rayne saw.

"Is that always a bad thing?"

Rayne nodded. "Pretty much."

When Rayne just continued to sit still and look straight ahead Haven placed a hand on her arm. "What do we do?"

"I'm not sure. He wants me to get out and follow him. But one, I can't abandon the car here, and two, if he is leading me to another body I will have no way to explain it."

"That is a conundrum."

"To say the least."

Cars passed them occasionally as Rayne debated her options. Haven unbuckled her seatbelt and then Rayne's. "Go on. I'll slide over to your seat and wait. If anyone stops to see what I'm doing I'll tell them my sister had to use the bathroom really bad and couldn't wait."

Rayne nodded. "Great idea. Embarrassing, but great." She waited for a line of cars to pass then swung open her door. After quickly exiting the car, she hurried to the other side and knocked on the window. Haven settled herself in the driver's seat then hit the electric button, taking the passenger side window down.

"I'll be as quick as possible. But if I'm not back in ten minutes, drive on up the mountain and find a place to turn around then come back. You'll have to go back some before you can turn around again, but I don't want anyone getting suspicious that you are sitting here for too long. Police do patrol these roads all the time."

"I don't like the idea of leaving you here at all. Just hurry. Tell Running Bear I said to make this fast!"

Rayne smiled though she was nearly sick with concern for Haven. Sitting on the side of the road was not the safest thing for her to do given the crimes that had, and were, being committed in the area. "I promise I'll be as quick as I can. But no more than ten minutes… Okay?"

Haven nodded and glanced at the dash. She stated the time then nodded to Rayne again. "Okay. Ten minutes."

Rayne headed in the direction of the tree line and shivered, knowing she and her sister would soon be out of each other's sight. She didn't know why that bothered her so much, other than the obvious reason of a serial killer on the loose, more people now being reported missing, and the such, but it was more than that, and she didn't know if her fear was for Haven or for herself.

Trying to ignore her sudden propensity for premonition, Rayne followed her friendly neighborhood ghost into the forest hoping he wanted her for any other reason than the one she feared. It surprised her to see him this far from the area where she, and the White families, lived, and she wanted to ask him about that but more than anything she just wanted to get wherever they were going, so she could hurry back. The further she got from Haven the more uncomfortable she felt about it.

It didn't take long before Qaqeemasq stopped and pointed to the ground. Rayne swallowed, preparing herself for the worst, then moved to the area he indicated. She looked down and saw a moss covered rock. She looked back at him and frowned. "What?"

Cold air circled her and he pointed again, jabbing his finger downward this time.

Rayne stooped down and looked at the granite stone then realized it was out of place with everything around it. She touched it and warmth flooded her senses. She glanced up at Qaqeemasq. "Is this a headstone?"

Warmth flooded her again as it always did when he was satisfied with her. She pushed at the moss to dislodge it before she examined the rock, but she still nearly missed the chiseled letters as time and weather had apparently worn off a great deal of the stone's surface. Getting on her knees, she placed her face close to it and rubbed at the green stain the moss left behind. She placed her fingers in the slight indentions and tried to determine what the letters were. It took several tries before she realized that it spelled out F-A-W-N-T-A-I-N.

Rayne's head jerked up and she swallowed. "Is this my ancestor? Is this Fawntain Cavanaugh?"

Excitement made her cry out as warmth flooded her. She shook her head. "But how? How did she get here? The books say she lived with a tribe of Indians on the East Coast the duration of her life."

As had happened only once before, Rayne's mind went

blank and the image of her grandmother of many generations before stood before her, a beautiful young woman, her belly very large with child, or in her case, children.

Tears poured from her eyes, washing her face in sorrow as she packed the weather-worn wagon that had been her mother's, and a part of her entire life. Faded now from years of use and storage, she finished placing the last item in the wagon and climbed aboard the splintering seat before lifting the reins. Fawntain glanced back once and Rayne felt the sadness in the faces of the tribe she had called family, and the devastation twisting her ancestor's soul.

Fawntain looked down at the three long fresh cuts made on both of her forearms, marring her perfect skin. She snapped the leather in her hands and the two old nags that had lived almost as long as her plodded forward carrying her away from everything she loved, save those growing in her womb.

More gently this time Rayne came out of the trance and her eyes filled with tears. She'd felt the sorrow of her ancestor and the sorrow of those she'd left behind. She glanced to where Qaqeemasq hovered in sparkling wonder. "She came here alone?"

Warmth flooded Rayne and she allowed the tears to increase, mourning for the young woman who must have endured untold fear and agony and ultimately the horrendous pain of giving birth thrice during the long trip from the northern east coast to the Blue Ridge Mountains.

"Is that why you're here, too? You knew her?"

Again warmth, although this time it was sharper. "You loved her?"

Qaqeemasq dissolved without answering, but she had felt his sorrow before he completely disappeared. She ran her hand over the stone again, this time lovingly. "I'm so sorry you had to endure all that alone. I hope you know that I feel honored to know you."

Thinking about Haven's questions regarding her ability to contact any spirit other than Qaqeemasq had Rayne closing her eyes. She concentrated on the woman who had continued their line all on her own, but when she opened them, she was still alone with the grave marker.

Rayne sighed. Of course she was still alone. Her grandmother of many generations and she were of the same bloodline, and therefore their hereditary gifts did not reach for each other.

She rose and looked around once more before heading back to the spot where she hoped Haven still waited, wanting to share the experience. Fortunately she *was* still there when Rayne emerged from the forest but, unfortunately, a police car was parked behind her.

Rayne stopped short when she realized it was the little fat man who made her feel so creepy when he'd arrived to investigate the pie-stealing break-in when she still lived at the cabin Haven and Logan now occupied.

"There she is."

Rayne took in the disgust on Haven's face and hurried to get to the car. "Hi. Sorry. Had to use the bathroom, bad." She rushed to get into the passenger seat hoping he would let them leave without delay, but he leaned into Haven's window causing Haven to lean toward Rayne.

"Well, be careful. It isn't safe for two such lovely ladies to be parked along this road. Anything could happen."

Rayne felt awash in ants and had to keep from squirming. "Sorry. I'll make sure to go before I leave home from now on. You have a good day," she said, hoping he would take the hint.

Burt Thompson nodded and stepped back though he remained bent over to look into the car. "You too, ladies," he said, smiling at them both. He looked over to Rayne and then at Haven again, and shook his head. "I would have never guessed who was who."

Rayne swallowed, not liking the hungry look in his eyes. "Well thank you for stopping, officer. It's nice to see you again," she lied.

He winked at her. "Call me Burt. And be sure to tell Mr. White to let me know if he learns anything new about his nephew. Would like to know the kid's okay, but had to hand that case over to take something the department felt was more urgent. I'm sure Mr. White wouldn't agree that anything was."

Rayne nodded, just wanting him to let them go, but she held her smile. "I sure will. Thanks again."

Finally he stepped back and Haven pushed the button sending her window up. "Get us out of here," Rayne said, barely moving her lips as she continued to smile at the creepy officer staring at them.

Once they were on the road Haven shuddered and frowned at Rayne. "Thank God you got back when you did. I thought that man was going to force me to get out of the car. I swear he wanted to put his hands on me! *I felt it!* How is that possible? That is Destiny's gift. Anyway," she shuddered again, "He scares me."

"I know. He creeps me out, too."

"But he knew you. He thought I was you until I told him I wasn't, and then he got even weirder. I think he actually believes women are attracted to him."

Rayne settled in the seat and tried not to let the encounter unnerve her. "When I first moved here, and Garrison invited me to a family gathering I made several apple pies. I left a couple behind when we left for the afternoon, thinking I would give one to Garrison and keep one myself. When we got back that evening someone or something had eaten them or at least eaten at them."

Haven slid her a concerned glance but said nothing.

"With all the craziness going on in the community, we thought it best to report it to the police. He was the one that came to the cabin and the entire time he was in the house, I felt sick to my stomach. There is something weird about him, and it scares me, too."

Haven pulled over at the next rest stop and she and Rayne quickly traded places before heading on again. "I'm thinking something that may be completely out of line, and you can take it or leave it, but I think you should say something to Garrison about checking out that officer's story.

"What if he wasn't taken off the case for something

bigger? What if he was taken off the case because they suspect him of something?"

What felt like a load of gravel landed in Rayne's gut and she nodded. "I don't know if you're out of line or not, but I think it is definitely something he needs to check into. Would you mind if we look into the crystals another time? I need to get home."

"Not at all. I'm not in the mood anymore either. And I have some serious apologizing to do."

Chapter Eleven

Burt Thompson sat in his captain's office and seriously thought about just pulling out his gun and offing the guy. But that would cost him more than a reprimand. That would cost him his freedom and a chance to fuck Martha's brains out while he thought of those two identical beauties. But his wife was acting so whacky that she was scaring his dick into noncompliance.

It was too bad he couldn't do the twins, as he'd be more than happy to tie them together and show them just what it was he had, and was. The fact the fantasy caused his dick to fill to maximum capacity just proved the problem was Martha and not him, and he sure did hate to waste a good erection.

"...so you are on temporary suspension until the review is completed."

Burt frowned. "What?"

John Grammar shook his head, obviously annoyed. "Have you been listening?"

Fuck, no! "Yes sir, Captain, but I think I must have missed something. Did you say I am suspended?"

"Yes. Without pay. Until the investigation has concluded."

Burt shook his head, panicking. "*What* investigation?"

John took his seat and put his hands together, making a steeple of his fingers. "I think you need to see a counselor to help you with this inability to focus. It will be a requirement of your reinstatement, *as well*." He opened the long thin drawer at his flat belly and took the top card from a stack. He leaned forward and held it out to Burt. "This is Dr. Victor's card. Make an appointment for tomorrow."

Burt took the card and looked at the captain. "I don't understand any of this." *As well as what?* "Why am I suspended?"

John hesitated then took a deep breath. "Because you unnerve people. Especially women. I've gotten several complaints about them being stopped, and all you do is chat them up like a stalker. That isn't in your job description, and given what's been happening in Mystic Waters, everyone is jittery. I warned you to follow the rules.

"And...there has been an allegation that you are abusive towards your wife. She hasn't corroborated the accusation, but we are required to follow up on that, too."

Blind fury almost caused Burt to lose control, but he took several breaths before asking, "Who made the accusation? When was my wife questioned?"

"Martha said she refused to talk to anyone about what she called your particular sexual needs. That wasn't exactly a denial and given the complaints, her wording concerns me. Like I said, see the doctor."

Burt couldn't move. It was one thing to live with his need for the painful and abusive. It was something else for the entire police department to know about it. He knew now why everyone looked at him as they did. He rose, took the badge off his chest and, more reluctantly, the gun from his holster and laid both on the desk.

Without another word, he turned and left the office. Keeping his eyes trained straight ahead, he made it to the front door of the police station without making eye contact with anyone. He didn't stop moving forward until he reached the cruiser then realized he probably had no right to use it.

Burt looked back and thought, *fuck it.* If they wanted the damned car, they could go to his house and pick it up later. But first, he had someplace to be.

He pulled out of the parking lot and headed out of town, ready to put his *emergency* plan in action. It was actually a good thing he had some time off, but he *was* going to get his position back when he turned out to be the hero for finding the *"killer"* of Grey and Joy White, once he set the freak up.

Burt drove to the storage building at the edge of town and punched in the numbers to open the electronic gate, before heading for the unit at the far end on the right side. After a quick look around, he slowed and stopped the car. It was a relief there was no one about—what he was about to do required complete secrecy, and a lack of witnesses that could identify him or report his actions later. But then, most of his life had been about secrets.

No one could know his mother left his father. No one could know that first his father and finally his uncle sexually abused him for years until they made him just like them. Only Burt was proud he'd never touched a kid, which was what he had been at the time.

He hadn't been about to tell anyone of his past or his present or he never would have qualified for the force. The psych evaluation required applicants for the police department to have pasts that were squeaky clean and without blemish, which he thought so unfair because what had happened to him had been beyond his control.

So he'd lied.

Even Martha hadn't known anything about the abuse he'd suffered, and until recently she had accepted him anyway, which was why he had protected her for so long, even committing murder on her behalf. Sometimes he wanted to tell her, because he deserved hero recognition, but then she'd know he knew about her not-so-squeaky-clean past. And he liked having the upper hand in *all* his relationships.

Burt gathered the materials he needed and loaded them in the truck, knowing he'd have to find a way to get them into the house without Martha knowing. He needed to solidify his plan, making sure he knew exactly where his target was at any given time on any given day, but most importantly, when he was not going to be at that little shack he called home.

Feeling better about his suspension more and more all the time, Burt finished packing the supplies he'd spent the last month gathering and then he reached for the most important item. The gun that took the life of the police officer and his wife once belonged to Burt's father. Since the pistol was never registered, no one knew of its existence.

He'd almost thrown it in the lake after the murders, but he hadn't been able to part with it. Not because it was his father's, as far as he was concerned dear old Dad could rot in hell. But because it was the only weapon he had that no one could trace back to him.

Now that he didn't have to punch a time clock, he could put a couple of weeks into establishing patterns, discovering associations and, most importantly, weaknesses. Then he would set his victim up and set himself up as the savior.

Of course there were still a couple of problems with his plan. One, there was someone out there committing multiple murders and the department believed Gavin White's kidnapping, the remains already found from those murders, and the death of the Whites were all related.

If he set his intended victim up to take the fall for the murders of the Whites and then the kid showed up, everyone would know he had killed them and Burt's ass would be in a sling ten times over. But even if the kid never showed up and more murders occurred after his victim was jailed, then the police would question if they had the right man, and they would look at Burt in a way that would still put his ass in a sling.

"Fuck!"

Burt threw the last of his things in the trunk, knowing he probably had very little time before someone was sent to get the cruiser. Of all the possible problems with his upcoming plans, none of them would matter if the game ended before it began.

He slammed the trunk and then closed the door of the storage unit. Even though it was now empty, he locked the unit back up. There was a chance he would need it again, maybe even to use as a hiding place temporarily, if something went wrong.

A man had to have a contingency plan.

****

"I'm sorry to bother you, ma'am. I'm Kathy Gishwell with the Mystic Water's police department. I understand you are in some distress regarding your husband?"

Martha Thompson frowned at the female police officer standing on her doorstep. "I don't know what you're talking about. I haven't called the police." She watched as the young woman glanced at a small spiral note pad before frowning at her.

"It seems someone called claiming to be you then refused to talk about anything. When that happens, we get concerned that a woman is being battered and she is too scared to come forward, even when she wants to. Would you mind if I come in and see if we can make sense of this?"

"It isn't really convenient right now."

"I really must insist, ma'am. It would be better to do this now, rather than after your husband gets home."

Martha hated pushy people and the officer was pushing hard. She didn't know what to do. The last thing she needed was someone trying to dig into their lives. But short of being rude, it didn't look like the woman was going to go away. "For just a minute then."

Officer Gishwell smiled and stepped forward as Martha pushed the door open further. She had to hold her irritation back as the officer seemed determined to look at every single stick of furniture, curtain, and trinket in the house, all while walking to the couch.

"Do you mind if I sit down?"

Indicating the couch, Martha took the chair Burt usually sat in. "What is it that I can do for you?"

"Like I said, we received a call, and the woman said she was you, and that there were some, well, sexual battery issues."

Martha tried to hold in her fury. Who could have done such a thing? She had never once told anyone about their sex life. And that only left Burt. But he would never tell. He would be the one to pay.

"I can't help you, Officer. I didn't make the call so I guess it was a hoax."

"I see." She studied Martha before making notes in that little notebook. "Well, since your husband is an officer of the law, and has been suspended pending the outcome of an investigation into the allegations, would you be willing to undergo an examination to help disprove this issue quickly?"

Her stomach churning, Martha just stared at the woman. Finally she shook her head. "I'm sorry, but no. You will just have to take my word for it."

Officer Gishwell rose to her feet after making one last entry into her notebook. Martha stood too, wanting to get the woman out the door but seriously terrified. *Burt was suspended?* That meant he could be home any time, and if he hadn't revealed anything about their sex lives, then he would assume she had.

"Thank you for your time, ma'am. I'll see myself out."

As much as she wanted to watch the door close behind that woman, Martha followed her. "Just one thing...."

Officer Gishwell turned, her brows raised inquisitively. Martha swallowed. "Was Burt suspended just because someone made a wild accusation against him about me?"

The officer's features relaxed into an almost smile. "I'm sorry, ma'am, I'm not at liberty to discuss that."

Martha nodded and watched as the officer returned to an unmarked car. Her heart pounded as the woman backed out of the driveway and then slowly drove away. She was still standing there trying to process what had just happened when Burt pulled in moments later. He spotted her and glared, making her stomach churn.

Smiling from behind the glass storm door in welcome took considerable effort as Martha's lips trembled, along with the rest of her. All her decisions to take control of her life depended on her actually getting to live it and knowing his temper, and that he was probably going to blame her for something as serious as getting suspended from the police force, made him more dangerous than ever. Worse still, if he didn't end up killing her she would have to figure out what she would do with him home all day. She wouldn't be able to take care of anything without him sticking his nose in it, and that just wouldn't do. There were just some things he couldn't know.

Mostly that she had rented a house, and that she was in the process of preparing to leave him once she had all her ducks in a row.

She backed away as he struggled to get out of the car, hoping she could get to the bathroom and prepare to deceive him before he demanded she submit to one of his sexual tantrums. Once inside the tiny restroom, she pulled a panty liner from the bowl she kept beneath the sink.

Martha searched with frantic haste for the tube of fake blood she had bought several Halloweens ago, certain she had seen it stuck up in the vanity's cabinet recently. As her desperate search failed to achieve the result she'd hope for, she opened the medicine cabinet behind the cracked mirror over the sink. The small bottle of iodine was her only hope.

She quickly poured a small amount onto the pad and lifted her dress. Within seconds she had the self-adhesive tape attached to the crotch of her panties. The feel of the cold liquid changed to a hot sting once she pulled her panties back up, reminding her that Burt's abusive sexual appetite often resulted in injuries that were now taking longer to heal.

And now she smelled like iodine.

With her eyes watering she took another foray into the medicine cabinet and grabbed the bottle that held only a few remaining drops of the perfume Burt liked her to wear. She just hoped it was enough to cover the strong odor of antiseptic.

As ready as she was going to get, Martha stored both bottles back where she found them and opened the door, fully expecting Burt to be just outside of it waiting. But he wasn't. He wasn't even in the house yet.

Torn between relief and curiosity she ran to the front

window and peeked out through the sheers. But he was no longer there. She made a quick but silent dash through the house, but still no Burt. Perplexed now, she went to the bedroom they had shared until she started sleeping in the other room, and looked out. Burt was in the back yard, closing the door of the small shed where he kept the lawn mower.

As he headed for the door off the kitchen, which was on the right side of the house, she hurried to beat him and was opening the refrigerator when he came through the door. She looked up, faking surprise, and slapped a smile on her lips.

"Hi! I didn't expect you home so early."

Burt just looked at her, his eyes hooded, but she couldn't gauge anything by that because age and gravity had caused his upper lids to droop.

"Hi." Holding his right arm down against his side he advanced into the house and walked past her, going straight back to the bedroom she had just left. She heard the door closing and was certain the lock clicked, too.

Martha exhaled heavily, realizing she had been holding her breath. She pulled out a bottle of spring water, the only thing Burt usually allowed her to drink, and took a long pull from it. She stood waiting, wondering what he was doing, and then decided he must be using the bathroom as he was taking so long.

She heard him returning and made herself busy wiping down the already pristine sink before turning to look at him when he reentered the kitchen. "Can I get you something to drink?"

Again Burt gave her a strange look before shaking his head. "No. I decided to take the afternoon off. I've got some other things to take care of today. What are your plans?"

In all the years she had known him, Burt had never once asked about her plans, or feelings, or anything for that matter, except when he'd been concerned about her fake period.

She struggled to find an answer, *any* answer to his question. "Just the usual. Cooking and cleaning."

Burt shook his head, his multiple chins dragging behind. "Go do something fun. Have your nails done or something. Take in a movie. You've earned it."

Now she was *really* scared. Not only had he lied about work, he was being nice. "Okay... Thanks."

Too uncertain to ask him all the questions bombarding her brain, Martha started past him, headed to her room, but he stopped her and she stiffened as she waited for a fist to the stomach. Instead he pulled her to him and kissed her with an unheard of gentleness on the lips.

When he was done and opened his eyes, his bushy brows drew together. "What? A man can't kiss his wife?"

Her stomach churning in earnest, Martha attempted a smile and nodded. "Of course." To her relief he released her, and she tried to casually walk on back to her room, although she wanted so badly to run.

Anger she expected. Abuse she expected. But Burt Thompson, nice man and loving husband, scared the shit out of her.

Chapter Twelve

Destiny hung up the phone and stared across the great vista laid out on the other side of the house's three stories of glass walling. She had always loved her hometown, if you could call Los Angeles that, and couldn't believe Rayne was marrying a man in the little town she had only gone to for a short reprieve almost three months earlier.

Now Haven was there too.

And they wanted the books: those great heavy tomes of the entire Cavanaugh history, including how their ancestors created potions and medicines and spells. She didn't mind sending them, as she had no use for them, but it just added to the feeling that everything that was once a staple in her life was deserting her.

And she was lonely. Not just for her identical sisters and the joy and irritation they brought to her, but also for those who came to her for help on a weekly or monthly basis. As a therapist she should have remained neutral, but her gift had given her the opportunity to really get to know people, so she had made some wonderful friends and had developed some close relationships. But now she avoided everyone, telling her secretary to tell her current clientele and any prospects she was on holiday, indefinitely.

Now she was alone, barely able to contact her sisters because the hick town they were in had bad cell phone service. And even more alone because her gift, which had weakened over the last few months, had finally abandoned her too.

But she refused to run away like Rayne and Haven. She would fix this one way or another, with or without their help. She'd start by going back to the clinic she and Haven had visited to have another cleansing. Maybe even set one up weekly for the next little while. The herbal tea enema had helped strengthen her chakra once, so maybe another one would again. Although this time it wasn't just weak, it was completely gone.

But in the meantime she would eat right and get plenty of rest. Go on hikes and exercise to build her strength. Meditate for hours if necessary. Anything and everything she could think of to get her system and her spirit healthy.

She glanced at the clock and stifled a groan and then shook her head. *No!* She wouldn't allow negative energy to take hold. That would only make things worse or at least not make them any better. And she was definitely going for better.

Destiny smiled as big as she could and then forced herself to laugh. She repeated the laugh and did so again until she was actually laughing at how silly she must look and sound. Since she did feel a little better, and her spirit felt lighter, she did it one more time, just for the heck of it.

That was good. Very good.

Now she needed yoga, or at least her version of it, to stretch out some of the kinks that were surely twisting and choking off her energy. Destiny began moving slowly, allowing her body's trunk, hands, arms, legs and feet to move and stretch and turn as far as they would, in every direction she could make them go. She continued the process until she made a seductive dance of it before settling on the floor facing the city and the ocean beyond.

Closing her eyes, Destiny began to hum a tune her mother taught her as a little girl so many years before. She remained there, the afternoon sun pouring over her, until she felt lighter and lighter...until she finally felt her spirit soar.

Startled, she realized she was *actually* soaring above the house!

With a bird's eye view, and the sun warming her back, she took off to the east and took in the patchwork quilt of varying shades of greens and browns, occasionally seeing great splashes of color where flowers grew wild or by design.

There were rooftops of red and orange terra cotta, or black, gray, or green slate. Some of the homes were surrounded by large areas of nature and others were grouped together in the grids that make up subdivisions. Many of the smaller homes had swimming pools. The blue or turquoise waters reflected her hawk-like shadow as she flew over. Nearly every larger home did as well, their elaborately designed concrete ponds in various shapes and sizes.

Treetops were darker dots of green. Sometimes they were singular and other times multiples clustered together. The flowering ones had tiny dots or clusters of red or yellow or orange. Ribbons of white concrete and gray or black asphalt made up thin roads, and thick highways, and the sky was reflected in tall buildings made of mirrored glass.

Destiny had never felt so free, so alive, and so filled with joy. She continued away from the bright ball of gas heating the earth and eventually the air around her cooled and the light of the sun waned.

Below, with vision that adjusted as available light did, she saw vast areas of sandy soil and sparse vegetation. Then salt soil and absolute desolation. And finally she was over green pastures again which continued for endless miles and miles.

No longer paying attention to the populace reflected by the number of homes, Destiny took in the wide winding rivers and the large forest-flanked lakes dotting the landscape before she flew above another line of mountains, this one covered in evergreens she could smell as well as see.

Though it was fully dark now and she felt as if she had flown for hours, her vision was still sharp and clear, and her energy high.

Abruptly she felt like a marionette, her strings being tugged by a puppet master, and she knew her spirit was no longer free. She sensed no threat, so she allowed the pull of the earth to bring her closer, though she knew what she felt had nothing to do with gravity.

Finally below the clouds, her spirit hovered over a plot of wooded land high on the eastern side of the mountain range. There sat a small house made of roughhewn logs topped with a green tin roof, and behind it, an upside down cone shaped building made of stripped tree trunks and the skin of animals long dead.

Suddenly she was sucked down through the opening at the top of the cone and felt the heat of steaming moisture sliding through her. Though not painful it disoriented her, making her have to gather her thoughts again before she was able to assess where she was and why she was there.

Knowing she had no form, she still felt she gasped when she realized she was with a man. Though large and heavily muscled, he sat hunched before his steam pit with his head down. His long silver streaked brown hair hung far down his hairless, muscular pectorals, to reach his flat dark nipples. He sat with his sinewy legs crossed in what was known as Indian style as he chanted in a language she didn't understand.

Because of his position and since he was completely nude, his hairless flaccid genitals were fully exposed between muscular thighs, but even though his manhood was currently lifeless it was obvious he was more than adequately endowed.

Destiny felt amusement filling her and knew if she was solid, she would be smiling. Or blushing. *Or both.*

She forced her thoughts away from his sexual dimensions and continued her perusal, taking in the strength of his form and the goodness that radiated from his soul as it met and mingled with hers.

He gasped and lifted his head and she could only stare in wonder at how beautifully made he was. His tanned face was all chiseled angles and straight lines. His forehead was high, his lips wide and full, and his eyes as light blue as a clear winter sky. He looked around the tent and she realized he was looking for her. That he somehow knew she was there.

She floated to him and brushed her essence against him, though she had no idea if he pulled her or she went on her own. She watched as he struggled with emotions so powerful they filled her and nearly overwhelmed her with joy.

Destiny stared, fascinated and aroused, as his penis filled and thickened, and rose to point toward the tent's ceiling. Want and need like she had never experienced pulled her against him so that she felt the length of him, the warmth of him, within her being.

She wanted to tell him she was real, she was there, that she would be whatever he wanted or needed her to be. He began chanting again as tears formed and slid from his eyes to create a river down his high cheekbones where they crested and then fell from his face as if flowing over a waterfall, pooling on his thighs.

The chanting continued, pulling her closer and closer into him and around him. He suddenly stilled and quieted before stating softly, "My destiny is foretold."

Like a movie played backward at warp speed, Destiny was yanked from him, pulled up through the tent's opening, dragged across the mountain and river and lakes and streams. She flew backward, spinning crazily, over farmland and housing developments and skyscrapers until she opened her eyes and took a shaky breath, realizing she was once again looking out her apartment window as the tip of the sun sizzled at the Pacific's horizon, and then was gone.

Dizzy, confused, she fumbled and stumbled her way to her feet. She looked around the room, her head still spinning, as chill after chill covered her body, making bumps rise on her flesh and tears form in her eyes.

"It was a dream?"

Distraught, disbelieving, she ran zigging and zagging into walls, unable to get her balance. She finally reached her bedroom and threw herself onto the bed where she gave in to the tantrum of hurt and anger that held her in its grip. Taking a broken breath, she quieted to stare at the ceiling, realizing she now knew what true disappointment, loneliness, and heartbreak was.

"It was only a dream.

"It was only a dream."

Dear God! It was only a dream!

****

Tom Whitehawk struggled to gain his feet. He was weak, disoriented, and confused, as well as a little sick to his stomach. *Was that real?* Was what he just experience real? Or had three days with no food and only water to drink thrown him into hallucinations?

Needing support, he grasped the closest pole supporting the sweat lodge he'd erected with his father's help. He stood there for several minutes to get his balance as well as give his body time to adjust to the new position.

He attempted to take a step, but his legs were numb and so shaky he ended up dragging one foot, waiting for balance, and then dragging the other forward to meet it. He repeated the process, all the while holding on to the tent's poles, until he reached the overlapping flap that led to the outside.

As the moon was beginning a new phase, it was fully dark, so it took his eyes a moment to adjust. While waiting he rejoiced the moment he had felt the spirit of the maiden and mourned the sudden loss of her.

She had not only come to him, she had caressed him, bringing his spirit as well as his body to life. It was without question the most amazing moment of his thirty-five years, and he hoped it was real. He needed it to be.

She was pure of spirit and held magic. Things he would need in the coming days. He would need her to guide him through the evil he had felt for weeks and then had seen coming early in his time of meditation.

Though he didn't know what form it would take in the real world, the visions were clear enough to let him know that danger lurked close by and it meant to consume him.

The vision of evil had manifested itself in the form of a great beast, able to breathe fire, bent on his destruction. And it hadn't been alone. There were other smaller beasts

146

around it, nipping and biting at him, tearing into his flesh.

His eyes were now able to see clearly, so he forced his body to remain erect while shuffling his way to the back entrance of his ancestral home. Though the main part of the structure was very old, with only the spaces between the weather-beaten logs repacked to keep out weather and bugs, the roof, which had been changed and replaced many times over the years, was relatively new.

Tom entered the wooden planked door, which was also newer but old enough that it matched the grayness of the rest of the structure. Once inside he walked to the corner he'd made into a kitchen when he had moved in three years earlier. He pulled wrapped venison slices and mustard from the small refrigerator, tossing them onto the little drop leaf table he used for both counter space and dining. He then retrieved the bagged bread his mother made for him, and his father had delivered when he'd arrived with the tools needed to build the sweat lodge.

Though he'd hated disturbing the ground and ruining the integrity of the historic location to have city water lines and plumbing installed both inside and outside of the cabin, Tom was grateful to have the running water now as he went to the freestanding sink to wash his face and hands.

Knowing he was about out of steam, Tom retrieved a cup of water, a tin plate, and a knife to slice the bread before settling in the only chair in the cabin. In moments he had a sandwich slapped together. After laying it on the plate he lowered his head, giving thanks for the visions, for the visit he was certain was as real as he was, for the earth which nourished all life, and for the food he was about to consume. The quick blessing done, it took six bites and a great deal of slow chewing before his meal was complete. He drank the entire cup of water in as many swallows and instantly felt his body's appreciation for the hydration.

Not satisfied, he grabbed an apple from the supply he kept refrigerated, snagged a towel and washcloth then headed back out the back door for a shower.

The shower shack, as he called it, had been a labor of

love for him and his father, built at the same time they'd done all the renovations on the old place. To keep the homestead looking cohesive, they found an old barn the owner wanted torn down in the next county over and had volunteered to disassemble it and haul off the old lumber for free. Though not as old as the cabin, it was old enough to fit right in, as nature had a way of balancing itself and the things man placed upon it.

The farmer had not only been grateful to have the spot cleared, he'd pitched in and had the privilege of listening while Frank Whitehawk recounted the history of their people and the origins of their tribe with a deep voice now a little shaky with age but still almost hypnotic in cadence. The next day when they returned to continue tearing down the old structure, the farmer's sons joined them too and, while working, listened intently as Frank spoke of the time the cabin was originally constructed and how he had gone from being a poverty-stricken youth born in those very walls to the owner of a large business that even now thrived though he was semi-retired.

Tom had listened as well, though he'd heard the stories many times. Verbal history had always been the way of his people, and he hoped it always would remain so, though he knew his lack of wife and children was a disappointment his father would never verbalize.

Smaller than the original structure, though not by much, the shower shack with its toilet stall was set back into the trees just enough that one would have to know of its existence to find it.

He finished his apple and pitched the core far into the trees, knowing animal or insect would benefit from the natural remains, before he entered the shack. He ignored the toilet as he was so dehydrated that it was an unnecessary luxury. He stepped into the large area they'd constructed for bathing instead.

Tom turned the faucet handles he'd carved into hawk's heads. He still loved the fierceness of their frozen gaze and was glad he'd decided to make them rather than attaching standard hardware to the well-hidden copper pipes required to bring the water in.

As warm water poured like a heavy rain over his head and body, he knew he could have stood there for hours, but he was a child of the earth, and respect and appreciation for Mother Earth and her resources were ingrained strongly during his upbringing. He washed his long hair quickly with the shampoo and conditioner his mother still made, even though they now owned a large earth-friendly factory that produced and sold the same products, as well as ancient holistic remedies.

The products, which made his father a wealthy man, had throughout history been the very things laughed at by others. Now they were considered the right things to use by a vast population of not only people in this country but in countries around the world.

He finished his hair and tackled his body with the same diligence until the soapy cloth met his groin. He inhaled a shaking breath, remembering the instant he had felt her presence and the moment when she had touched his spirit with the soft glide of her soul. Her appreciation for his hereditary features had filled his heart with adoration and his desire with heat and blood, until he had wept with the joy of her.

Tom continued washing himself, this time more slowly as he was once again unbearably erect. Though it would have been so easy to pleasure himself with thoughts of her on his heart, he chose to honor her and remain celibate until he found her and could pleasure her as well.

Knowing she was real, as her spirit had not been like the vision foreshadowing evil but rather a living entity, Tom vowed his life and his honor to her for all time. That done he moved past the pain of need and scrubbed the remainder of his body until his form was completely pure.

Feeling so much better after the refreshing bath he walked back to the cabin, allowing the air to dry his body as he often did, using the towel to rub the water from his hair. He entered the door and stopped, taking a moment to look around. Though he could see nothing out of place, the skin on his body rose in alarm, as he was certain someone had been in his home, touching his sparse belongings.

Chapter Thirteen

Haven settled back, so stuffed she was embarrassed, but rather pleased with the way the day had ended. She and Rayne had hurried back to Garrison's cabin only to find the men gone. But the trailer they had loaded earlier was still there.

At first Haven feared she had sent Logan to the emergency room as Rayne had suggested, but a quick trip back down the mountain and to the hospital had nixed that notion. Then she thought maybe they went to the cabin she and Logan now shared. So they drove back up the mountain, but the men weren't there either.

It totally sucked that she had little to no cell phone service on the eastern side of the mountain range, and Haven knew she would have no choice but to change carriers as her cellular phone company was a small locally owned carrier based in Los Angeles. Up until now there hadn't been a need for anything national so she had been able to avoid signing a service contract, which was required with all of the larger carriers.

It would have been nice if Rayne had gone on and gotten another phone from a local or national carrier since she had decided to make Mystic Waters her home permanently, but Rayne avoided electronics of any kind as if they would give her cooties. Once she lost a phone her sisters had forced upon her to begin with, which she had done very recently, she wouldn't get another one on her own. Other than the aunts and her sisters, there had never been anyone Rayne would talk to on the devices anyway.

In essence, they were just out of luck.

Every time Haven tried to call Logan or Garrison, the bars indicating signal strength would drop drastically or disappear altogether whether she moved or remained in the same spot. When she finally did get a bar or two, the screen blinked with a ROAMING warning then NO SERVICE. Of course she had never foreseen these things being a problem, as it hadn't occurred to her she would one day end up on this side of the country.

It was a little startling to realize the longer she was in Mystic Waters the thought of staying seemed more and more attractive, especially since her gift had reactivated. In a strange way, yes, but still it was stronger than ever. Haven was curious to discover just how strong, and she desperately wanted to learn how to control it. After all the years of fearing it, and being lazy about learning anything more than necessary about it, she knew her gift was a treasure and not something to be ignored. Just like realizing Mystic Waters wasn't just some little dot on the map.

The area was aptly named. Mystic Waters was a region filled with the mystical. And as soon as she could, she wanted to check out the large lake it was named after. She'd been frustrated at having to drive around to locate men who should have been where she and Rayne had left them and to have a cell phone that was nothing more than a useless bill to be paid.

After an irritating amount of time of driving to one place and then another, she and Rayne realized they should have just gone on and investigated the crystals. They were both feeling very put out when the guys finally arrived back at the cabin a couple of hours later.

Irritation turned to contrition when it turned out they'd gone to the White farm where Garrison's mother had packed Logan with ice bags to help bring down the horrible swelling Haven had caused to his genitalia. As embarrassing as that was, even while in pain, Logan had gone to the trouble of baking Rayne and her an amazing chocolate cake that was so sinfully rich she would have killed for another slice even though she was already full from devouring the meal Garrison and his mother put together.

"I'm sorry."

Rayne, Garrison, and Logan all stopped moving at the same time and seeing that their forks were at identical levels midway between their plates and their mouths almost made Haven smile. But she had been eating and mentally practicing her apology all the way through the meal so smiling didn't seem appropriate.

"Okay."

Haven frowned at Logan. "That's it?"

"Yes. Are we done fighting?"

Haven glanced at Rayne. She shrugged. Then she looked to Garrison who quickly stuck the chocolate confection in his mouth and began chewing in earnest. Finally she looked back at Logan.

"You aren't going to call me names, or throw things, or anything?"

He took a bite and chewed slowly as he watched her, never breaking eye contact. Once he swallowed he set the fork at the edge of his saucer. "Well, I'm not going to have sex with you, obviously."

Snickering from her sister was completely ignored, or at least mentally filed away for another time. "Is that a temporary thing or are we talking *ever*?"

Logan stretched his legs out beneath the table, winced, and then pulled them back up a little. "Depends on, I guess, if the cantaloupes you created ever go back to just being walnuts."

Haven took a deep breath, ready to slap Rayne if she didn't get control of herself. "Since I'm a nurse, I guess I could check things out for you and see if you need additional medical attention."

"I made you chocolate sin and you are just going to check me out to see if I need someone else to fix me, *Nurse*?"

Haven lifted a brow. "Just what exactly is it that you want me to do, *Doctor*?"

An easy grin settled across his lip. "Kiss it and make it better."

This time Haven had to glare at Garrison as well as her

sister when he choked on the cake while chuckling. She turned back to Logan as she forked a large bite of the chocolate sin directly from the large amount of remaining cake sitting in the center of the table.

Locking onto Logan's gaze, Haven placed the thickly coated icing covered confection between her lips and past her teeth then closed her mouth to pull the fork out a millimeter at a time. She chewed very slowly and watched his lips fall open slightly as he watched her mouth. She finally swallowed and leaned toward him. "Is that what you want me to do to you, *Doctor*?"

Both his inhaling and exhaling were audible and Haven knew she had him until he slowly shook his head. "No. I want you to kiss them, not consume them."

Garrison laughed outright at that and she felt her hands warming. She slid Garrison an evil smile. "Would you mind taking my sister for a walk?"

The laughter left Garrison's eyes as he slid an uneasy glace at Logan and then Rayne. Finally he turned back to her. "Sure."

Rayne dropped her fork, grumbling about them always having to leave their own home, as Garrison quickly grabbed a couple of flashlights from a kitchen drawer then guided her toward the front door. Haven ignored them, already knowing Garrison would do anything for his friend, even give up eating that sinful cake. Rayne was not going to be as gracious about it, but she'd just have to get over it as far as Haven was concerned.

Once she felt they should be far enough away she stood. "Okay, big boy, let me see them."

Logan was careful while pushing back the chair. He rose and unbuttoned and unzipped his jeans. He pushed them down below his knees before reaching for the band of his boxers. He pushed them down as well and stood there before her.

Haven watched his every move then sent a quick look to his face. She immediately looked away, horrified and regretful at what she had done. She had never harmed another living thing in her life, and she had really done a number on him.

His testicles were huge and his penis black and purple and possibly swollen too, though she didn't actually know for sure.

The pain he must be in took her breath and she knew it was something she could have fixed once upon a time, if she'd been willing to expose herself and her hereditary gift.

For now the warmth in her hands felt more normal, heating as they always did when someone or something was in pain, but did she dare trust them? The last thing either one of them needed was for her to scorch his boys. Or burn them clean off.

She moved to him and put her arms around his neck gently, making sure her hands didn't touch his bare neck exposed above his collar. "Oh, Logan. I am so sorry."

He was as gentle in putting his arms around her waist and pulling her closer. "I know. Me too." He grinned, looking intently into her eyes. "I shouldn't have forced you. I don't do that. I want you to know, really, that I have never manhandled a woman in my life. And it won't happen again. Please forgive me."

The warmth in her hands increased, though not alarmingly. She closed her eyes and laid her head on his shoulders and just allowed him to hold her. She wanted so badly to heal him, to touch his mind with healing because she feared touching his body. She fantasized what it would be like to surround him with healing light and heat and actually felt both his body and hers enveloped in warmth.

She mentally pictured his genitals cooling and the swelling decreasing until, though not completely back to normal, they were no longer as bruised or swollen. She heard his sharp intake of breath as his head whipped around and he buried his face in her hair. The fantasy dispersed into fragmented pictures that continued to shatter until they no longer existed as their bodies cooled rapidly, returning to normal. She lifted her head from his shoulders and turned to him, taking his lips with all the passion the experience had ignited in her.

He responded with as much ardor, his mouth a magic wand that had her dancing and floating in air. When their lips finally parted, Haven was dizzy, glad for the support of his solid form.

Breathless, Logan continued to hold her tight until both could breathe normally again. He pulled her away just enough to look into her eyes, his own liquid filled. "You slay me. Everything about you takes my breath away. Don't ever get mad at me again. I'll screw up. I'm human. But please don't get so angry you leave. Hit me or bite me or turn that fire you have inside of you on me, but don't stay mad at me, I can't take it."

Haven stared at him helplessly, slain as well. She didn't know what to say, not knowing if he was actually acknowledging her gift, or if he was only speaking metaphorically. Either way she didn't dare confess or deny, so she said nothing, instead she took his mouth again, this time pouring not want, not need, but love into the kiss.

They were both shaking when they finally stepped apart and Logan looked down for the first time since dropping his pants. She looked as well and had to silence her reaction, as everything she had envisioned had come to pass.

He looked up her and smiled as he pulled his clothes back together. "Looks like Mrs. White's ice packs worked pretty well. Maybe in a day or two you will still kiss it and make it even better?"

Haven laughed, relieved and disappointed at the same time. They were back to normal as far as their relationship was going, and he hadn't realized his healing was not a result of ice, but of fire.

But in the depths of her soul, the relief was bittersweet. Yes, her secret was still safe, but for the first time in her life, she really wanted someone outside of the family to know who and what she really was.

"Maybe…though I've never done that before, either. I may need some instruction." She grinned at him. "You may have to do me again first…just so I can study on it."

Logan laughed. "Deal! I have no trouble playing teacher." He shook his head in wonder, his eyes shining with admiration for her. "The only thing I can't figure out is how some other man has not been privileged enough to touch you before now."

Haven shrugged, knowing he would probably never know the honest answer to that question. Her fear of touching had made it impossible for her to allow herself to be touched in the past, it was only with him she'd ever been able to be close to her real self.

"Those other men weren't you," was the most honest answer she could give him.

He moved forward and pulled her back into his arms. "Thank you for that. Let's go home…I may be able to work up a lesson or two."

Haven looked at the mess they were leaving behind and lifted the glass topper to the cake stand Garrison's mother had sent to hold the cake. Then she quickly carried the dirty saucers over to the trash and raked out those needing it before setting them all in the sink. She looked back at the confection once more as they headed to the door, hoping she got a chance to get back before Rayne finished it off. But for now, she had something as sweet to look forward to.

****

Rayne finally pushed away her irritation and smiled at Garrison. "Those two make us look like an old married couple."

He laughed. "Oh, the feelings are there, sexy lady, and I'd be glad to prove it anytime you have doubts." He advanced on her and Rayne squealed and took off at a run. He chased after her, and soon caught her, but only because it was dark and the flashlight wasn't bright enough to give her confidence she wouldn't trip and fall.

Garrison nailed her with a kiss that started out rough then settled into seductive. She smiled at him when he lifted his head. "Now that's what I'm talking about!

"I wonder how long we have to be gone. That cake could give a woman an orgasm. And I'm up for a couple."

He laughed too, and kept her in his arms as they continued their stroll. "And here I thought it was me you desired."

Rayne punched him in the abdomen lightly. "I did say a couple. I was figuring on the cake taking care of only one."

Garrison grabbed her around the waist and spun with her a couple of times so Rayne was dizzy and laughing hard when he stopped. She swayed as her equilibrium settled and she gave him another hard peck on the lips before turning to walk some more, but she couldn't take a step unless she wanted to walk through Qaqeemasq.

She looked quickly at Garrison, but he wasn't looking at her, he was stooped down with the flashlight held on one spot, studying the ground intently. She looked down as well, and a chill ran over her skin. On the ground was a footprint in an exposed area of mud. It was bare and long and narrow and was headed in the direction they had just come from.

Without knowing how, she was certain it was Gavin's. She glanced back up but Qaqeemasq's glittering form was gone.

"I would know that foot anywhere," Garrison finally said, emotion making his voice coarse. He looked up at her and then back down as she knelt by his side. He pointed the flashlight and then a finger from his free hand at the toes. "You see that crook in the pinky toe? How it bends outward then the tip back in? My brother Grey always told Gavin that toe was special, that it had been kissed by an angel in his mother's belly, so that he wouldn't ever feel self-conscious about the small deformity, especially after he got older. It was like that at birth."

They both stood and Garrison searched for quite a while until he found another spot where the ground wasn't covered with dried leaves and there was evidence of two shod feet, as well as the bare ones. Excitement and fear wrapped themselves around Rayne, but she could see the stress it was putting on Garrison. "Those tracks can't be very old, can they?"

Garrison shook his head. "No. They probably would have been washed away by the last rain or would be overgrown like everything else. They can't be old at all." His eyes filled with tears, and he went to his knees just inches from the evidence his nephew was still alive or had been very recently.

Rayne went down as well, stooping to put her arm around his shoulder and hold him as he quietly fell apart.

She kissed the top of his head before they both stood. "Let's mark this and get the police." At the mention of the law, Rayne's heart kicked up a notch.

"I forgot to tell you; that officer that came to the cabin when I first moved here and something ate my pies? Haven and I saw him today. And we both thought you might want to have him checked out.

"He told us that he was taken off Gavin's case because he was needed to do something more important." At the fury that crossed Garrison's features, she held up her free hand. "I know. Just listen though. This might be important. The only thing that is as big to everyone else right now is all the bodies being found, but we thought what if he wasn't taken off for that reason. What if he was taken off for another reason? What if he had fumbled the investigation or something?"

Rayne didn't want to add what was for her a real concern. What if that strange man had anything to do with Gavin's kidnapping? It would make it so easy for him to lead an investigation and keep everyone from the location where the child was being kept.

Garrison nodded. "Let's mark this so we can find it again quickly. As much as I want to follow the footsteps right now, it makes more sense to have real light and more help. We just have to be careful not to step on any on the way back. Let's mark all that we find.

"And let's hurry."

Chapter Fourteen

As he'd been watching it all afternoon Gavin turned down the television and listened for any sounds in the rest of the house for a long time before getting up to go to the bathroom. He had made several cloaked attempts to find where the camera was kept, but he was afraid to be obvious about it so he really hadn't gotten anywhere.

He relieved himself and took a shower, all the time trying to decide what to do. If he just gave in and did as she told him he felt he would live a long time, possibly the remainder of his life imprisoned in the room. On the other hand, if he was caught snooping or trying to escape, he would likely wind up dead or back in conditions that were not nearly as nice, and those months in the dark, dank, and dirty were enough to last him a lifetime.

It was amazing to be clean all the time and to know nothing would attack or bite him during the night. And he felt so much better now that his fever was gone. He dried off and hung his towel and washcloth over the bars provided so they would dry without mildewing, and so *she* would be pleased with him.

Ma'am hadn't been back, as far as Gavin could tell, since the afternoon before. He was hungry as his food ran out hours earlier, but he was just hungry, not starving. He now knew the difference. He wasn't as concerned about water, as he had the sink to refill his bottle any time he wanted. In fact, he didn't have it all that bad now that he thought about it. But he was going to have to resume working to reshape his body. He was glad he was no longer chubby, but being rail thin wasn't attractive either.

He heard the sound of his door opening so he quickly grabbed a fresh pair of cotton pajama pants from the bathroom closet. In seconds he had them on and was walking from the bathroom into the bedroom. He stopped and smiled at her as if surprised and pleased to see her. "Hi!"

Though the netted hat was back in place, he could tell his greeting was met with approval when she stood up a little straighter. She moved a little farther into the room and sat a large rectangular tray on his table. He was aware she watched him the entire time as her body went in one direction and her covered head stayed turned toward him. He pretended not to notice the device in her other hand, though he was certain it was a stun gun, as he stayed where he was and remained perfectly still.

He didn't want her to feel threatened in any way and hoped one day she would actually relax enough to believe she had him under her control.

"Hi, yourself, Jimmy."

Gavin blinked several times, wondering if she was messing with him or if she really thought he was someone else. If that was the case then Jimmy, whoever he was, had dodged a large bullet, and Gavin hadn't been her intended victim all along.

"My name is Gavin. Gavin White."

The netting swung back and forth as she backed to the door. "No. Your name is Jimmy. Now say it."

Gavin's heart pounded as he stood staring at her, but he couldn't make himself say the name.

"*I said say it!*"

Jumping at her outburst, Gavin nodded and swallowed, both the lump in his throat and his pride. "Jimmy."

She stood there, visibly shaking, and he was glad he had only just relieved himself, as he was certain pee would be running down his legs. There was something terrifying about seeing her shake like that. He didn't want her mad enough to shake like that. Ever.

She took a moment and then seemed to settle down. This time her voice was softer and higher though in its own way still coercive. "Say my name is Jimmy."

Gavin licked his lips and nodded. "My name is Jimmy." The netting bobbed up and down and he exhaled.

"Good boy.

"Say it again."

"My name is Jimmy."

"What is your name?"

Tears formed but he held them back, making his throat tight. "My name is Jimmy."

"Good boy."

She reached back and opened the door behind her as she continued to watch him. She backed out slowly; the stun gun held in such a tight grip her knuckles were white. "I'll see you in the morning, Jimmy."

Gavin hope the expression on his lips was a smile, but he seriously doubted he had accomplished making one as he struggled to keep from crying in front of her. "Good night, ma'am," he choked out, barely above a whisper. She hesitated and Gavin was afraid she was going to force him to say it louder, but she finally pulled the door closed, taking her from his sight.

He nearly slid to the floor. The relief that she was gone was so great his legs felt boneless, but Gavin held himself together enough to make it to the bed. Without touching the tray that smelled distinctly like roast beef, he turned on his side, away from the door, and closed his eyes.

I will not cry. I will not cry.

He silently repeated the litany until he was certain he wouldn't, fearing she had gone straight to her monitor to see what he was doing. Once he could breathe without his breath coming in great shuddering waves, he sat up and pulled the sliding table in front of him, over the bed and his lap.

After lifting the lid he looked at what was unquestionable the best looking and smelling food he had seen in months. Though he had no appetite at all, he ate the entire plate of roast, potatoes, carrots, green beans and the two rolls.

If he was ever going to escape, he needed all the

strength she was willing to provide for…and a cunning she would never know he possessed. Until it was too late.

****

The hat was a bothersome necessity, so she was happy to take it off and placed it back over the Styrofoam dummy's head. She glanced into the monitor and was satisfied to see he was eating, and was glad she had seen the dog being trained that morning in the park across from the grocery store. Though huge and ugly, its master rewarded it each and every time it obeyed him, so the dog did exactly as he was told.

It had given her an idea.

Her newest Jimmy would be trained in the same way. After all, had she had a mother she was certain the woman would have told her the way to a man's heart was through his stomach. And though not yet a man, Jimmy was getting closer every day, and if his appetite was any indication, she would have to consider getting him longer pajama's soon. As tall as the kid already was, chances were he'd still add another inch or two before he was done growing.

She just needed patience, both to give him time to mature and for her to recalculate just how she wanted to handle things on the outside. Her plans weren't working out exactly as she had hoped, but she would figure out what to do next eventually, as long as the kid wasn't a distraction. Thankfully he was so grateful to be in a nice room with all the amenities that he was being a model pet.

Renting the house was a stroke of genius.

Humming to herself, she changed once again into the outfit that virtually made her invisible to those whose attention she didn't want to attract. She laughed at the idea of being invisible, and even better, *invincible*, delighted it made her feel she had super powers.

Now all she needed was a cape to go along with her mask.

Wouldn't that be fun?"

Chapter Fifteen

Though he would have rather been searching, Garrison sat with Rayne in the back of a large room filled with Mystic Water's finest. At the opposite side of the room, Captain Grammar stood beside the podium where the spiffily dressed FBI agent he'd introduced as Special Agent Bret Thorne showed charts and pictures being relayed to the overhead projector from his laptop computer.

The meeting had started shortly before they arrived at the station, but Garrison had called ahead and the captain had left word for them to be sent on back to the conference room upon their arrival. Although it was unusual, and not normally something family members were allowed to be included in, John Grammar had made them the exception because of his close relationship with the White family, and Garrison and Rayne's involvement in furthering the case.

Images of the remains already found flashed across the screen as Agent Thorne recounted the details the locations revealed, followed by detailed autopsy reports and the speculations that resulted.

It was difficult to look at the images they had mostly already seen and hear the horrors that preceded the deceased's demise, but Garrison appreciated being allowed to attend.

He inhaled sharply when his cousin's photos and information were revealed and was thankful for Rayne's support when she took his hand to comfort him. He tried not to react a second time, but when Logan's younger brother's details proved he had suffered an even harsher death than Tony, Garrison thought he would be sick.

Everyone's relief was obvious when the screen went black, and the room filled with the sounds of air leaving a vast number of lungs.

The agent stepped back from the podium and gave everyone a moment to gather themselves before he continued talking. He retrieved a large leather binder from his open briefcase and looked out at the crowd before laying it on the podium.

"The profile we have for the individual we will call the *Unsub* is likely somewhere between thirty and sixty years old, male, has never married, and has few or no close friends. He was likely abused as a child and a target of bullying while in all levels of school, though it's doubtful he graduated from high school. He would have hurt, maimed, or killed small animals when he was younger just for the experience and fantasized about doing it to someone bigger than him when they hurt him in some way.

"He will most likely live in virtual seclusion, avoid conflict though he will certainly have weapons, and can probably live off of the earth's natural resources for long periods of time.

"He is quite possibly someone you have seen or even know of but he would never draw your attention to him. He may or may not originally be from the area, but has lived here several years and knows the mountains intimately, or those bodies would have been found long before so much deterioration had taken place.

"Although we are looking for an individual for the three bodies recently found, as they all fit the same MO, there may or may not be more than one individual associated with those murders, Gavin White's kidnapping, and his parents' deaths.

"For now we need to go on the assumption that they are all related, as I just learned that there is new evidence that Gavin White was recently alive. But I'll get back to that.

"We believe the most deteriorated victim may have been accidently killed or was killed in the heat of the moment and became the catalyst for those that followed. Though the Unsub would have been horrified at first *if* it was an accident, the experience of taking a life with violence, and being the one in control—quite possibly for the first time in his life—may have given him a thirst for blood that, although already a part of his physiological makeup, would likely have never manifested itself beyond his imagination.

"That is pretty much all we have right now as I am not fully apprised on the new information. Are there any questions?"

Several hands were raised and Agent Thorne pointed to a person several seats ahead of them. Garrison processed the information as a short-haired woman stood up. When Rayne gasped at his side, he looked at her questioningly, but she only shook her head and turned her attention back to the woman.

"Thank you for the information, Special Agent Thorne. I was wondering if you could tell us why you believe this is a man and not a woman."

Since a woman asked the question, there were a few male groans. After the officer sat back down, the agent ignored the sexist response and repeated the question in case anyone had missed it. "Though we can't guarantee that we are looking for a man, a woman serial killer is nearly nonexistent. There have been a few throughout history, and are still three currently on death row, I believe, but the overwhelming majority of these types of murderers are men.

"Added to that, the victims are all at least average size, though young, men. It would take an incredibly strong woman to kill them the way they were killed. Not only would she have a fight on her hands, the depth of the hatchet wounds once they penetrated bone would have taken a great deal of strength to push on through, even from a man."

He pointed to another officer and this time a tall gray-haired man stood. "I know that there is a popular television show out there that calls their criminals Unsubs. Who had the term first?"

Agent Thorne pressed his lips together as the room filled with laughter. Garrison didn't get how they could find laughter in the midst of so horrible a situation. He glanced at the captain whose face was stone cold and he felt a little better.

"I don't actually know the answer to that question. It isn't one I've ever thought to ask. However, for anyone who may not know, the reason we call them Unsubs is to keep from giving them a tag name that will make them famous like the Unabomber, or the BTK serial killers. The media fed their thirst for publicity. The term Unsub literally means unidentified subject of our investigation."

He pointed to another officer, who stood. "Agent Thorne, how heavily involved will the FBI be in this investigation?"

Agent Thorne stepped back and looked to the captain. John stepped over to the podium and looked at the officers and Garrison and Rayne. "We've asked the FBI to take over the investigation. Our department will simply be here to support them from here on out."

There were whispers going on around the room following the captain's announcement, which stopped when the FBI agent was once again at the podium. "Thank you all for your time and attention. Please feel free to see me directly if you have further questions."

He stepped down and began the process of gathering his presentation materials as Garrison led Rayne from the room. "If you want to go on back to the cabin I can talk to the captain and Agent Thorne by myself. I'll have one of the officers bring me home afterwards."

Rayne nodded slowly, her eyes searching his. "Okay. I'll see you later then."

Garrison kissed her quickly and softly, grateful for her understanding and lack of questioning. He knew she'd stay if he wanted her to, but he needed to speak to the men alone. He turned to reenter the conference room and the door nearly hit him. He grabbed the handle and held it open for the woman officer who had asked the first question of the FBI agent before he moved forward and allowed the door to swing shut behind him.

****

Rayne turned away, but the woman Garrison had been gentlemanly to ran and caught up to her. "Hey! Hi. I just wanted to tell you when I was questioning you about the first body that you found, that it was nothing personal. It was just business. I got the impression the second time I saw you that you didn't like me."

Rayne couldn't believe the officer would care one way or the other, but southern manners dictated she respond kindly. Too bad she wasn't a southerner. "Thanks. That's great. Have a good day." She started walking on, but the woman followed her again.

"Look, I don't know why you think badly of me. I'm a nice person."

Rayne stopped again. She planted a smile on her face. "I'm sure you are. But I just came out of a room where the man I love had to watch family members and family members of friends horribly disfigured remains being plastered on a giant screen, as well as listen to the horrible ways in which they died. I'm sorry. But I'm not feeling all that social at the moment. *Please*, excuse me."

Rayne attempted to leave again, uncertain why the woman agitated her as badly as she did. But the fact was she was burning mad. And if she had to have one more conversation with the officer, she would probably end up in jail.

She made it out of the double doors and instantly sighed in relief, even though she was horrified by her behavior. She was never rude. Ever. "What the hell is wrong with me?"

"Are you all right, miss?"

Rayne looked up and had to take a moment. The man standing before her was perhaps the most beautiful human male she had ever laid eyes on. She smiled and felt foolish. "I'm just talking to myself. Sorry."

He grinned, his wide full lips stretching across his face.

"You know what they say...."

Rayne laughed. "Yes. Unfortunately I couldn't swear under oath that I don't ever answer."

He laughed too and held out his hand. "Tom Whitehawk."

She took it. "Rayne Cavanaugh. I'm engaged to the man who made your kitchen sets. He's inside, actually."

Tom glanced at the doors of the police station then at her. "Any news on his nephew?"

Rayne didn't know if she was allowed to say anything or not, so she just mentioned the FBI was heading up the investigation now.

He nodded. "Well, I was headed in there myself. I think someone broke into my house last night."

Rayne shook her head. "I've only lived here a short while, but the crime rate in this area is horrible."

He nodded, studying her closely. "It hasn't always been that way.

"Do I *know* you? Have we met?"

Smiling, Rayne shook her head. "No. Never saw you before in my life. I'm sure I would have remembered."

He grinned, though it wasn't reflected in his intense, ice blue eyes. "Yeah, me too. Well you take care, and be careful when you are out alone. Strange things are happening around here."

Rayne nodded. "Yeah. You too. Bye now."

Rayne waited for a patrol car to pass by before heading to Garrison's truck. She opened the door to get in and glanced back to see Tom Whitehawk staring after her with a perplexed expression. He waved when he realized she was looking and she waved back, thinking, *Yeah, strange....*

The trip back to the cabin gave her time to think but her mind wouldn't focus on anything but the questions filling her head regarding Gavin White's current circumstance. *Was he still alive since being moved from wherever it was he'd been hidden? Had they stumbled close to the area where he was held and he'd heard them but had been unable to call for help? Where could he have been taken? And who would kidnap a kid his size and for what purpose?*

None of it made sense.

A sick feeling hit the bottom of Rayne's stomach. It didn't make sense unless the man holding him was a sexual predator....

There was no way she could ever tell Garrison of her thoughts and fears. It would completely destroy him.

****

Garrison listened to the FBI agent while his stomach rolled over and over again. None of the possible reasons for Gavin still being alive made sense, particularly since there was no ransom demand. The officer spoke of things Garrison wouldn't wish on his worst enemy, much less a beloved nephew.

John Grammar stood behind him, his friend's big hand clutched Garrison's shoulder in acknowledgement of his pain. As much as he appreciated it, he was chomping at the bit to get the search started. The day was getting away from them! But when he said so, he only got sympathetic nods.

"It's taken all day to get the manpower here that we need to do this right. And now it's getting late. These agents don't know the mountains and there isn't enough time to get everything set up before the light starts going."

"I know this is frustrating for you," Bret Thorne began, "but we need to see every possible clue so we can try to track where Gavin was being held. It may lead us to where he's been taken. But we will have the agents and the dogs out first thing in the morning. I promise. And I'm hopeful that if we can find a location, we can get an idea on how he's been treated so far."

Garrison was afraid to ask, but he had to know. "What will the area tell you if he is no longer there?"

Concern that had already cloaked the agent's eyes now sharpened them. "If there is evidence it may tell us how well or poorly he was fed. We may be able to determine if he was locked inside somewhere or attached to something to keep him from running away. We'll gather samples of anything that looks like bodily fluids to analyze any blood, urine, vomit, or anything else, as well as clothing if there is any. Even stool samples if we find them.

"There could be a lot or no evidence at all, depending on how cunning the kidnapper is."

Garrison nodded and rose. "Excuse me," he said gruffly, before nearly running from the room. Fortunately he knew exactly where the restroom was and barely made it into a stall before everything he'd eaten earlier came back up his esophagus and out of his mouth.

He continued retching for several minutes. When he finally stopped, he grabbed the wet cloth being held just inside the stall door. He placed it over his mouth and nodded his thanks to John, knowing his sore throat would prevent him from talking.

"If he's alive, we will find him," John vowed quietly. "And I'm willing to tear this town apart if I have to."

Garrison nodded again and walked out of the bathroom when the captain stepped back. He glanced around the squad room, puzzled to see Tom Whitehawk sitting and talking to the woman police officer, but he didn't try to get his attention. Right now all he wanted was a ride home so he could get back into digging through Gavin's things, knowing he should have already finished the job, but he hadn't really seen the point once the bodies started turning up. Though he had tried to convince himself and Rayne differently, Garrison knew in his heart he had already given up on finding his nephew alive.

Until he'd seen those footprints.

He looked back over at Tom and then went on to let the officer who would take him home know that he was ready. Tomorrow would be another bust in getting Tom's furniture delivered, but he knew the man would understand.

****

Leaving out his visions of dragons and demons, and his visit from the ethereal female, Tom began relaying as many of the events as he could about the break-in. He knew he was fumbling the entire interview, as he would

171

start to say something, realize it wasn't anything he wanted to share, and then start to say something else. By the time he stopped talking, he wasn't really sure what he had or hadn't told because his concentration was shot and had been since running into Rayne Cavanaugh on the sidewalk. There was something about her that felt familiar. Though like her, he was fairly certain they had never met.

If it had just been that she was beautiful, Tom knew he could let thoughts of her go as she had *clearly*, and he was quite sure, *purposely*, stated she was engaged to Garrison White. But it wasn't about her looks. It was something—a familiarity…or something—he couldn't quite put his finger on, but it was there, and it was consuming his thoughts.

"Mr. Whitehawk?"

Tom nearly groaned when he realized he'd been lost in thought over her again. "I'm sorry. Yes?"

Officer Gishwell looked at her notebook then at him. The skepticism was plainly written on her features.

"Is there anything else you want to add, Mr. Whitehawk?"

"I'm not sure what else to tell you."

She nodded and looked at the little notebook again. "So, let me make sure I have all of this straight.

"You were in your sweat lodge—"

"Tent."

She glanced at him with a frown that clearly said *whatever.* "Okay, your sweat *tent* last night, and then you were done sweating so you went to your house and got something to eat and then went to take a shower. When you came out of the shower you walked *back into your house?*"

Tom nodded. "It's an old cabin. I built a shower building outside."

Just short of rolling her eyes, she nodded. "Okay. And were you nude the entire time?"

Tom frowned at her. "What difference does that make?"

She grinned. "None I guess, just trying to piece

together the facts.

"So…you walked back in your back door and you didn't see anything missing, or moved, but you are sure someone was in there touching your things, which you say are of no monetary value."

Tom nodded. "Yes. That's pretty much it."

She leaned to the right side of her office chair and placed her elbow on the high arm, then played with her lips as she studied him. Finally she sat up and opened the desk's file drawer where haphazardly thrown large zip-lock bags filled with capped cups laid. "Mr. Whitehawk, if I were to give you a drug test right now, would you be able to pass it?"

Tom looked at her in disbelief. "Excuse me?"

She slid the drawer closed and shrugged. "Just checking. Of course I can write up the report and come to your house if you want me to, but if there is nothing missing or even out of place it's really a waste of everyone's time. We would end up having to dust the entire place to look for fingerprints."

The last thing he wanted was her in his home, or anyone else for that matter. "I don't need anyone to come out there. I just want to have a report filed in case anything else happens."

She nodded. "Okay. I'll need your full name, address, social security number, birth date and contact numbers."

Chapter Sixteen

Haven left a naked and snoring Logan in the loft as she roamed around the main level of the cabin before heading to the refrigerator. After they returned from Garrison and Rayne's cabin the night before, he had talked about being incredibly tired, reminding her all her patients had fallen into a deep sleep soon after she had healed or cured them with her gift.

Before Logan entered her life, it had been so long since she'd last touched anyone she had nearly forgotten the toll it also took on her. She had slept a good part of the day away and she felt terrible.

Haven pulled bottled water from the refrigerator and took a long swallow and then another. The incredible thirst would likely last for another twelve or so hours then her system would recharge and she should be fine, if that was the way her recovery system still worked.

She walked over to the bowl of crystals and looked at them for long moments before lifting the bowl and studying them more closely. The bowl started vibrating almost immediately and the crystals lit up but weren't throwing off lights like they had when she first felt their power. Haven wondered if her own weakened strength was reflected in theirs, or if they'd weakened because of her use of them.

It was something to ponder and investigate.

Haven settled on the couch and placed the bowl on the cushion next to her as she went over the events that had resulted in Logan's genitalia nearly healing. She'd been filled with sorrow and was contrite over injuring him and had feared touching him. So she had fantasized his healing, and to the extent the fantasy went, so went the repairs to his body.

It was an exciting new discovery she couldn't wait to share with Rayne. Since they had talked about the possible evolution of their gifts, Haven was dying to get her hands on the books Destiny was supposed to have sent. But in the meantime she wanted to learn as much as she could on her own.

Unfortunately, it still didn't solve the issue of touching Logan. Both times her hands met his skin, first to stop the bleeding where she had bashed his skull and then again when he sent her to the moon and back with an orgasm that took her breath away, she had managed to fry him.

That would not do.

There had to be a solution, or one of these days he would finally grab one of her hands and the resulting zap would not be easily explained away. It was just plain luck she had gotten away with what had happened so far. And it shamed her to realize just how often she had harmed the poor man.

Two out of the three times had been deliberate acts born of fear or anger, even though the first time she'd had a legitimate reason as she had believed him to be an intruder. Still, she was not meant to harm. It went against everything she'd been taught as well as against her natural ability to heal.

So…there had to be a resolution. She just wished she had some idea where to begin looking for it.

"Haven?"

She stood and looked up to the railing lining the loft. Logan leaned against it, looking like he had a serious hangover. "Are you okay?"

Logan nodded. "I just got a text message from Garrison's phone, but I think Rayne sent it. She needs us to come back over. Fast."

Haven smiled, delighted to be going back. There should still be cake and she could get Rayne off to the side and let her know about the healing. "Okay."

He stretched and turned around, and the fading handprints on his back reminded her she needed to lose the excitement and get educated as quickly as possible. Then she looked lower and wondered...had the healing continued while he rested or was it as it was when he'd conked out? Haven grabbed the bowl and speedily replaced it on the mantle and then stopped.

She recalled she'd been some distance away, at least a half mile by her calculation, when they were at the other cabin. Maybe distance from the power source would help temper the fire it enhanced...but then again, maybe not. She just didn't know. Sadly it was something she didn't have time to investigate at the moment.

She ran up the stairs hoping to get a quick look at Logan's genitals but he'd already pulled on boxers and was in the process of pulling up his jeans. Disappointed, she stood waiting until he was dressed. "Did Rayne say why she wanted us to come back?"

Logan nodded, his gaze serious. "Yeah. I called her and heard thumping sounds and Garrison in the background shouting. She must have stepped away from him because it got quiet and then she told me that there are a lot of new developments, and some so scary that Garrison is hysterical." He looked at her, worry causing lines on his forehead and at the corners of his eyes. "I've known Garrison White since we were kids. He's a rock. If he is this torn up, whatever is going on is really bad."

Chills lifted the hair on Haven's arms and ran up her back. Logan finished dressing and walked over to pull her into his arms. He held her for a moment, and she held him back. "What haven't you told me?"

He sighed heavily. "Rayne said they've found evidence that Gavin was alive at least recently, and the FBI believes, since there was no ransom demanded, the only reason he may still be alive is because he's being sexually abused or tortured for some sadistic person's pleasure."

Nausea hit her stomach. "Oh, no... We need to get over there."

"Yeah."

They took Logan's rental car and were at the cabin in

minutes. Rayne met them at the door, her expression sad, her eyes wet. She looked at Logan. "He's back in Gavin's room, tearing the place apart."

Logan nodded and walked past her and headed back toward the bedroom as Haven stepped over to pull Rayne in for a hug. "What can I do?"

Rayne shook her head. "I don't know. I don't even know what to do for him. Garrison's lost it. He's completely lost it."

Haven nodded and walked Rayne back to the bedroom door. Logan had Garrison pinned tightly against him as Garrison struggled and talked at warp speed, but he was basically incoherent, and inconsolable. Logan looked at them and threw his head slightly, asking them to leave.

Haven felt Rayne's hesitation so she gently pulled her away. "Let Logan handle this."

Tears poured from Rayne's eyes as she allowed herself to be led to the couch. "He's finally reached the limit of what he can take. And I don't blame him. But he won't let me help. He doesn't want me to touch him. I'm sorry I dragged you all back over here, but I didn't know what else to do. He thinks so much of Logan, and they are such great friends, it was the only thing I could think of."

Haven took Rayne's hand. "It was the right thing to do. Those two are closer than brothers. Even in the little time I've been here, I can see that. And don't ever think you can't call for my help, any time, day or night. I love you. And I am so sorry—" Haven's eyes filled then spilled and she had to take a moment before speaking. When she could finally speak, both sisters had tears racing down their cheeks.

"I am so sorry that Garrison is going through such a terrible thing. I can't imagine how he feels, and hope I never have to, but we will do whatever it takes. Okay?"

Rayne nodded, and held on tight to Haven's hand. "Okay."

"Haven?"

Both women looked up and then stood when they saw

Logan standing behind them. Haven walked to him sniffing and scrubbing the tears from her cheeks. "Yes? What can I do?"

He pulled his car keys from his hip pocket and handed them to her. "I need you to get the black bag out of the trunk for me, please."

Rayne joined them. "Your doctor bag? Is he hurt?"

Logan nodded. "He's found a picture and I think that's what set him off. I don't know the significance of it yet, but he's cut his hand pretty badly on broken glass lodged in the shattered frame."

"Why is he so quiet now?" Rayne asked, looking behind Logan.

"I finally got him to calm down enough to hold the wound while I get medical supplies. Do you have any first aid materials?"

Rayne nodded and headed to the bathroom. Haven placed her hand on his back, still too afraid to touch his exposed arm. "I'll be right back. Are *you* okay?"

Rayne returned with a large first aid kit, several rolls of gauze, tape, alcohol and peroxide and handed them to Logan.

"I'm fine... In doctor mode. Just get the bag for me. I've got a vial with a strong sedative in it. If Garrison will allow it, I'm going to knock him out for a few hours. His mind needs a rest." He nodded his thanks to Rayne for the supplies as he turned to return to Garrison, but she placed her hand on his arm, stopping him.

"Can I help?"

Logan smiled at Rayne sadly. "Not right now. Let me get this taken care of. Hopefully he's gotten himself under control for the moment."

Logan left the room as Haven headed to the car. She had the bag out and was back in the house in less than two minutes. She opened his bag and pulled the plastic box containing three vials and opened it. She read the first and returned it. The second one was what she was sure Logan was after, but just to be sure she read the third one then returned it to the box, too. Varying sizes of paper and plastic packed syringes were in a side pocket and she pulled out a few before finding the one she knew he would need.

She glanced at Rayne who stood watching her silently, her arms wrapped around her middle as if holding herself together. Haven smiled at her gently. "He's going to be okay."

Rayne nodded almost desperately before looking back in the direction of the bedroom. Unable to see so much pain tearing at her sister, Haven opened the package, screwed the needle on the syringe, pulled the plastic cap off, and then pushed the needle in the bottle's rubber stopper to pull out enough of the sedative to knock Garrison out for a good while.

She turned to her sister, her heart breaking at the fear she saw in Rayne's eyes. "Stay here. I'll help Logan."

Rayne nodded and collapsed on the couch, her eyes going distant and defeated.

Haven hurried back along the short hallway, and then slowed her steps as she approached the door where Logan's soothing words were met with silence. Garrison was on the floor, his back propped up against a closed closet door, his arm stretched out to Logan who was wrapping bandages and chatting in a low monotone voice.

She stepped into the room and approached the men slowly, not wanting to startle either one. Logan glanced at her and then the device in her hand, and he nodded with a slight smile. He turned back to Garrison who was staring blindly into space.

"Hey, buddy, I'm going to give you an injection. Okay?"

Garrison said nothing. Heaving a sigh, Logan held out his hand to Haven. She nodded as she turned the syringe so he would have it ready to inject.

He turned his gaze back to Garrison and started talking again, about the time Garrison's mother had to bandage up both boys when they decided to wrestle close to a briar patch. Haven listened to the story and couldn't help but smile. Garrison's expression didn't change, and she wondered if he was in shock and unable to comprehend what Logan was saying.

But she knew it didn't matter, as he was completely motionless through Logan swabbing the arm with alcohol, biting off the needle's plastic protection, then injecting the drug. When Logan pulled the needle out, Garrison finally flinched and his gaze landed on Logan.

"It's a cop. I think it's the cop who led the investigation."

Haven watched Logan purposely not react, though she knew he was quaking inside, just as she was. A police officer? The one who had harassed her and Rayne? She wanted to ask questions but knew now was not the time to say anything.

Garrison turned to her as his head fell back against the door, and she knew the sedative was already taking affect. "Where's Rayne? I need her."

Haven turned immediately but didn't even get to take a step as Rayne flew past her to get to Garrison. She was on her knees at his side before her body had completely stopped its forward momentum so she swayed into him and wrapped her arms around his shoulders and held him.

"I heard," she said to the room at large. "We have to call John Grammar. He's the captain of the Mystic Waters police department," she said, looking to Haven and Logan.

Garrison nodded as his eyes closed, and Haven moved forward at the same time Logan did. "Rayne, honey, let us have him. We'll put him to bed. And in the meantime, you use his phone and call the station."

Rayne reluctantly released Garrison and moved back before Logan maneuvered Garrison so he could stand and lift the lifeless body. "Okay. Just put him in Gavin's bed. It will be too hard to get him up to the loft."

Logan nodded, and with Haven's help they stepped over the broken glass still lying about and placed him on the bed. When Haven turned, Rayne was already gone. She turned back to Logan who was staring down at his friend.

"Do you think it will disturb him if I clean this glass up?"

He turned to pull her against him. "No. You prepared slightly more than I had planned to give him, but I think it will help if he's out for as long as possible. It won't hurt him, but jackhammers won't wake him right now."

He turned his face into her hair and kissed the top of her head. "Thank you for having it ready. I think we could make quite a team."

Haven snuggled against him. "I think we already do."

"The captain is coming and he's bringing the FBI agent with him. They'll be here shortly."

Logan held onto Haven as they turned to face Rayne. "We're going to clean this glass up. If he wakes up before we expect, he could step on it. Would you mind making some coffee?"

Rayne looked at them, and then at Garrison, then back up again as she nodded her head rapidly. "Of course. I'm sure all police officers drink coffee. I will. I will...."

She turned and left mumbling to herself. Haven watched her go, and sighed. "She's barely holding it together."

"I can see that. After we talk to the police, I'll give her a mild sedative too and you two can go up to the loft and get some sleep. I'll take the couch."

Haven snuggled into him. "Thank you."

He nuzzled against her hair then kissed the top of her head again. "For what?"

"For being such a great guy, even after I've been such a witch."

He pulled back and grinned, adoration and affection in his eyes. "You have certainly cast a spell on me."

****

The officers looked worn out, as Logan figured they all did at this point. He shook hands with John Grammar, a man he had known from way back when but hadn't seen in years, then with Special Agent Bret Thorne, a man he figured he'd rather have in his corner than out of it. The agent's intense scrutiny could make a man confess to something he hadn't ever thought of, much less done.

They settled in the living room, Rayne between Haven and Logan on the couch, and both officers of the law facing them in rocking chairs Garrison had no doubt made. Logan looked from one to the other, already knowing a little of the day's events as Rayne had filled them in as much as she could. Since both men had gratefully accepted black coffee they sat back in the rockers holding their cups, occasionally taking a tentative sip until Rayne settled on the couch.

"Thank you for coming," Rayne began. "I know what we learned while the meeting was going on, but when Garrison got home he went straight to Gavin's room and started tearing into it.

"What happened after I left?"

They looked at each other as if to see who was going to speak. Finally, Agent Thorne deferred to John. He nodded.

"As you know, it's been months now since there was any indication that Gavin was still alive. Honestly, the department had already been expecting to recover a body, if that, even before the other remains were found, indicating the possibility of a serial killer."

Haven took one of Rayne's hands, and she immediately took Logan's. He glanced at her, in appreciation. Whether he had ever had a relationship with his brother or not, Danny *was* his brother, and knowing he'd been victimized and then murdered was sickening for them all.

"But we knew that already. Rayne told us about the meeting. What set Garrison off to the point that he has trashed Gavin's room and was so...hysterical, is the only word I can think of? Garrison doesn't get hysterical," Logan added.

John nodded. "He got sick at the station after we told him that we have pretty much concluded that the only reason he is being kept alive is because he's either a sexual slave or something equally as bad. Any other reason wouldn't make sense. There's been no demand for a ransom. No demand for publicity to make any kind of statement."

Logan looked down at his and Rayne's joined hands. He cleared his throat. "Do you believe that this is the same person who killed all the other young men?" He looked back up at John, and, as he feared, he got a nod.

"We believe it is a very real possibility."

"And the person or people who killed Gavin's parents?"

Agent Thorne spoke up, "I thought this afternoon that was a possibility, but I've had a couple of hours to pour through the files Captain Grammar provided and now I'm thinking *not*. The MOs are too different. If the person who shot the Whites is the same one who took these young men, they would most likely have shot them, too, not take what appears from the forensics report to be a hatchet to them.

"The shooting was a preplanned act that was quick and simple, and possibly, given Grey White's position on the force, a result of an arrest or to stop an ongoing investigation. We are examining his files, especially his most recent cases, and looking into what he was working on when he was killed to see if something may have been missed before.

"The chopping up of the other victims—" Bret looked at Logan. "I'm sorry. One was your brother."

Logan swallowed the bile lodged in his throat. He couldn't open his mouth to speak so he simply nodded, hoping the agent would get it all out on the table.

Apparently getting the message, he continued, "The way in which the other victims were killed indicates an act of rage. So we believe they all must have either tried to escape or fight when they were being…handled."

Logan could barely stand to hear more, and understood why Garrison had gotten sick and then lost it. He wanted to put his fist through something. But he had to know everything. If Gavin had a chance at surviving, he couldn't hide his head in the sand. "So you are saying, as long as Gavin cooperates he will live?"

Bret nodded. "That is what I believe, yes. The fact that he has been moved, and is able to walk, is a good sign given the amount of time he's been missing. But, as you can imagine, we are very concerned what his state of mind is at this point.

"There's still one scenario we can think of, that keeps me from discarding the possibility of it being the same Unsub, I'm sorry, unknown subject of interest... And that is if Grey White had some knowledge, or even suspected something about the crimes against those young men, and the Unsub realized he was being investigated."

John held up his free hand to draw all eyes to him before he spoke. "I don't believe Grey could have known much. If he did have some idea this person was kidnapping and killing these young men, he would have shared it with me. Or with the officer who had been assigned to assist him."

"What was the officer's name?" Rayne asked, her voice tight.

"Burt Thompson."

Rayne shook her head. "*That's* the man who was assigned to assist him?"

John looked at her hard, his brows pulled together. "Yes. He was always following Grey around asking if he could help him, so Grey finally started sending Thompson to check out this or that, I think mostly just to get him out of his hair.

"It's pretty much what we've all done with the guy at one time or another. I wanted to fire him a long time ago, but I needed concrete justification or I'd have to deal with lawyers.

"He's suspended without pay now because he's finally doing things that people are reporting back to the station. I just needed a little more, and he was gone.

"Do you know this officer?"

Haven spoke up quickly and told them about the

incident on the mountain road, and Rayne followed with the break-in at the cabin, then finally Logan rose and went into the room where Garrison was still out cold and picked up the torn photograph of the Mystic Water's Police Force. He returned with it and handed it to John. "This is what Garrison had in his hands when I got here. He was in a rage. Which guy in this photograph are you talking about?"

John looked at the crumpled and bent portion of the photograph that remained. Someone had torn off the right side of it. He looked at the faces of the men and women he worked with every day and then looked for the one he had just suspended.

"It isn't who is in it, but who isn't. And that would be Burt Thompson. He's been torn off. I remember he was on the outer edge a little away from the rest of us when the photograph was being taken because the photographer kept telling him to get closer. After about the third time, he finally just took the picture. Thompson's always been a little odd, so I didn't think much of it.

"Damn!" He dropped the picture and stood, setting his coffee cup on the fireplace mantel. He pulled out his cell phone to punch at the screen, looking at them all as he spoke. "This is Captain John Grammar, MWPD, Badge number 1722. I need every available squad car sent to Burt Thompson's house. The address is in the employee database. No sirens, no lights. I want everyone armed and silent and to wait outside until I arrive.

"And get me Judge Maddox's number. I need him to sign off on a warrant. Tell him we have probable cause to believe Burt Thompson is involved in the crimes regarding Gavin White. If he has questions, tell him to call me. Call me back and let me know where we stand." He snapped the phone closed and headed for the door.

Bret Thorne stood and handed his cup to Rayne. "Thank you, ma'am. My people will be out here to set up the search early. Will you and Mr. White be ready?" he asked, before pulling out his cell phone. At her nod he started punching its screen as he turned and left too.

Logan hurried to follow them out, going to the driver's side where John was already starting the car. "What do we do?"

Talking on his phone quietly, the agent got in the car on the opposite side as John's window slid down. "Stay put. This will take some time. Most likely the rest of the night. I'll call Garrison's phone first thing in the morning."

The window went up as he was backing out. Logan watched them leave torn between obeying and following to get a look at the man who may have raped and killed his brother, glad Garrison was passed out. Logan had taken an oath, and couldn't break it to break a guy's neck, but Garrison was under no such restraint. If *he* had any idea they were going after the man who had something to do with hurting his family, Garrison would likely end up in jail for murder, too.

Chapter Seventeen

Burt couldn't sleep with so much to think about. Getting suspended had pissed him off, but he had turned lemons into lemonade and the nice cool drink was settling in his stomach pretty well.

He'd been really careful and hadn't actually touched anything except the bottom corner of the weirdo's bed. He had even thought ahead enough to have on latex gloves and the disposable shoe covers hospital staff wore. And a ski mask, just because he'd liked the idea of it.

But the longhaired freak hadn't made things easy for him. Burt had expected to have ample options to hide the gun and dope, but the guy took being a minimalist to a whole new level. And he'd had to watch while the freak walked around his yard naked.

Who did that?

It had pissed him off to have to look at the other man's body when his own hadn't ever been one that women wanted. But then he thought about what other men would do to that sissy boy with his long hair and long dick when he went to prison for killing a cop and his wife.

Yeah, they would tear that boy a new one.

The pleasure that thought brought got a rise out of his own dick and he rose from his bed and walked to Martha's room. She was sound asleep, her still young features angelic in slumber. But he didn't want an angel tonight. He wanted screaming and crying and he didn't care if he was the one doing it.

She still thought he didn't know about her past. Because that was the way he always wanted it to stay. If she ever found out that he had saved her from a life in prison by killing the cop who was investigating her, she would be forever grateful. But he didn't want grateful. He wanted her to always be as she had been when she first came to him. Scared and alone. And willing to accept whatever he did.

It irked him she sometimes got sassy and threatened to expose him for sexual battery, especially after all he had done for her. More than once he had almost given himself away by telling her he knew her real name and had the mug shots that had once been in Grey White's possession.

It was just a good thing for both of them that White hadn't known he was showing Burt pictures of his own wife. If he'd given the mug shots that came over the fax machine to anyone else to look into, then Martha would be behind bars and Burt would be lonely again, just like he had been all his life.

Burt crawled onto her bed and knew the instant she was awake, although she didn't move or open her eyes. Smiling, more than willing to play her game he slowly pulled back the covers and placed them on her other side.

He pulled up her gown and approved of her bare bottom and then remembered she said she was on the rag. He slid her legs apart and saw there was no string to indicate she wore a tampon, confirming his suspicion she had lied to him. He knew when she started her period and he knew when it was done, as he'd charted it for years.

But two could play games.

She knew what had to happen if he wanted sex and she was bleeding and protested him taking her vaginally. If she wanted to fake being on the rag, then so be it. Only this time she would be punished for lying to him. He would take her without lubrication. And he dared her to make a sound in protest.

Burt jerked her hips upward and ignored her fake mumble as she continued to pretend to be asleep. He grinned as he held her by her pubic bone with one hand and massaged his dick into a hard weapon with the other. He had a second of self-doubt when the picture of the freak's much larger dick came to mind, but he pushed it away.

What woman would want that up her ass?

He rose up on his knees and pulled Martha's hips up further and aimed before ramming into her. She screamed her head off and fought to escape him, but he held tight and laughed as he pushed his way home.

The shout of *"Police"* coinciding with the crashing windows and doors caught him by surprise, and he froze as the men and the one woman he had worked with filled the room, their flashlight topped automatic rifles pointed at his head, body, and back.

His dick deflated inside of Martha and she jumped forward playing the hysterical victim to the hilt. He was dragged backward off the bed and held face down on the floor while they cuffed his hands at his back and shackled his ankles together.

While his Miranda Rights were being read, Burt lay there dazed yet coherent enough to be mortified to have his bare ass and his sexual needs exposed for the department's amusement. The only thing he could be thankful for at the moment was he had already ditched the gun.

When the officer asked him if he understood his rights as they had been read to him, Burt nodded, knowing he was off the force now for good.

****

"Are you sure you don't want to go to the hospital, ma'am?" the emergency management technician asked for the fourth time.

Martha shook her head, tired of repeating herself. They couldn't make her go, and there was no way she would do so voluntarily.

"It would go a long way in convicting your husband for the assault," Kathy Gishwell inserted, drawing Martha's attention back to her.

"He wasn't assaulting me. We were having sex. You all breaking apart the house scared the hell out of me and I screamed."

"I don't believe you are being completely honest with me, Mrs. Thompson."

Martha was allowed to dress, but she still felt

completely exposed as several of the officers going through her and Burt's things had seen every private part she had. There was a time when that wouldn't have bothered her as much, but times had changed and her body wasn't what it once was.

And it only made it all the more embarrassing that anytime one of the male officers looked her way they wouldn't make eye contact but would quickly look away again. Except for the female officer who invaded her doorstep the other day, that one was staring at her like she could see right through Martha, all the way to her bone marrow. If she wasn't afraid to expose any more of herself and her past by drawing additional attention to herself, she would tell them they had no right to be in her house, going through her things, and demand they all leave. But asserting herself now could open up doors she'd rather remain shut.

"I am ashamed," Martha said, deciding to play the victim...to the extent it suited her, knowing that telling Officer Gishwell that she had no intention of being honest with her wasn't in her best interest.

The officer nodded and wrote in her little notebook. "I can understand that, but you could have avoided this humiliation if you had been honest. Will you be honest with me now?"

Furious that the woman was determined to make her feel as small as possible, Martha ignored her. It was already hard to pay attention while her personal things were being pulled out of cabinets and closets. She swallowed, wishing she could go back to her bedroom and make them leave everything alone. If anyone looked too closely in her bedroom closet, humiliation would be the least of her problems.

She turned back to Kathy Gishwell. "Please make them stop going through my things. I didn't do anything wrong."

Kathy pressed her lips together and sighed. "I'm sorry, but the warrant covers the entire house."

Martha frowned. "Just what are you looking for?"

"I'm not at liberty to say. Your husband is being taken to the station now. His rights have been read to him, and the captain has forty-eight hours before he has to officially charge him with anything. But we have probable cause to believe he is involved in some criminal activity."

Martha shook her head. "That is ridiculous. I thought this was about someone calling the other day pretending to be me, and reporting that Burt had sexually assaulted me. Which I already told you didn't happen."

What the hell has Burt done?

Martha was seriously concerned now. She definitely didn't need these people investigating him to the extent it pulled her in as well. It would ruin everything she had worked so hard to set up. She tried not to let her fears show though she was pretty sure they would be attributed to her being sexually assaulted by her husband, as the officer's expression clearly showed she didn't believe Martha had willingly participated in Burt's rough, and some would say disgusting, sexual behavior.

"Mrs. Thompson, Martha, you don't have to cover for him anymore. He isn't going to be able to hurt you if you will let us help you. Go with the EMT to the hospital. Let them do a rape kit and examine you so we can get the documentation we need to keep you safe."

"I don't want to leave my house while so many people are in it. Please, make them stop going through my things. Nothing in my room belongs to Burt!"

The officer studied her, and Martha was afraid her tone was too insistent, but then she rose and walked into the bedroom where Burt *had* assaulted her. It was a great relief when not only Kathy Gishwell emerged, but the other two officers appeared as well. Martha expelled a deep breath, relieved they were no longer looking through her things.

She tried not to look *too* relieved though, as that could cause suspicion. When Officer Gishwell settled back on the couch at her side, she knew she was going to need to find a way to get the woman off her back. "Thank you."

Kathy smiled, but her eyes held determination. "Now, how about that trip to the hospital?"

****

After being hauled out of the squad car with only the blanket they had quickly thrown around him back in Martha's bedroom, Burt was walked to the interrogation room and placed on the side of the table that faced the wall of mirrors. The handcuffs were removed and his wrists were then re-shackled, this time with the cuffs that had a long chain, which ran through two upside down horseshoe shaped steel U-bolts attached to the table's surface. With the blanket now wrapped around his waist, he was left alone.

Burt knew there were several people on the other side of that mirror watching him and talking about him, probably calling him a freak, and worse, but he knew he had to pretend he was confused about being hauled in. Anything else was an admission of guilt, and he wasn't admitting to anything. What went on in a man's home was his business and no one else's.

Three men in identical black suits walked in, their starched white shirts nearly blinding under the fluorescent lights, their thin black ties perfectly straight. Unease tingled down his spine, as he was sure the strangers were federal agents.

Two stood at his back on either end of the room, and the older, more distinguished one laid a thick manila folder, a legal pad encased leather binder, an ink pen, and a tape recorder on the table then sat in the interrogator's chair facing him. Burt's stomach rumbled loudly, and he knew it wasn't from hunger, as the man pushed the button on the device.

"For the record: I'm Special Agent Bret Thorne from the Washington D.C. branch of the Federal Bureau of Investigations. I'm here to investigate several murders that have taken place in Mystic Waters, West Virginia, over an as yet undetermined amount of time, as well as the current kidnapping of the minor child of two of the victims, seventeen-year-old Gavin White. The minor was sixteen when he was kidnapped nearly six months ago.

"With me are Special Agent Cameron Fain and Special Agent Richard Hume, also from the DC Branch, as well as the interviewee, Burt Thompson."

He looked up from the notepad he had been reading from and lifted the pen before he looked at Burt. "For the record: Burt Thompson, are you aware that this interview is being taped?"

Burt nodded.

"For the record: Mr. Thompson nodded.

"For the record: Please state out loud, *sir*, that you are aware that this interview is being taped."

Burt kept his mouth closed as he seriously considered telling them he wanted a lawyer, which would put a quick end to the interview. But he knew firsthand what law enforcement thought about that. He would be branded as guilty from the get-go and treated as the enemy once he was back in a cell.

"For the record: Mr. Thompson is refusing to cooperate. Special Agent Cameron Fain, please state for the record who is in this room and where the electronic tape recorder is sitting."

The agent stepped up to the table. "For the record: I'm Special Agent Cameron Fain, Washington D.C. branch of the Federal Bureau of Investigations. With me, conducting the interview is Special Agent Bret Thorne. Special Agent Richard Hume is also present in the room. Sitting at the table with Special Agent Bret Thorne is Burt Thompson. Between them on the table is a Kiko Sounds brand tape recorder, which is currently running to record what is being said in this room."

Bret Thorne nodded and the agent returned to his corner of the room. Then the head agent turned to the other one. "Agent Richard Hume, would you please come forward and state for the record who is in this room and where the electronic tape recorder is sitting."

The agent moved forward and Burt had had enough.

"Oh, hell. I'm here. Burt Thompson. The damned interview is being recorded.

"Satisfied?"

Agent Hume returned to his corner without another word, and Burt glared at the man before him just waiting for the guy to smirk. But his serious expression never altered and that had Burt's stomach churning again.

"Thank you, Mr. Thompson. Please state for the record your full name, address, social security number, and your badge number with the Mystic Waters Police Force."

Knowing he had no choice, Burt grudgingly gave up the information and watched as the agent wrote it all down on his tablet, though Burt knew he already had the information. It was a stall tactic used to give the one being interviewed time to think about the fact that he or she was in custody, and to hopefully scare them into compliance.

Well he wasn't going to give them the satisfaction.

"Thank you, Mr. Thompson.

"For the record: Mr. Thompson was apprehended tonight at his home by the Mystic Waters Police Department headed by Captain John Grammar. Mr. Thompson was allegedly sexually battering his wife of nearly eight years at the time of his apprehension but put up no resistances, so no lethal force was necessary nor used to extract him from her person or the home.

"For the record: Mr. Thompson, from your standpoint is this information correct?"

Burt fumed, shaking with anger. "Hell no, it ain't right! I was having sex with my wife. She likes it in the ass and she likes it rough. But that ain't none of your damned business."

"For the record: Mr. Thompson denies sexually battering his wife.

"For the record: Mr. Thompson, are you personally familiar with the currently unresolved case regarding the murders of Grey White, a Detective with the Mystic Waters Police Department up until his death, and his wife, Mrs. Joy White?"

Burt knew he had to cool down and play right. The last thing he needed to do was screw this up. "I am. I was White's partner."

For the first time Agent Thorne's features altered. *Slightly*. Then his mask of superiority was firmly back in place. Burt waited as the agent made several notes.

"For the record: Mr. Thompson, you state that you were Detective Grey White's partner. Was this a regular partnership that was established by Captain Grammar or his superiors?"

Burt shook his head then frowned when the agent just sat looking at him. "No. It was a partnership that came from White needing additional help and me having time on my hands. Mystic Waters wasn't exactly a metropolis of criminal activity back then."

The agent looked at him for long moments then made notes on his pad.

"For the record: Mr. Thompson states his, quote, partnership, end quote, with Detective Grey White, now deceased, was not an officially appointed position.

"For the record: Mr. Thompson, were you involved in any investigations with Detective Grey White immediately preceding his murder?"

Burt hesitated, knowing he was heading into a trap. "I was sent here and there for him, not on anything important. Most of the time I felt I was wasting my time. It's embarrassing to admit, but I was little more than a gofer. He liked brown mustard on his corned beef sandwiches." Burt laughed at his own joke but the other faces in the room didn't alter.

"For the record: I will ask again. Mr. Thompson, were you involved in any investigations with Detective White immediately preceding his murder?"

Burt's cheeks heated, but he was determined to win this battle of wits so he shook his head and lied. "No. Nothing specific. As I said, I was his errand boy. But to my knowledge he wasn't working on anything important. Just the usual car break-ins and home invasion stuff. But those were usually just kids making trouble."

"For the record: Mr. Thompson states that he was not working on any important investigations with Detective White preceding his murder.

"For the record: Mr. Thompson, have you ever been in the home of Detective Grey White and his wife, Mrs. Joy White?"

Burt hesitated again and then nodded. He was certain he had left it clean that night, but there was always a chance a hair fell from his increasingly balding head. "I was sent there once not too long before they were killed to pick up his briefcase. He had forgotten and left it at home. His wife invited me in while she fetched it.

"But that was the only time."

"For the record: Mr. Thompson states he was in the home of Detective Grey White only one time, to retrieve the detective's briefcase from Mrs. Joy White.

"For the record: Mr. Thompson, do you recall the date you were sent to the White home to retrieve the briefcase?"

"No."

"For the record: Mr. Thompson states he does not recall the date he was sent by Mr. Grey White to retrieve the briefcase he states he was sent to retrieve.

"For the record: Mr. Thompson, on the day that you went to retrieve the briefcase for Mr. Grey White, was Mrs. Joy White the only person in the home?"

Burt shrugged. "I don't know. I didn't leave the living room. If there was anyone else there, I was not aware of it."

"For the record: Mr. Thompson states he was unaware if there was anyone else in the home of Detective Grey White other than himself and Mrs. Joy White."

"For the record: Mr. Thompson, have you ever met Gavin White, the minor child of the deceased's, Detective Grey White and his wife, Mrs. Joy White?"

Burt shook his head in denial but then remembered the kid sometimes went into the station to see his dad. "Uh, yeah. I almost forgot. I saw him a couple of times at the station, but I was never introduced to the kid."

"For the record: Mr. Thompson states that the only time he has ever been in the presence of the minor child Gavin White, son of the deceased Detective Grey White and his wife, the deceased Mrs. Joy White, was at the Mystic Waters Police Station where there was no direct contact between Mr. Thompson and the minor child Gavin White.

"For the record: Mr. Thompson, have you ever met or had any contact with Anthony White-Taylor?"

Burt huffed. "How long is this going to take?"

"Please answer the question."

"No. I don't know him."

"For the record: Mr. Thompson states that he has never met the deceased Anthony White-Taylor.

"For the record: Mr. Thompson, have you ever met or had any contact with Donald Hanson, Junior?"

Burt shook his head, wondering if they were going to try to pin every murder as well as the kidnapping on him. "No."

"For the record: Mr. Thompson states that he does not know and has not had any contact with the deceased, Donald Hanson, Junior.

"For the record: Mr. Thompson, have you ever met or had any contact with Samuel Paine?"

"No."

"For the record: Mr. Thompson states he has never met or had contact with the deceased, Samuel Paine.

"For the record: Mr. Thompson, are you currently suspended from the Mystic Waters Police Department?"

"Yes."

"For the record: Mr. Thompson states he is suspended from the Mystic Waters Police Department.

"For the record: Mr. Thompson, did you kill Detective Grey White and-slash-or his wife, Mrs. Joy White?"

The abrupt question caught Burt by surprise and he laughed. "Does anyone *ever* answer that question with anything other than a resounding, 'No!'?"

Burt rolled his eyes at the stone cold gaze of the agent.

"No. A *resounding* no!"

"For the record: Mr. Thompson states he did not kill Detective Grey White and-slash-or his wife, Mrs. Joy White."

"For the record: Mr. Thompson, did you, or do you now, have knowledge of the whereabouts and-slash-or condition of the minor child, Gavin White, son of the slain Detective Grey White and his wife, Mrs. Joy White?"

"No. And my answer to all the rest of the names you plan to mention is a no, also. Are we done here?"

Special Agent Bret Thorne ignored Burt's outburst and repeated his last question and Burt's response, *for the record,* and then went through the list of names of the serial killer's victims again.

Burt gave up, wondering if the interview would ever end. He was certain it had to be way up into the morning hours by now and he wanted to sleep. Finally the agent seemed ready to be done with it all, too.

"For the record: Mr. Thompson, do you so swear that all the answers, statements, and denials that you have made during this recorded interview with myself, Special Agent Bret Thorne of the Washington D.C. branch of the Federal Bureau of Investigation, and in the presence of both Special Agent Cameron Fain, and Special Agent Richard Hume of the same branch of the same agency, to be, to the best of your knowledge, the truth, the whole truth, and nothing but the truth? If so, please so swear."

Burt grinned at the agent, relieved the interview was finally over, and though exhausted to the bone, he felt he'd done quite well. "I so swear."

Special Agent Bret Thorne rose and tilted his neck one way and then the other, making audible cracking sounds. He punched the stop button on the recording device and closed his leather notepad holder then began stacking everything into his hands. He and the other agents headed to the door, and Burt couldn't believe they were just going to leave. He had some questions of his own!

"Excuse me!"

When the agents turned to face him, he held up his hands as much as the restraints would allow. "What is it I am being charged with?"

Special Agent Thorne looked at him, his deadpan expression still in place. "Captain Grammar will be the one to inform you of that."

Burt sat there as the men left and then turned to glare at the mirrored wall. In seconds the door reopened and Captain Grammar and two of the officers he'd known for years entered the room. The captain set a tape recorder on the table as the two officers walked to stand behind him, just as the agents had.

Fury filled him, replacing exhaustion, as the captain took the seat facing him, lifted a legal pad and pen, and pushed the record button.

Chapter Eighteen

"Good morning."

Logan opened his eyes and looked up from his bed on the couch. Garrison was looking down at him holding a cup of coffee in each hand. He struggled to sit up on the end of the couch and took the cup offered. Garrison dropped down on the cushion on the opposite end.

"Thanks."

Knowing Garrison was talking about the night before, Logan nodded, took a sip, and swallowed. "Welcome." Then he held the mug out. "Thanks, too."

"Welcome. Girls?"

"In your bed."

"Guess I looked a little crazy."

"Yeah."

"Okay."

Logan grinned. "Better?"

"Yeah."

"Okay."

They sat there sipping coffee silently for a couple of minutes. Then Garrison sighed. "Call John?"

Logan nodded. "Yeah, he came out here with an FBI agent."

"Bret Thorne?"

"Yeah. Think they arrested that cop last night. He will call this morning sometime with an update. FBI is gonna start the search too, once it gets light."

"Good."

"Yeah."

Garrison glanced over, paused, and his lips almost formed a smile. "You look like hell."

"Feel like it, too. Took a long time to fall asleep after everything."

Garrison took another sip and then set his cup on the table next to him before he rested his head back against the couch. "Should have given yourself a shot too."

"I think that's how junkies get started."

"True."

"They can't tell for sure, because all the remains are so deteriorated, but they think the guys were probably sexually molested."

"I know."

"Made me sick, still does."

"Me too."

"I didn't like Donny," Logan said, his voice shaky. He set his cup on the table next to him, not sure it wouldn't spill with his hands trembling so much.

Garrison nodded, his own emotions still too close to the surface to respond. After a few breaths, he could. "That wasn't your fault. You were just a kid. I hold your parents fully responsible for the relationships that existed."

"Me too. Mostly. But I should have gotten over it at some point."

"Not possible when nothing ever changed. This isn't your fault either. Donny getting caught up in it, I mean."

"He died thinking I hated him."

"Maybe. Maybe not. Never saw any indication he thought about you one way or the other."

"Thanks. I needed to remember that. Still, he was my brother."

"Then mourn him. But don't blame yourself."

"I've been more upset about Gavin and the others than my own brother. I think that's what bothers me the most. That and the fact that I know I should be helping my parents through all this, but I can't stand the thought of being around them."

"Understandable. Are you going to tell your parents what we've learned so far?"

Logan shook his head. "There isn't any point. It will only make it worse for them."

"You're a good man."

Logan laid his head back and closed his eyes, wishing he could drift back off to sleep. "So are you."

Warm wet lips brushed his and his eyes fluttered open telling him he had indeed fallen asleep. Haven's chin was at his eye level as she had leaned over his head and was kissing him upside down. He tilted his head back and to the side to allow her better access. When she finally stood back up, he realized Garrison was getting the same treatment.

"What a beautiful way to start a day."

As Rayne stood and both girls moved around the outsides of the couch wearing nearly identical thigh length football jerseys—Haven's a Tennessee Titans in light blue with darker blue trim and white lettering with the number thirteen on the front, and Rayne's a West Virginia Mountaineers jersey made of navy blue with gold designs with the number twelve—to climb onto their laps, Garrison agreed and then added, "I feel like I'm in a Wrigley's Doublemint Gum commercial."

The girls' laughs were as identical as they were, but Logan knew he'd never mistake one for the other, absolutely certain he could find Haven in a crowd of a thousand, blindfolded. And he knew right then he didn't want to live the rest of his life without her.

"Marry me."

Her quick intake of breath was matched by the couple's sitting next to them, but he only had eyes for her. "I'm serious. Marry me."

She trembled in his lap but he held her securely, since her hands were twisted together, and not on him. He wanted them on him. *Really* wanted them on him. But he knew the coming day wouldn't allow any of them to have privacy.

"You aren't saying anything."

"Let's get some clothes and hit the shower," Garrison said, lifting Rayne as he stood. She looked down at them, smiling at Logan and sending a look of concern at her sister. But Haven hadn't moved and was still looking at Logan.

Garrison set her on her feet, and they made a beeline for the loft only to pass by a moment later with clothing in hand as they headed back to the bathroom. Logan waited, hoping Haven would speak once they had some privacy.

"No?"

Haven slid from his lap and walked to the kitchen to pour herself a cup of coffee and then held the flask up, offering him one silently. Logan shook his head and continued to watch her. "I didn't know you drank coffee."

"I usually don't. This is an emergency."

"Because I asked you to marry me?"

"Because I couldn't get to sleep until late and I'm shot."

"So bad timing on my part, or you're just not interested?"

She smiled at him from across the room. "Oh, I'm interested, but there are complications."

Logan felt every inch of his body relax. He smiled and rose to his feet, grabbed his cup and went to join her. "I can move to California."

"You hate California."

"I love you. Location doesn't matter in the end."

She stared at him as her eyes filled and threatened to spill over. "I hate California, too. I love Mystic Waters though, and my sister is here. I want to live here."

"More than you want to be with me?"

"That isn't fair."

He smiled. "What do you feel for me, if anything?"

She was silent for a while as she looked into his eyes, then she frowned and it felt as if his heart had stopped.

"Everything."

Surprise had his heart pounding again. "Then that's all I need right now. Marry me and we'll play doctor and nurse until I grow too old to get it up anymore."

Haven laughed. "That's crude."

He grinned. "I wanted to see you smile when you tell me I mean everything to you. So tell me again, now."

Haven moved to him and put her arms around his

neck though he could tell she wasn't touching him with her hands. Before he could comment that she rarely ever did, she gave him such a brilliant smile that it took his breath.

"You mean *everything* to me," she said, her green eyes shining with the truth of her words. Then she frowned. "But we hardly know each other."

"I know all I need to know. You?"

She grinned. "Maybe." When his brows shot up, she laughed. "Okay…you still do mean everything to me in spite of that, if that helps."

Logan took her lips, intending to make her as sure of what she was saying as he was of his own feelings, but she turned the tables on him, and he forgot about everything else as he got lost in the wonder of her kiss.

****

Since Rayne and Haven were the same size and Logan could wear Garrison's shirts and shorts as length didn't matter, Logan and Haven headed for their showers as soon as Garrison and Rayne were done.

Haven was relieved the FBI agent called before they could make it into the bathroom to let Garrison know the search teams and dogs were already in route, so she didn't have to make excuses about not touching Logan's body.

Other than a few long kisses and several quick ones, and Logan taking the time to lick the water pouring over her breasts then suckling from them until her knees nearly melted, he was in a frenzy to hurry washing as much as she was.

They had laughed at each other and themselves throughout the entire process and were still smiling after hurriedly dressing in the borrowed clothes. The smiles melted off both of their faces when they stepped into the living room and saw Special Agent Thorne sitting on a tall bar stool at the island sipping coffee and talking quietly to Garrison and Rayne.

They approached, and caught the last of what he was saying.

"…so we'll start there and have one team work in the

direction of the site we hope to find, and another to go in the opposite direction, though my guess is that a vehicle was waiting and we'll lose the trail at that point."

Haven glanced at Garrison who looked a lot better than he had, and noticed Rayne was rubbing his back in circles for comfort and support. A part of her envied her sister, knowing Rayne could even do that when he wasn't wearing a shirt, but another part of her celebrated the gift she had feared gone forever only a short time ago. Especially since she had taken the opportunity to look at Logan's groin in the shower and saw he looked completely healed.

She'd fought to hold in her smile since Logan caught her looking and his shaft rose to the occasion. He'd sent her a warning with his eyes that said he was ready anytime she was. Only their time constraints had prevented her taking him up on it.

It was a good thing she hadn't. It was obvious when the agent rose and headed to the door that everyone had just been waiting for them to appear, to get the day started.

The FBI agents came prepared with long automatic weapons they slung over their shoulders and were dressed in black helmets with face shields, heavy black vests adorned with the three large white initials of the agency on both the front and back of the protective gear, which was worn over black jumpsuits, and tall black combat boots.

From a long line of black Hummers, they unloaded the trailers carrying up to four single passenger four-wheelers each, and were nice enough to provide a four-wheeler each for Logan and Haven. Garrison had his own four-wheeler and an extra one that Rayne had apparently ridden before because she jumped right on it and took off after he pulled them from out of the back of his workshop.

After a short lesson and little trial and error on her part, Haven decided she liked the vehicle much better than walking, and it wasn't long before she and Logan were bringing up the tail end of the large group of agents following Rayne and Garrison into the forested mountainside.

All too soon they were slowing down and those who had already stopped were dismounting. Haven and Logan turned theirs off and walked up to the back of the group where Garrison was stooping down. Though she wasn't close enough to see, she was certain he was showing the agents the footprints Rayne had told them about the night before.

After telling the others to remain still and look around them for additional footprints, Rayne and Garrison led the lead agent and both squad leaders to another location about twenty feet away. They all stooped down there as well and Special Agent Thorne pulled a short straight wire with an orange triangular flag attached from his vest pocket and stuck it in the ground.

Haven glanced back and noticed the first location where they had been also had one of the flags. Then she looked at the twenty or so other agents and realized they also had them either in their hands or sticking out of vest pockets.

She looked over at Logan and her heart broke. He looked upset again, and she could only speculate that he was thinking about his brother. There would be no flags for Donny.

"Hey! You okay?"

Logan smiled at her, but it wasn't a smile of joy, just one people pasted on when they didn't want anyone to know they were feeling less than happy. Of course she knew better and wanted to fuss at him for thinking he had to hide his feeling from her. But that was a conversation for another time.

After living her entire life in the fear of being found out, Haven had had enough. Now that she had found the man she wanted to spend her life with, she knew she would have to be brave and chart new waters as she needed to be able to comfort Logan when he needed comforting.

Like now.

Her mostly sleepless night hadn't been all about what

was currently happening around them. That was part of it, yes, but not all. She'd also pondered over the way in which she'd been able to heal Logan without touching him and a theory took hold. But like all theories there was only one way to find out if she was right. And that was to test it.

Now that she had time to concentrate, and with the confidence borne from her last experience using her imagination to control her gift, she stepped closer to him and took a deep breath.

Haven envisioned holding ice cubes in her hands. At first they melted quickly, sizzling and popping as steam rose. Refusing to accept defeat, she mentally added more. This time the melting slowed and the cubes lasted longer, but eventually water slid through her fingers. She repeated the mental image again and again, each time attaining an additional degree of success until finally she was able to smile when they all held, and were solid cubes of ice chilling her hand.

Not overthinking what she was about to do, she held the image of solid cubes as she reached over and slid her fingers between Logan's. When the image held without any effort on her part, she was able to breathe easier, and she was actually relaxing as he curled his fingers around the back of her hand, bringing their palms together. Logan looked down at her and smiled. Elated with her success, she smiled back at him brilliantly, as they moved forward to join the others.

Special Agent Thorne introduced the two squad leaders, and the agents divided into two groups as did the K-9 agents and their dogs. Both groups started out back to back and studied the ground before they stepped forward going in opposite directions.

Haven and Logan followed the group heading away from the road. Since Agent Thorne, Garrison, and Rayne led their group, she and Logan followed behind the line of men and women and brought up the rear once again. It was a position she liked as the two of them could hold hands and walk at their own pace.

Though no one spoke, the snapping twigs and dried leaves crunching beneath several feet, the variety of birds singing, calling, and whistling, the squirrels hitting branches as they jumped from one branch or tree to another, and the chirping, clicking, high-pitched rattle of male cicadas looking for love were a symphonic racket Haven knew she would have to learn to like.

She squeezed Logan's hand tightly and he looked down at her. She smiled up at him, just happy to be able to touch him. Of course she couldn't tell him that so she leaned toward him and he leaned down for a quick kiss.

Hands swinging, they continued to follow the others for what seemed close to an hour before the dogs started getting antsy. Less than a minute later the German shepherd, bloodhound, and two beagles were dancing in circles then jerking and pulling against the restraining leashes.

Everyone was moving faster, trying to keep up with the men who were being dragged by the excited animals. Haven's heart pounded at the indication they were close to the area where Gavin White was once held. She and Logan picked up speed, wanting to keep up with the others, until they all reached the spot where the German shepherd sat quietly, and the other dogs barked uproariously.

When the barking dogs started pawing at what looked like a waterfall of thick vines coming over one of the mountain's many tall jutting rock formations their squad leader moved forward and spread the plants apart. He walked forward and disappeared behind the vines, then returned a few minutes later. Haven and Logan made it to her sister and Garrison's side as the squad leader walked back to them. He nodded to Special Agent Thorne, his gaze sharp and serious. "This is it."

Chapter Nineteen

Gavin pretended to watch the television as concern ate at him. Ma'am hadn't been back since the afternoon before, and his hunger was getting the better of him. He'd already had his shower, had again made a cursory inspection of his room looking for the camera, and had settled in to watch both the morning news, and two Sci-Fi movies on the FX channel.

She was making a habit of not coming as often and he wondered if her life outside of this house was causing her some problems. He hoped so. He hoped she would disappear forever, but then he would have to take more chances.

So why not now?

Feeling she would understand he was just hungry, or at least hoping it since he was breaking a rule, Gavin walked to the door and knocked. And waited. After a minute he knocked again. And waited. Fear and excitement set in as he stood staring at the knob.

Do I dare touch it?

What if she has electric current running to it? Will it kill me?

What if she's really out there just waiting to see what I'll do next?

His stomach hurt with all the possibilities, so he backed away and went to his bed. He flung himself backward and barely stifled the growl of anger at himself for being such a coward.

He wanted to be brave. He wanted to go back to his Uncle Garrison's cabin and be the kid he should have been when he was taken in. He wanted to see his Gramps and Grandma, Granny and Pa, and he wanted to see Kaylee Timberwolf, because he would be brave enough now to go up to her and tell her how much he liked her.

After what he had survived, talking to the prettiest girl in school would be a cakewalk.

His parents were gone forever. He had known it then, but he hadn't accepted it. Being a prisoner for all this time and being treated so harshly the first few months had given him a lot of perspective.

And a lot of time.

He'd had little to do over that period other than to grieve and to think about every minute of the life he'd lived. He had some great memories of his years with his parents. He missed his dad every second and his mom every day. They had both been decent people, community leaders, loving parents who had loved him enough to teach him right from wrong. Good from bad. And given him every opportunity to become the guy he wanted to be.

But mostly they wanted him to know he would always owe something back. Not to them, but to the community they lived in. Service to others had been their life's mission.

His dad hadn't even minded that Gavin hadn't wanted to be a cop; instead he'd supported his son's every athletic desire, saying Gavin would find his own way to contribute when the time was right.

Gavin was so thankful for parents who had made him their priority and thankful too that they came from an extended family who cherished each other above all else.

His dad coached in one capacity or another from Gavin's pre-school years until he reached high school, when Grey White, father, finally got to just sit in the stands and cheer Gavin on. He never once complained about what pursuing Gavin's dreams had cost him, in time or money, even though Detective Grey White put in some long hours, sometimes only stopping his work long enough to catch a game, and then he would have to return to handle whatever crisis was going on at the time.

His mother had been as giving in her own way, taking him wherever he needed or wanted to be, babying him when he'd get sick, and listening and only offering advice when he'd asked for it when he'd liked a certain girl or had fallen out with one of his friends.

But the greatest gift they had given him was their love for each other. Tears came to his eyes as he remembered they couldn't be in the same room without loving looks or gentle touches passing between them.

They had laughed often as a couple, and as a family, and he missed them so much he felt broken inside. But he was their son, and he would survive because they would want him to.

So for now he would wait and do as he was told. It wasn't worth the risk of getting himself killed, or moved. He was a White, and the Whites took care of each other. Even after all this time he was certain the rest of his family would never give up until they found him.

The sound of the door being unlocked had him scrambling to his bed. He looked at the door expectantly as it slid open, relieved he hadn't tried the doorknob. She walked in with a large box and set it down and then stood with her back to the open door. Since she usually shut it behind her, he wondered if she would even stay the short time she usually did.

"How are you today, Jimmy?"

Gavin didn't allow himself to hesitate. He smiled at her as he always did, and apparently she bought that it was real. "I'm fine. I was hoping you would come. I missed you. And I'm hungry."

White flashed under the netting. "That pleases me. And that's why I brought you lots of supplies that you can stock on the shelf in the closet. Sometimes I get too busy to shop for food, so this time I just got a lot. But I'll still bring you hot meals when I have time."

Gavin nodded, as his stomach rumbled. She laughed at the sound, startling him. He looked at her and then allowed his lips to fall into the first real smile he had for her. "Like I said, I'm hungry."

"There's a hot meal in there now in Styrofoam, from the steakhouse. Enjoy it while it's hot. I have to go now. Be a good boy. Remember I'll be watching."

Though she said the last teasingly, Gavin knew it was a threat. He nodded, holding his smile in place, though now it wasn't as real. She started to back out and then stopped.

"Who are you?"

He didn't miss a beat. "I'm Jimmy."

"Good boy."

She left, and Gavin ran to the box and lifted it, thrilled with the weight of it. He sat it on the bed and opened the top, and was even more thrilled to see that it was tightly packed. First he lifted the steak house's white plastic bag, careful to keep the Styrofoam container level as he set it on the rolling table, and then pulled out a couple of dozen individual size cereal boxes. The variety had cereals he loved and some he didn't, but he knew he wouldn't waste a one of them. There was a large plastic bag of glossy red apples, and he felt his mouth water. He hadn't had fruit in forever. Bananas and another bag filled with oranges were next and he almost cried with excitement. A variety of chips, and packages of cheese and crackers and peanut butter and crackers were pulled out and placed on the bed. Three six-pack boxes of fruit cocktail, two large bags of beef jerky, five little cans of Vienna Sausages—he turned his nose up at—and a plastic-wrapped 24-pack of bottled waters later, and he had the box empty.

He tried not to think back to his time in the dark dank place, but it snuck in when he realized this was just a better variety of the same routine. But he pushed those thoughts away. Ma'am had said she would still bring him meals. Which meant these things were just extra, not all he would have to last him a week.

He hoped.

****

It made her feel good to know he was really embracing his new situation. It was worrisome to think she would have to find a way of disposing of another body and then turn around and capture another candidate, as Mystic Waters was no longer a good place to hunt for her Jimmy.

If this one didn't completely convert before she could

find a safe way to get them both out of town, she would have to find a new town and start all over again. And she wasn't getting any younger.

A convoy of Hummers filled with FBI agents now filled the town. *That*, coupled with everything else that had gone on recently was making it increasingly harder to get the supplies she needed to train her new pet. The cashier at the grocery store had looked at her and laughed after she had placed all her groceries on the conveyor belt, and then had asked if she was headed to a liquor store next.

When she had given *Sally* what she was sure was a confused look, the young woman had said for the party she was obviously throwing. She had laughed and thanked the girl for reminding her. Only she hadn't thanked the nosy little bitch for reminding her to get liquor, she had thanked the clerk for reminding her she was doing something someone would notice.

She wouldn't make that mistake again.

Between now and the next time she took Jimmy a large supply of anything, she would have time to make several small purchases from several different places. And hopefully by then she could also be looking for a new town to move to.

But now she had to get back to her fake life, and take care of a little business. Too bad she couldn't take the night off, even though there was nobody expecting her to come home.

Chapter Twenty

Garrison, Rayne, Haven and Logan were all made to wait outside with the majority of those who had come to find the location where Gavin was once kept, as only two of the agents were allowed inside. Although Haven knew it was to protect any evidence that might have been left behind, it was hard for them all to comply, especially Garrison, who kept pacing in large circles with Rayne right on his heels.

Haven sat waiting on a fallen log with Logan by her side, but her happiness of earlier was now replaced with concern for the man she loved. It hadn't occurred to any of them before Bret Thorne's explanation, that there was a good chance more than just Gavin White's DNA might be found behind those hanging plants. Garrison was fit to be tied he was so angry, but Logan's reaction was worse. The color drained from his face. His eyes were vacant. His skin pale and cold.

So they sat waiting, her wanting to comfort, him brooding and lost in thought.

After nearly three hours the two men came out carrying the large plastic black boxes that carried their forensics tools as well as any evidence they might have found. They removed the coverings on their boots before nodding to Special Agent Thorne. Without making eye contact with anyone else, they walked to their four-wheelers and drove away.

Logan jumped to his feet and headed for the head FBI agent. Haven had to run to keep up with him, and by the time they reached him so had Garrison and Rayne.

"What did they find?" Garrison demanded before anyone else could speak.

"I don't know yet. They will head straight for the

airport where our plane is waiting and will be in DC an hour or so later. We've got a team in place waiting for the evidence. We should know at least a few answers by morning."

Haven envisioned the ice and this time it only took two tries to keep it in place. She took Logan's hand and he held to her tightly. She squeezed back wanting him to know she was there for him as Bret Thorne continued talking.

"They'll have a report emailed to me within a few hours detailing what they have and what they saw. As of right now this area is quarantined until we're certain we don't need to go back in there for more evidence."

He looked at the two men, and then at Rayne and Haven. "I know this is hard for you, but it's necessary. Those men are trained not to disturb evidence over and above what they are collecting, and they had on gear that leaves nothing new behind.

"If we are going to have a good shot at finding your nephew, we have to do this as cleanly as possible."

Garrison nodded, though Haven could tell he wasn't satisfied with the information. She understood his need to *see* where Gavin had been kept. If it had been one of her sisters, she would have clawed the agent's eyes out to get inside.

"There will be guards posted here in shifts until we are satisfied there is nothing useful left to find and no reason for us to continue looking here. I promise to keep you apprised as the information comes in, but you have to promise me that you won't do anything to taint the evidence that may still be waiting to be found."

Garrison nodded, this time with resignation. "I promise. Just please let me know something, *anything*, as soon as you do. Even what the other agents may have discovered."

"Deal." The agent held out his hand and Garrison took it.

"How will you know whose DNA is whose? I mean, I know you have the bodies of the others, but what about

Gavin?" Rayne asked.

Bret smiled at her with approval. "Good question. Thankfully Detective White had a file in his desk that had an identification card with Gavin's picture on it. Captain Grammar had it in his files on Mr. White's murder. At the time it was made, Gavin was six years old, so it may have been a first grade project at his elementary school. Though the boy's features will have changed as he grew, the large spot of dried blood encased in the plastic bubble should be enough for a positive identification." When no one commented, he continued. "A lot of parents have those made in case their children ever go missing or are kidnapped. Of course they hope they'll never have to use them."

Rubbing Garrison's back, Rayne thanked the agent and he nodded before turning to assign the first two agents their watch. The four of them headed back to the four-wheelers without talking, and Haven knew each of their heads were too full of unanswered concerns to make light conversation.

When they stopped next to the small vehicles, Logan lifted his arm and looked at his watch, taking her hand up with his. "I can't believe it's only one-thirty in the afternoon. It feels like it should be getting dark soon."

Haven nodded, exhausted herself, thinking the same thing. "A bed sounds really good to me."

****

As tired as she was, Haven couldn't fall asleep. The events of both the day and all the days since her arrival in Mystic Waters filled her head with thoughts both good and bad. Although the FBI agent thought they'd had a good day, all she could think about was what they *hadn't* learned as she stared up at the point in the cabin's ceiling.

There was so much to celebrate, yet Haven hesitated to think in those terms. She was so happy to be able to touch Logan, so happy to be in love with such a wonderful man, and more so to be loved by him, but the very air around the mountain felt tainted with evil and she shivered beneath the light covering.

"Come here."

Haven sighed and looked over to see his sleepy smile. "I'm sorry. I didn't mean to wake you."

Logan pulled her close and she wiggled her way under his arm so she could lay her head on his chest. He kissed the top of her head then she felt him settle back.

"I'm not. I didn't mean to fall asleep on you to start with. What man does that when he has the most beautiful woman in the world in his bed?"

Haven smiled and kissed his chest. "One who is completely, and understandably, exhausted.

"And I can't be the most beautiful woman in the world. Rayne and I are identical." She grinned to herself and kissed his chest again, determined to let him find out about Destiny later.

Logan ran a hand down her face before running his fingers through her long hair. "True, but you are more beautiful to me. Although I'm sure Garrison would disagree, and he has the advantage."

Haven pulled back and looked at him, feeling a little hurt. "Why does *he* have the advantage?"

Logan shrugged, moving her slightly with him. "Because the woman he loves has agreed to marry him. You never answered me."

Relaxing into him but still keeping her head up so she could look at him, she nodded, trying to look very serious. "Ah… That is true.

"Of course I will have to give it considerable thought," she said, grinning, before quickly brushing her lips against his. By the time he reacted to kiss her back, she had already pulled back.

He grinned at her teasing. "How much thought?"

Still grinning she nuzzled her way under his chin and nibbled at his neck until she felt his lower body squirm. She rose up and returned to her former position where she could look down at him. "I'm thinking several hours. At least."

Logan laughed and grabbed her to him before rolling them over so that he was on top. "I would be more than happy to use my powers of persuasion. For as many hours as it takes."

She laughed as he raised and lowered his eyebrows in opposing directions and she squirmed as he tickled her into screaming hysterics. After he stopped, and she settled, he captured her mouth for a deeper than deep kiss that left her sighing and smiling a little drunkenly. "And I will be more than happy to let you."

In her opinion, and it was the only one that mattered to Haven at the moment, over the next hour and a half Logan did an *amazing* job of convincing her she couldn't live without him for the rest of her life.

His lips knew wicked tricks she doubted even her ancestors had thought of, as they were everywhere at once it seemed, teasing and taunting, tasting and tantalizing until she was screaming for mercy.

His hands held their own magic as they molded and mastered her body to his will, sending her soaring beyond the planets then plunging her into mind-spinning helplessness until she was senseless and nearly unconscious.

He was a Master Wizard, his powerfully magnificent rock of a body fitting hers to perfection, making her his Yang, to his Ying. They were two halves of the same whole, incomplete individually, but seamlessly flawless when joined.

He made her laugh and he made her beg as he took her to heights she never knew existed. He touched her heart and soothed her soul and took her body beyond the galaxy and back three times before she was certain she could stand no more. But he was determined to dot all her I's and cross all her T's so he took her up and over the edge again, this time joining her, and holding her tightly as he filled her with his seed.

Recovering took time, and the sheets had to be pulled from the bed when they could finally gain enough energy to rise. Logan balled the cotton up and threw the sheets over the lofts railing before he pulled her against his sweat-soaked flesh for another kiss that curled her toes.

Weakly they made their way down the stairs and he grabbed the sheets on their way to the bathroom where he dropped them in the hamper before pulling her into the shower stall.

Warm water poured over them as he reignited the flame within her, only now she didn't fear that it would scorch him in return. She allowed the power within her to build only enough to give her the strength she needed to give him as good as she was getting.

She tasted and tantalized inch after inch of his flesh, then boldly took him fully into her mouth. He moaned as if in agony before pulling her away to lift her into his arms. He held her bottom as she clung to his neck, her womanhood poised over his shaft. He held her there as water rolled down both of their faces while he stared lovingly into her eyes.

Shaking with the necessity for completion, she wiggled to get closer until the hard length of him filled her, but Logan shook his head slowly.

"Say it."

Haven fought for the breath required to speak as she trembled uncontrollably in his arms. As no doubts remained she opened her mouth to answer, but he must have taken her delay as reservation, and he took her lips again for a toe-curling kiss while rubbing his shaft at her opening.

If she wasn't so lost in lust, she would have laughed at his antics, but she needed him inside of her and she needed him there fast, so she broke the kiss. "Yes!"

He plunged into her and she screamed the word again and again as waves crested and crashed repeatedly throughout her body and mind. When she was finally spent and he allowed her legs to slide down his body, they stood under the cooling spray fighting for breath while holding each other up.

****

Haven opened her eyes and realized darkness had fallen, and that they had slept the day away. She quietly slid from the bed, not wanting to disturb her fiancé. Thinking of him in those terms should have terrified her, but now she understood why Rayne was always only filled with joy rather than fear of the future.

Though there was a long history of Cavanaugh women who had set the examples of all the reasons to never marry, those lessons seemed silly now. Times had changed and people, at least in North America, weren't condemned so harshly for being different. So she need not fear being stoned to death, or hung, or beheaded.

But more than that she felt it was safer now because she was learning to control herself and as long as she and her sisters kept their gifts a secret there was no reason to fear loving a man. And if down the road there was a chance, maybe they could even share their true selves with the men who loved them.

At least she hoped so.

"I'm starving."

Haven turned back and smiled at the long naked male in her bed. "Me, too. Do you want to see if Garrison and Rayne are up and hungry? We could all go out."

Logan grinned at her. "You look good enough to eat, my future wife. But my stomach wants steak, so that sounds good. I'll give them a call."

While he rolled over to disconnect his cell phone from its charger, Haven pulled on a clean bra and panties and then shorts and a top. She headed down the stairs to get them each bottled waters to quench their thirst, and when she returned, he was rising from the bed. She couldn't help but smile at his perfection.

"Garrison said they were getting up too, and steak sounded good to him. When we get there we'll call and see if Bret Thorne has any news."

Together they straightened the sheets and pulled the bedspread up to make the bed before heading down and out of the cabin. The sun had set but just, so the twilight sky gave them plenty of light as they walked to Logan's rental.

The ride over was always short so they were at Garrison and Rayne's door in minutes. Rayne met them on the porch and smiled at their joined hands before sending a wink to Haven. "Told you."

She turned to reenter the house as Logan sent Haven a curious look. She shrugged, acting dumb, not able to tell him Rayne had predicted she'd find a way to keep from harming him with her super powers.

Though they hadn't been able to get through to the FBI agent, and there was still an air of fear and concern that filled the air around them, the large dinner turned into a celebration when Logan announced their engagement. Drinks were ordered and toasts were made in both directions as they found an island of joy in the sea of disaster.

The sisters hugged and whispered as the best friends pounded fists and tried to outdo each other as they bragged about their prowess in capturing their ladies. When they were told they'd closed the place down they headed back to the mountain to continue the celebration, hopeful the glad tidings would continue come morning when they called Bret Thorne again. Because the only thing that could make their lives more perfect was for Gavin to be well and headed back to his family soon.

Epilogue

Burt Thompson fumed, and pulled on the bars of his cell. He wasn't going down for what he'd done, and he sure as hell wasn't going down for what he hadn't.

It burned his ass that Martha hadn't been to see him, though he knew she might not have been allowed until they charged him with something. Well now, as far as he was concerned, they had and he had no choice but to play his ace in the hole. He just wished he knew how to do it without making it obvious he was setting the freak up. He looked through the bars at the man he used to work for, knowing he'd have to be careful. John Grammar was no dummy.

"I need to see my wife."

John stared at him then shrugged. "That will be up to her. But I'll let her know you asked to see her."

"And I want a lawyer. Need one appointed since I'm pretty sure I don't have a job anymore."

This time John nodded. "I'll send word to the judge that you are requesting a public defender, if and when we charge you."

"You do that," Burt snarled, hating the superior SOB. "And while you're at it you might want to consider you've got the wrong man. I didn't do what you are accusing me of.

"Where's the evidence?"

"We haven't actually accused or charged you with anything."

"You think I'm stupid? You think I don't know that those questions the FBI and you asked all damn night long were to trip me into confessing to something I didn't do?"

"I asked during that all night interview where you were the evening Grey and his wife were murdered."

"Yeah, and I told you. I was home with my wife!"

"That isn't checking out."

Burt froze. "What the hell are you talking about?"

"Your wife said, that you said, you were working that night. All she knew was that you were not home until very late."

Fuck! What the hell is wrong with her?

"Well she is mistaken. She isn't that smart anyway. I only married her because she likes it dirty and rough, and so do I.

"But the entire department knows that now, don't they?"

The expression on John's face didn't change. "I told you to talk to the psychologist, and you never did, which gives me grounds to officially fire you. Your suspension is over. Consider yourself fired."

He turned and walked away as Burt cursed him then cursed him some more even though Burt knew the thick steel door John Grammar walked through soundproofed the rooms on the other side.

He turned and went to the long cold steel bench of the holding cell, wondering what to do. His only hope for a quick release had been Martha giving him an alibi, and him finding a way to direct the police to that longhaired freak.

Kevin Hellerman entered the door John Grammar had exited. "Captain says you can make your phone call now."

Burt smiled as he rose to his feet and allowed Hellerman to handcuff him through the rectangular opening of the cell door. He didn't speak to him though he'd known him for all the years they'd been on the force together. Instead, he stepped back until the door was open then preceded the officer to the pay phone just outside the cell. He waited as Hellerman dropped the coins in the machine and stepped away.

"I'm going to talk to a lawyer. I'd like some privacy please."

Officer Hellerman nodded and walked to the far end of the long hallway that held all the barred, open-faced cells. Burt turned his back to the officer and lifted the heavy black handset and tucked it between his ear and his shoulder and then turned his cuffed hands so that he could punch the numbers no one ever needed to look up. But before he did that, he had to remember what the numbers were that blocked caller identification. It wouldn't do him any good at all for Emergency Management Services to see he was calling from the Mystic Waters Police Station.

Burt searched his memory and knew he was just going to have to go with his gut, hoping he wasn't about to waste the only option he had. He gritted his teeth and punched in star-six-seven then nine-one-one.

"Nine-one-one. What is your emergency?"

Burt nearly laughed but he controlled himself and whispered in as high a pitched voice as he could, "I know who killed all those people in Mystic Waters, West Virginia. His name is Tom Whitehawk!"

He hung up before the operator had a chance to ask any questions, the handset making a loud banging sound as it fell into the holder. Burt didn't care. He had done all he could do. Now they would have no choice but to investigate. And then, he would be set free.

THE END

Take a sneak-peek into the Third Book of the
Cavanaugh Sisters Trilogy!

Tempest's Embrace

A Mystic Waters Book

JC Wardon
www.jcwardon.com

Tempest's Embrace

Cavanaugh Sisters Trilogy
Book Three

Prologue

Blood froze in Tom Whitehawk's veins when he opened the back door of his small cabin as more than a dozen automatic rifles were quickly raised to point at his head and nude body.

"Put your hands in the air!"

"Put your hands up!"

"Get them up high!"

Tom lifted his hands quickly, his gaze darting from one combat-clad FBI agent to another as their hysterical shouts ricocheted and echoed around the mountainous terrain. His ears ringing, Tom stood there fully exposed as his heart pounded painfully against his chest wall. Stunned speechless, he forced himself to remain where he was as two agents advanced on him rapidly though everything inside of him screamed, *Run!*

With a black leather-clad hand, one agent cuffed the back of his neck and roughly pulled him forward so he was standing just outside of the doorway while the other instantly grabbed his wrists and swung them out and down to secure them together behind his back.

The only things keeping him from shouting in indignation and anger as his shock wore down were the remaining weapons still pointed at him, and the fact that he couldn't seem to breathe. Denying the panic building, Tom closed his eyes to block the sight of those who had trespassed literally and figuratively against him as he sought strength from a lifetime spent in rumination and prayer.

He silently called to the heart of Mother Earth for inner peace and sanctuary, and her response was as it had always been. He inhaled her serenity and let tranquility wash through him as each tension-strung muscle relaxed one by one. The tightness of his lungs loosened as well, allowing him to breathe evenly. Renewed in spirit, calmer, he opened his eyes to look once again at those who had no right to trample what he and his people considered sacred ground.

With his head held high and his shoulders pulled back, Tom studied one agent after another to calculate their strength, and touch their minds with his. Relieved to sense none were trigger happy, he kept his feet planted firmly apart giving them the show they had apparently come to see. Satisfaction gripped him as a couple of agents broke eye contact and looked away, though their guns remained on him all the same.

For the first time in his life, Tom understood what it felt like to be one of his people faced with an army of aggressive white men, though in this case there were also women present. But he would not cower, nor would he be embarrassed that they had come at him before he could relieve himself. Despite the chaos they had made of his rising, his morning hard-on stood proud and unapologetic.

A shiny black SUV pulled up and a tall man dressed in a black suit and tie, covered with a vest displaying the large white initials of the agency he worked for, emerged to walk by the agents targeting Tom. He looked at Tom, frowned, looked back at the armed agents and began shaking his head. He stopped in front of Tom and removed his sunglasses, uncaring that the weapons were now aimed at his back. "I'm Special Agent Bret Thorne of the Washington DC branch of the Federal Bureau of Investigation. Are you Thomas Whitehawk?"

"Yes. What is this about?"

Agent Thorne pulled an envelope from his vest before opening it and pulling out a piece of paper. "This is a search warrant for your home and property. Is there anything you would like to tell me before we commence?"

Completely confused, Tom could only shake his head as Agent Thorne turned to another agent. "Go inside and get this man some clothes!"

The barked command told Tom two things and he relaxed slightly; the superior agent had figured out their mistake, and was now going to fall all over himself to fix things, and the man sent to retrieve his clothing was completely intimidated by the more seasoned agent standing before him.

Agent Thorne turned back to Tom, annoyance written in the set of his mouth. "You have been identified as a suspect in crimes committed in Mystic Waters. Do you have anything to say about this accusation?"

Not expecting those words, *ever*, to come out of anyone's mouth regarding him, Tom shook his head. Not in denial. In disbelief. He drew in a deep breath as the lead agent's statement had knocked the air from his lungs. Unblinking, he looked the man straight in the eyes. "I say that is ridiculous. Anyone who knows me, knows better. I would never hurt another living thing."

"Here you go," the agent said, holding out the clothing to Agent Thorne.

Thorne didn't bother to look anywhere but at Tom's eyes. "Unlock his hands."

The younger agent looked at his superior with brows drawn together. "Sir?"

Agent Thorne finally glanced over at the retriever agent, his mouth set with grim purpose. "Unlock Mr. Whitehawk's hands, *now*," he said quietly, through clenched teeth.

The underling quickly pulled out keys and walked behind Tom. In seconds he felt one, then the other wrist being released. He rubbed his wrists and took the clothing the agent now held out to him. Tom could feel the younger agent's fear masked anger but he wasn't certain if it was directed at him, or his boss. Keeping his eyes on the young man, he bent and pulled on the jeans and then the T-shirt before turning his attention back to the man in charge.

"You could have knocked on the door."

Agent Thorne sighed. "You must have come out

before I had a chance to get here." He glanced over to an agent standing apart from the others, his eyes holding retribution. "My orders were to wait until I arrived to engage the suspect."

Tom watched as the man who held a look of defiance turned and walked to stand by another agent before he turned back to the man who was obviously in charge. Tom knew that one was itching with nervous energy. It radiated around him in colors of red and black. He turned back to the lead agent again, hoping this farce was about over before someone did something stupid—like shoot him.

"I think you will find that you have made a very big mistake. On several levels."

Agent Thorne nodded. "I am aware of the laws governing the lands in this area, and your special rights *here* on this mountain, and as a Native American on these lands. I take full responsibility and I apologize for the mistakes made here today, by my agents. *However*, we do have a Federal warrant, which supersedes your ability to stop us from searching the premises. Nothing that is not relevant to our investigation will be disturbed. And your land will be treated with respect and, to the best of our ability, without harm."

Though his heart was pounding again, Tom didn't allow himself to react as he took the paper and looked it over. Once he was done reading, he handed it back. "I would have been more than happy to cooperate with you, assuming that you are also searching every home in Mystic Waters.

"Unless that *is* your plan, I will have no choice but to look at this as a direct and prejudicial attack against my people as well as myself, and I'm sure charges will be filed on our behalf against the United States Government for yet another broken treaty."

Agent Thorne nodded once. "I understand. I've had the opportunity to read the treaty, and as such, I am trying to make sure that you and your ancestral lands are treated with the proper respect.

"Again, I apologize for the inappropriate way in which you were...handled." He remained facing Tom, his gaze assessing and unwavering, as he addressed the others. "Put the damned weapons down!

"Henson, Parks, get inside and look around and make it quick!"

Tom stood there trying to come to grips with what was happening while he opened his mind to rescan those around him, starting with the one directly before him. The senior agent gave off an even vibe. Though his irritation at his agents was obvious, Thorne's sense of authority and perhaps even his personality didn't lend itself to spikes of heated aura or even an increased heart rate that would normally be apparent in someone given the volatility of the situation.

Thorne's calm demeanor wasn't common at all, which piqued Tom's curiosity. He put what was happening around him aside as he focused, delving deeper into the agent's psyche. What Tom found fascinated him: absolute calm. Purity of purpose. A hard line dividing the agent's sense of right and wrong.

Because Tom could read such things in people it calmed him further to know the agent wasn't faking his ability to completely handle the situation and that he was a man of integrity. But what the agent may or may not have known was that Tom's threat hadn't been idle. The Council would be up in arms and be ready to spend whatever it took to handle this insult to their spiritual leader.

Tom hoped it wouldn't come to that. If he was ever needed to physically fight for his people and their rights, he would be there in a heartbeat, but until that time came he planned to continue living the life that had chosen him. That meant peace and solitude. The last thing he wanted was to become a public spectacle.

"It won't take them long. I live a minimalist lifestyle."

Agent Thorne said nothing as they waited, and Tom realized while he'd been assessing the agent, the agent had been assessing him. Neither broke eye contact, until a minute later when one of the agents who went to inspect Tom's cabin returned to stand next to his superior. He had a pistol dangling from a gloved finger on his left hand, and a plastic wrapped brick of what was obviously a dried green plant in the other.

Tom looked at both items and then at the agent as real anger gripped him. "We both know that isn't mine." He turned back to Agent Thorne. "*You* know that isn't mine!"

Thorne looked at him a few seconds more then turned and walked around Tom to go into the cabin. He was gone only a few minutes before returning to address the agent still holding the contraband. "Bag those and get a detailed report to me within the hour." He turned to the others who stood waiting for instruction. "Search the area. You have one hour. Leave everything as you find it unless it is relevant to the investigation. And I want a report on what you find, if anything.

"And I had better not hear that one word of any of this has been leaked privately, or to the press."

Finally he turned back to Tom. "I'm going to have an agent re-cuff you. It will go a lot better for you if you cooperate."

Tom shook his head, unable to believe what was happening. "It isn't mine," he reiterated from behind clenched teeth. Agent Thorne nodded so slightly Tom was sure he was the only one who saw it.

"Just cooperate. You will ride with me."

Tom put his arms behind his back although it went against every fiber of his being. Something about the senior agent's demeanor made him want to trust the man, but he wasn't sure he trusted his own judgment at the moment. Physical violence was foreign to his spirit, yet everything inside of him screamed for retribution. He called once again to his mountain mother and was relieved when the alien feelings seeped away. Tom remained silent while being re-cuffed and while being led to Agent Throne's SUV.

The agent directed to lead him to the vehicle touched the top of his head as he was seated inside, then a seatbelt was placed around him and locked into place. The sound of the lock went through him and he wondered when, if ever, he would ever be free again.

Within minutes, Bret Thorne was buckling his own seatbelt, telling another agent he could ride with someone else. The look on the underling's face said it all, and Tom was getting more concerned by the minute.

After they pulled away from his home, Tom couldn't hold back the question. "What's really going on here? Do you really think I've done something involving that gun?"

Thorne shook his head as he looked in this mirror. "No. I'm going against every protocol there is by doing this, but I'm going to ask you to work with me."

Tom locked onto Thorne's gaze reflected in the mirror, although the agent continued to look between him and the road. "What are you talking about?"

"There isn't an FBI agent worth his salt that couldn't see what we just found is a set up. My guys laughed at how easy it was to find the gun and the drugs. Unfortunately for the person who put it there, they forgot to take the evidence sticker off.

"I'll have to have you piss in a cup, so I hope you don't have anything in your system, but I would stake my badge on your fingerprints being nowhere on that gun."

Tom hung his head as the air left his lungs. "Thank God! I was sure your guys were setting me up. I just didn't know why.

"I can guarantee you there isn't anything in my piss. As for the gun, I've never touched it. Where was it?"

"It was under the mattress, at the foot of the bed closest to the wall. It was obvious that it had been shoved there quickly, with no concern to hide it. In fact the butt of the grip was visible and I'm thinking that was on purpose."

"So, in spite of finding a gun and drugs at my place, you believe me?"

"I'm pretty good at what I do, Mr. Whitehawk, which is why I'm leading rather than following this task force. And my gut is telling me several things. One is that leaving a weapon where it can be found quickly isn't something a man as smart as you would do. Not to mention you have thousands of protected acres—that would take us *years* to search—at your disposal to hide things that could incriminate you, should you ever decide to become the criminal I doubt you are.

"I had an agent pull your life history as soon as we got the report that there was something to investigate at your address, an address by the way that has no actual physical address on a Federal level. So the caller who blocked the number they were calling from knows something the average person wouldn't have known, and will turn out to be the one who is trying to turn the attention away from them, and towards you.

"And even if I didn't know all that, there was the fact that although you were angry about what was going down, you were calm, which I have to give you credit for. No way could I have stood there naked and been more intimidating than the task force of agents holding their automatic rifles at me."

Tom couldn't help the smile that crinkled the corners of his eyes. He'd never thought of himself as intimidating on any level, and he wasn't about to admit he'd been shaking on the inside like a little girl. He held his thoughts without sharing them as the agent seemed willing to talk and the more he talked the better Tom felt.

"Knowing how easy it was for us to find condemning evidence would have had a guilty man sweating at the very least, and talking his head off to try to divert our attention. There are other things I can't disclose at the moment, but put your mind at ease. This all smelled worse than two day old fish lying in the sun."

The agent's eyes glimmered as he looked back. "I just bet you were calculating how much you were going to sue the government for when my agent walked out with the contraband."

Tom almost smiled at that, too, but this time didn't. "What can a report on me tell you? I live too simple a life for anyone to know anything about me unless they know me personally. I don't use the Internet. I don't get involved in politics. I am a spiritual man who seeks a higher power to help those who ask it of me, but I don't advertise myself in any way."

Agent Thorne made a sweeping turn before bringing the SUV to a standstill at one of the mountain's lookout rest stops. He undid his seatbelt and turned in his seat. "Unfortunately for us all, the government knows a lot more than they should about pretty much everyone. But I don't have time or the authority to go into that.

"This is the thing: I'm taking a big risk here not only with my superiors, but with you as well if by some chance you aren't who I think you are, by telling you what I already have. But I'm going with my gut on this, and it tells me you are innocent. But more importantly, it tells me you can help us catch those who are responsible for the deaths of those young men, and possibly the White kidnapping if you're willing.

"But for now, publicly, I'm going to have to treat you like a serious suspect. The only people who know any differently at this point are the two agents who went inside your cabin expecting to find something because I told them to, and you and me. Those men are worthy of my job and can be trusted. If you are willing to help us, we may be able to save Gavin White's life. I believe that kid is still alive and the sooner we get to him the better his chances are of staying that way. I just hope he holds on.

"I know I'm asking a lot of you. Your reputation will suffer for a while. Your family will be hurt and angry. But I promise you in the end everyone will know of your innocence. You'll never be convicted of this."

Tom didn't know if he had any choice, but he needed time to process what was happening. "Can you give me a few minutes?"

Agent Thorne nodded as he put his seatbelt back on. "That's all I can give you. If I take too long getting you to the Mystic Waters police station to be booked questions will be asked that I don't want to answer yet."

He started the vehicle and pulled forward, then turned as he backed up, before dropping it back into drive and pulling out onto the road in the direction they'd originally traveled. Tom knew he couldn't pass up an opportunity to help the White family; though very distant, they were a part of his own, but he didn't know how he could stand the hurt to his parents or those who trusted him with their spiritual cares. His parents would be devastated for him over his arrest, although they would know he wasn't capable of what he was about to be charged with. It would be the same with all those who knew him, and it would be a black eye to his people when they were all committed to fighting old prejudices by the ways in which they lived their lives.

"Will I have to remain in jail for long?"

Thorne glanced in the mirror. "That will be up to the judge. As soon as I can get clearance for all this, I'll let him know you are actively cooperating with us and are not a flight risk. We'll get you bonded out as quickly as possible, but you may be safer locked up. People can get pretty daring when a child is involved."

"So everyone will think I've committed these crimes."

"Unless they know you well, and maybe even some of those folks will be unsure for a while, but if you can get the man that's currently being held to talk to you, I think there is a pretty good chance we can wrap some of this up fairly quickly.

"I'm going to keep Captain Grammar in the loop because I can tell he's a good man, but no one else in the force because, at this point, I believe there are two different people committing these crimes, and I believe one is a dirty cop. He's the man being held now, but we can't charge him for any of this yet. I'm hoping Captain Grammar has charged him with domestic assault. It will buy us some time."

Tom took several deep breaths as he processed Agent Thorne's information. "I don't really have a choice. The Whites are good people and have been family friends for generations." He didn't mention the several generations' back blood relation. There wasn't any point.

"I hate that they will think I had anything to do with any of this. And it will kill my father and mother. They're pretty old. If I do this, can you at least let them know the truth? It will save both of us a lot of trouble: me worrying about my parent's health and you not having my very powerful father fighting what you are planning."

Thorne looked in the mirror as they approached the town. "I don't know…but not yet. I'm usually a by the book man, but there are always shades of gray in these cases and my immediate superior had my position before her promotion. I expect her full cooperation and support on this.

"But until I get clearance from the Director, I'm powerless to do anything more, so from here on out I have to follow protocol. I believe it would go a long way with her superiors if your father is willing to stand up against any tribal or racial fallout that may result. This case is complicated enough with what I believe are at least two, and possibly three, different criminals committing these crimes. The last thing we'll need is an uprising.

"If I can get approval to carry this forward my way, your father would have to be willing to do it without letting anyone else know, and that could cause him problems."

Tom nodded. "I understand that more than you do. Can you get us alone with him where no one else can hear or record us? I think I can take care of all of that."

Thorne drove for a minute before nodding. "Once I have the go-ahead, I'll make it happen."

ACKNOWLEDGEMENTS

I would like to send out a special Thank You to all who have embraced the Cavanaugh women. May your lives be as enchanted!

To my lovely sister, KT, who catches every word I misspell and offers endless sisterly love and support!

And my editor, Kim Jacobs, for taking me on and putting up with my wild imagination!

Thank you all so much!

JCW

ABOUT JC WARDON

JC Wardon loves writing fantasy and spends her days weaving stories for those who love it as well. Though she has great appreciation for romances, a juicy and complicated plot is what she holds most dear. Danger, mystery, and magic are the life's blood for her Mystic Waters Books. She hopes you are captivated, and stimulated, and that your hearts become engaged. Visit her at jcwardon.com.

The Cavanaugh Series Books Now Available!

(The Cavanaugh Sisters Trilogy)
#1 Mystic Thunder
#2 Touch of Lightning
#3 Tempest's Embrace

(The Cavanaugh Series continues!)
#4 Jewel of the Nile
#5 Sapphire Blues
#6 Diamond in the Rough
#7 Luna's Landing
#8 Celestial Liaison
#9 Zeus: *Unbound!*
#10 Apollo: *Unleashed!*

The Cavanaugh Series Books still to come!

Heracles: Undone
Soleli's Secret
Gavin's Ghosts

The Blood Moon Chronicles

Blood Moon Rising

Read on…

Available now in ebook at Amazon!

BLOOD MOON RISING
JC Wardon

In the beginning, before the time of man, there was a great battle between those angels who believed in One True God, and those who did not. At the battle's end, those who did not believe were damned by the Creator, destined to a life in the pits of despair with the leader of the revolt, the master of vanity, Satan.

But there were those angels who realized their mistake immediately. Filled with regret and repentance, they begged an audience with the Creator, prostrating themselves as they asked His forgiveness, even if they remained damned for all eternity.

The Creator looked upon those who had followed what was once His most beautiful angel into ruin. A God of mercy, as their repentance was sincere, He forgave all. As a God of justice, He knew a price was still required. But instead of damning the repentant, God gave them a sentence of eternal life in service to Him, cleaning up the wreckage He knew Satan would design.

Those few angels who had repented would be known as The Brethren, sheathed in physical form, commissioned to reproduce, and capable of magic. They were to become an elite army of guardians who would watch over and protect the Creator's newest creation. *Man.*

Now, many generations later, Satan's son has risen to a power so deviant even Satan fears him. Natas, the ultimate spawn of evil, is master-mining the cataclysmic destruction of mankind to prove he is greater than his own father, and of God Himself.

With the battle for all mankind rapidly approaching, The Brethren are desperately seeking the destined mates the Creator designed just for them. These women, once the mating ritual has occurred, enhance The Brethren's powers and become the vessels to reproduce the Creator's future warriors.

But the prophesied blood moons approach, the mates have all but disappeared, and evil is gaining ground on the earth. With so much at stake The Brethren know they must prevail with all haste, as time is rapidly running out for all.

Prologue

Riagan Absalom flew low over the ocean as fast as his large wings would carry him. His heart beat at dangerous levels, not because of his always heightened need for haste in the sleek hawk's body he preferred for solo flight, but because she was calling to him in a panic that terrified him.

For centuries, no, *forever*, he had waited for her, looking for her on every continent, in every time period, until finally, only a decade or so before he had come to the conclusion that he, the hereditary Prince of his people, was meant to spend an eternity alone, without his destined mate.

It was happening too often now. The Brethren never knew who their mate was, or what her gift was, they only knew that a life with that one special female was their required destiny. Together they were both stronger than apart. Their individual gifts, once harnesses and sharpened, not only doubled in strength, their lives were almost always instantly enriched with offspring which would bear one or both of the talents of their parents.

The lack of mates and offspring for centuries had seriously depleted the army. An army needed to protect those to whom the Creator gave the earth. With reports that Natas was raising his own army for a major onslaught against all humankind, and with the majority of his own brothers-in-arms still without their mates, he feared the world in gravest danger.

Riagan didn't know what had happened. His father, the first of the original fallen who had repented, had been promised by the Creator that mates would be created, one each for every one of the brethren. Since he didn't doubt the Creator for a moment, it meant that Natas and his *vamphere* were getting to the mates first.

It made him sick to think of it. The mates were pure. Females who would instinctively know that to lose their purity before mating with their destined master would cost them their place in paradise. Such degradation would be worse than death to these women. And the loss of them would be worse than death to each male.

Age held no meaning to the brethren except it was a burden to spend century after century in limbo while risking their very lives. Waiting and wanting that which they were designed to crave. Alone and lonely. With nothing more than an entire existence filled with nothing to look forward to; with only pursuing evil to pass the time. These burdens, after centuries, would destroy the spirit, slowly, until one after another of his brothers had sought the only escape available to them. They would seek that which they were sworn to destroy, and allow themselves to be slain.

Until recently.

Natas was as wicked as his father, or perhaps even more wicked as he'd been the spawn of two evil souls. Satan had once been God's beloved servant, and though he had done a stellar job of tempting man to sin, even he hadn't gone to the lengths Natas had to destroy that which the Creator made into flesh.

Now, somehow, Natas found a way to destroy the reprieve of death for the disheartened brethren by keeping them barely alive until continual exchanges of blood from those demons known as vamphere would turn his brother's silver blood, black. The brethren would then turn into creatures that needed human blood to exist. To deny the need would mean certain death and an eternity in Hell, with all the other forever damned.

Accepting that he would never give in to such a fate, thus accepting that he would spend eternity alone had been a bitter pill to swallow for Riagan. He, as Prince to his people had a duty to perpetuating his breed. To create a successor should he fall in battle. To help his brothers find their own mates even if he could not find his. And he had done his best to do his duty. To be obedient. To remain humble. To ignore that need that sometimes made him forget that his first and only real purpose was servitude, first to God Almighty, then to mankind.

The irony that the Creator had made him and all his kind with a physical need that was as strong as it was powerful sometimes felt like a mean joke. The need to breed, to share his seed, was absolutely necessary for his, and the brethren's happiness, he knew, and for all their well beings. Sure, he was capable of dalliances with human women if he felt so inclined, but none of those encounters would ever produce offspring, as children could only result with a true mate. And those encounters would not satisfy in any way that mattered. Only his destined mate could satisfy his needs, as he would be the only one ever able to satisfy hers.

But after thousands of years, she'd failed to appear. She'd never sought him. Had never even given him a hint that she existed. And now, after he had all but given up she summoned him. Not with the subtle scent he'd expected, but with so many pheromones filling his senses, as well as the universe, he feared that Vamphere would find her, too. Which meant he had to hurry.

Now that he'd found his way to her, there was no way he'd lose her.

Not to man.

Not to beast.

Not to the devil, himself....

About JC Wardon

JC Wardon loves writing fantasy and spends her days weaving stories for those who love it as well. Though she has great appreciation for romances, a juicy and complicated plot is what she holds most dear. Danger, mystery, and magic are the life's blood for her Mystic Waters Books. She hopes you are captivated and stimulated, and your hearts become engaged.

If you enjoyed **Touch of Lightning**, please consider telling others, and writing a review.

Website: **www.jcwardon.com**,

Facebook pages: **www.facebook.com/jc.wardon** and **https://www.facebook.com/JCWardonNovelist**

Tweet me: @jc_wardon.

Thanks for sharing my world. I'd love to hear from you!

JC Wardon